M000306950

A NOVEL

Eve, First Matriarch

Ancient Matriarchs Book 1

Angelique Conger

SOUTHWEST OF ZION PUBLISHING / LAS VEGAS

Copyright © 2017 by **Angelique Conger**

All rights reserved. No part of this publication may be reproduced, distributed or transmitted in any form or by any means, without prior written permission.

Angelique Conger/Southwest of Zion Publishing
7401 W Washington Ave
Las Vegas, NV 89128
www.AngeliqueCongerAuthor.com

Publisher's Note: This is a work of fiction. Names, characters, places, and incidents are a product of the author's imagination. Locales and public names are sometimes used for atmospheric purposes. Any resemblance to actual people, living or dead, or to businesses, companies, events, institutions, or locales is completely coincidental.

Book Layout © 2014 BookDesignTemplates.com

Eve, First Matriarch/ Angelique Conger. -- 1st ed.
ISBN 978-1-946550-00-2

For all the daughters of Eve, who strive to be honorable matriarchs.

CONTENTS

Prologue

People came from all around, many traveling for days to reach the family gathering. Many had not returned to Home Valley for years, others never visited the venerable family home. Excitement filled the valley as brothers, sisters, cousins, aunts, and uncles met, some for the first time.

They traded goods and food brought from their far away homes, along with stories of their lives. Through the days they together, they visited, ate, and playing games.

Women dressed in brightly colored robes brought their younger children and older girls to a meadow surrounded by tall pines to hear the revered matriarch speak. Most had not heard her story. Few of the young ones had met her before. Some older matrons waited many years for the opportunity to be with her, share in her love, and hear her story.

Ruth stood and the gabble of multiple voices silenced while the last of the sisters settled their offspring comfortably around them. Birds sang and a slight wind blew the fragrance of roses and violets from under the trees. Robes rustled, small ones hushed, and then a silence fell, as all waited to hear from the withered, ancient woman at the center of their attention.

"Grandmama Eve," Ruth said in a ringing voice, loud enough that all could hear, "we are here to be with you."

After looking around the circle of daughters and their young ones packed into the meadow, Eve lifted her tremulous voice loud enough to be heard by all. "This is as it should be. We, the Ministering Sisters, have met to share and to learn from each other."

"Ganet, Rebecca, and the others can teach us of organizing, working together, and caring for one another," Ruth said, waving her hands toward the other matriarchs. "But Grandmama Eve, there is one thing you can do for us. Only you can share your story."

A soft hum rose from among the women as they nodded and shared small words of agreement. After all, this is why they were here.

"You want to hear the story of an old woman?" Eve straightened in her chair, her face brightening. "Why would you want to know my story?"

The buzzing voices silenced, listening for the answer.

"All of us have other sisters in our lives to help in the birthing of babies. We have others to teach us how to cook, weave, and make pottery. With the Ministering Sisters, we have others to share in our sorrows and joys."

The group nodded and buzzed in anticipation.

Ruth raised her hands for attention before saying, "Grandmama Eve, you were alone. How did you do it? Where did you come from? Where did you live before here? What was it like to be alone with only Grandpapa Adam? How did you manage?"

The surrounding trees rustled as if in agreement. The women settled themselves as the old woman coughed deeply and drank from the tall, yellow, clay cup, covered in painted green leaves. A wolf pup peeped from behind a leaf. Eve took a deep breath, looked around at the expectant crowd and spoke, her voice ancient and dry, "I do not know where I lived before I came here. I lost the knowledge in my coming. I woke one morning to …

CHAPTER ONE

Eden

Green light filtered through the foliage in every shade. As my eyes adjusted to the light, flowers of every color filled my vision and sounds overwhelmed me.

Everything around me shimmered in newness and difference. My thoughts whirled as I attempted to sort out my location, or even my name.

A hand reached out, warm and inviting, and helped to lift me from my bed on the earth. I rose to see more wonders; creatures of many kinds and colors stood around me, as if they expected something to happen.

Who is this? What are they expecting of me? Dizziness filled me as I attempted to understand.

Squawks, chirps, brays, and rumblings filled my ears while a mixture of unnamed scents invaded my nostrils.

I stood, embraced by the overwhelming colors and sounds. I scanned around me, becoming aware of the beautiful man attached to the hand that had helped me up. He stood tall, with deep blue eyes and shoulder length, white hair. Beside him stood his mirror image, an older, wiser man. Both glowed. Did the light surround them? Or did it come from within them? I could not tell. Their clothing of the purist white, almost too white, shone, adding to the radiance. The cacophony of noise quieted, as though waiting to hear from my escorts.

I wondered who these beings were. The brilliance surrounding them made me want to look away from the bright light, yet kindness and love emanated from them. No reason presented itself as to why these blindingly exquisite beings were with me in this strange place. I did not think of them as strangers, strangers would not care.

I puzzled through this until the truth broke through. These were my creators! Creators? Yes. My Gods.

The one who helped me waited for me to solve my puzzle, and then spoke in a deep, resonating voice, "Are you ready?"

"Ready?" To explore? To discover?

"To meet your mate," he said.

Mate? What did *mate* mean? The word sounded familiar, and a memory stirred, warming me. Was I ready for a mate, one given to me by my Gods?

"Is it right that I should?"

Together, my creators nodded and smiled before turning to lead me a short distance around trees and past bushes. Animals trailed behind and beside me, while birds flew from branch to branch. We entered a glen, divided by a trickling brook, where another man with dark hair and penetrating blue eyes, stood tall and strong. My eyes were drawn to his. They showed kindness—and loneliness. Another elegant man, similar to the Gods in many ways, but different, somehow.

"This is Adam," the older God said.

Adam looked at me. A slow smile grew, leaping into his eyes. Nature released a collective breath and small noises surrounded us again.

"We are your Gods, but you can call me Father." The older God gestured to the younger. "This is Jehovah, my beloved son."

Jehovah stepped forward. "Adam, you were charged to be lord of this earth. Have you named the animals?"

"Yes, Lord Jehovah. Each has a name." He dragged his eyes from me to point to an animal. "Giraffe." He pointed another direction. "Dog. Over there are cats: lion, puma, and tiger." After he pointed to the animal, Adam glanced in my direction.

I tracked his hand to see strange and marvelous animals, amazing in their difference to the others. I stood, awed by their beauty and the immensity of the project Adam had completed. Would I be able to do the same, given a similar assignment?

"In the tree is a parrot, a bird. The smaller bird is a robin, and—"

"That is good," Father interrupted, "but do they provide you with companionship?"

"No. No they do not," Adam replied with sudden hesitance. His arm fell to his side. Excitement dropped from him like falling stones. "I am busy, but I am lonely. How can that be?" He gazed toward the Gods as he gestured about him. "In such a magnificent world?" His arms flopped to his sides again.

As Adam's words trailed off, I finally realized the difference between the man, Adam, and the Gods—no brilliance. I could look at the man easier than I could look at my Gods.

"You are not meant to live alone," Father replied, his gentle voice heard above the sound of brook and animals.

Adam looked up, biting his lower lip. Sadness and loneliness filled his face, dancing with hope as he darted a glance my way.

Alone? He had been alone? And my purpose here, to live with him? Who else? Only Adam and me, alone and together in this place, this world? I felt an important loss, a heaviness dropped on my heart. Could I live with the overwhelming loneliness as Adam had? Did I have a choice? We would be together, after all, not completely alone.

Father continued, "We know your needs. For this reason, we caused you to sleep while we created this woman. You named all the other creatures of this earth. What will you name her?"

Adam reached a strong hand toward me. I realized at that moment I could choose. I chose to accept my place. I placed my smaller hand in his and he drew me close. I inhaled his scent, his warmth. The noises silenced.

What name will Adam give me? Who am I?

Adam turned and stared into my eyes, I could see him thinking. Did he think this much to name the animals? I would ask later.

"Eve," he said at last. "The mother of all living.

It felt so right. My chest expanded as I opened myself to the name. Adam's intense gaze never left my face, willing me to accept the name and the honor of mother. Acceptance came. I felt a thrill zip down my spine, down my legs, and back into my heart. Eve, mother of all living. I smiled and laughed a tiny laugh.

Bird songs filled the air. Other animals added their voices in a hymn of adulation. A faint memory stirred and faded, leaving me with an understanding of the importance and specialness, somehow, of my name.

"Eve will be your mate and helper. Together you will live in this new world."

I looked up at the man standing beside me. What is this *mate* word they keep saying? Two of us together? Is that mate? Could I be his mate? A distant memory reminded me. I agreed to this place and to be his spouse. I could do this.

Father and Jehovah led us along a path. Adam held my hand as we followed through trees from the outer world into a verdant, ordered garden. I walked beside Adam. His eyes widened in surprise, viewing a place and things new to him. I felt his shiver of wonder as we traced the path of our Gods into a quiet, green clearing. Animals and birds accompanied us.

"You will be joined in a covenant of marriage," Father said. "Please kneel."

"Father?" I asked. I hesitated until He looked my way. "What is this marriage? Or mate? I do not remember."

An incandescent smile filled his face. "No, Eve. You would not remember. You and Adam will agree to love one another and care for one another for all time and all eternity. You will become one in purpose, as Jehovah and I are one. Together, you will face the challenges and the joys of this new world. That is marriage. We will covenant, or promise, to help you, and you will promise to help each other, to love each other, and to cleave to each other."

Did I trust this man, this Adam well enough to covenant with him in marriage? I raised my hands as I spun in a slow circle, taking in the beauty of the garden and thinking. Alone here, Adam and me, with no others, no other choices, for either of us. And I agreed to be here.

Adam caught my hand, stopped my spin, and stared into my eyes with an earnest longing. I saw the onset of love shining through; his powerful hand, full of promise, confidently clasped mine. Gazing into Adam's eyes, I chose togetherness with this man. The memory of his naming me stirred within my soul. Maybe I did not yet love him, nor he me, but love grew.

I thought of Adam's beauty; his gentle, though strong touch. Could I trust him to treat me well? I gazed into his brilliant blue eyes and found gentleness and hope. Yes, our love would grow. I would join this man in marriage.

Animals surrounded us in silence, watching and listening as we knelt, facing the other, both hands joined, eyes intent on the other as Father spoke the words joining us as husband and wife. After the last amen, I experienced a quiet peace dispelling my fears. Love and support emanated from our Gods.

Father and Jehovah looked at each other, a knowing look passed between them, before Father turned back to us, speaking in His gentle, but stern, voice.

"You are to multiply and replenish the earth."

"Yes, Father," we said together, glancing into each other's eyes before fastening them again on our creator.

"You may eat freely of the garden. All is for your use." He spread his arms wide, indicating the trees and plants in the Garden.

My eyes followed his arms, noticing heavy fruit dripping from almost every tree. All this? Ours to eat? Such abundance, and for us alone?

"You may not eat of that tree," Father added, pointing to a medium sized tree, filled with small, purple fruit, "for if you do eat that fruit, you will die."

Die? That sounded ominous. I shivered. I would not eat of that fruit. Adam nodded and I knew he felt the same way. My attention shifted back to our creator as he spoke once more.

"Go. Eat freely of the Garden. Explore. Discover the life within. We will return to teach you more later."

With that in mind, we gazed about us in wonder. Our Gods withdrew without our noticing. Alone together for the first time, Adam grasped my hand, keeping me close as we explored.

"I have not been here before. I did not know this Garden existed," he said, verifying my earlier suspicions.

He pointed to the animals, sharing the names he had given them. I laughed as spider monkeys hung by their tails and begged for the fruit in our hands. Parrots squawked in the trees and eagles floated in the sky. Small creatures, such as slugs, crickets, ants, and worms hid in the bushes, trees, and along the ground. I stared at every one, trying to remember the names of so many new creatures. I shook my head at the difficult task of trying to keep so much new information in my mind.

Adam plucked a sweet smelling pink flower and tucked it behind my left ear, stroking his hand through my long hair. I enjoyed his soft, gentle touch. It did not surprise me that I liked it, it felt so right. He stayed near touching me often. As he did, his face displayed his wonderment.

He stopped occasionally to pick a new flower for me to carry as we explored. Soon my arms were filled with dozens of fragrant blossoms, overwhelming in color and beauty. Among all this beauty, our love grew.

We picked fruits, vegetables, and nuts from trees, bushes, and the earth and marveled at the flavors, many new even to Adam. Sticky, sugary juices covered our faces and rolled down our arms. We ran laughing to a nearby stream to wash beside colorful fish. Insects buzzed through the air and in our ears. I gazed down at our reflections.

"We are different, you and me." I tilted my head to the side.

"Different in many ways, some more obvious than others." Adam reached toward our reflection. "There is a red to your brown hair while mine is dark."

I ran my finger down his long, straight nose then touched my nose while still gazing into the pool. "My nose turns up on the end."

"Your dark brown eyes almost match your hair—"

"—And yours are a brilliant blue." I reached out to touch his cheek.

Adam playfully splashed, disturbing our reflection. "We may be different, but we are together."

I washed the stickiness from my face and hands, then took a drink. With the water dripping from my chin I asked, "Does this magnificent garden have a name?"

Adam looked around at the garden around us. "I did not hear a name." He paused in thought a moment. "I know. You give it a name."

"Me?" I stared at him and plucked a blade of grass, twisting it between my fingers and inhaling the pungent aroma. My eyebrows lifted. "How will I name this? Are you sure? Naming was given to you to do. Will Father be unhappy if I name it?" Excitement and nervousness filled me.

"I named the animals. Father will understand. You name home."

I nodded and thought of names, rejecting several. Not Zoral nor Amat, nor any of the others I tried. Adam watched me in silence, knowing the challenge of choosing names. I felt a smile lift my face as I finally found the right name.

"Eden. This is Eden."

"Eden?" He scrunched his eyebrows close in thought, then smiled. "This is the Garden of Eden."

I stepped close and he pulled me into his arms. I welcomed his ready support. We embraced, recognizing the rightness of name—Eden, a paradise. We stood for a time, holding each other, enjoying the closeness.

When the light dimmed and the sun fell behind the trees, we found a place beneath a towering catalpa and laid down to sleep in each other's arms.

"How long did you live here alone? Before today?" I asked.

Adam stared into the darkening sky, his arm tightened around me. "I do not know. I did not count all the days. I named many animals, it took time to name the individuals." He shrugged. His free arm stretched wide, indicating the world around us. "The animals in the sea took longer. I stood on the seashore as each came to be named. It took many days."

He squeezed my hand, turned and faced me. Tears glistened in his eyes. "I thank Father you are here now, here with me."

We gazed silently into the heavens, my head on his arm, listening to the crickets' chirp, as a large, white circle began to rise, clear and beautiful. I lifted my arm and stretched it toward the white circle, then dropped it in awe.

"Oh, it is beautiful," I whispered.

"The moon," Adam whispered to my unasked question.

"It is so close. I can almost touch it."

Bits of light appeared, joined soon by larger splotches.

"What are they? I breathed.

"Stars."

I became aware of an order to these stars, identifying shapes in their outlines.

"A bear!" I cried, pointing.

"An eagle!" He pointed another direction.

"A chipmunk."

"Look, a fish."

Adam pulled me closer into his arms and I laid my head on his chest, enjoying his warmth, his closeness, and his scent as we watched the huge moon climb into the sky above us. Lying together, I slept until sunlight streaming through the trees woke me.

~

The next morning, I woke startled. I struggled to remember what happened. Questions about the differences in sounds and other sensations filled me. A fragrance behind my ear reminded me I lived in a new world. I turned my head to gaze at Adam. A smile creased my face as memories of the day before filled me: our marriage, our explorations, and the moon. Most of all, I remembered Adam's kindness.

He lay now with his arm thrown across his eyes to keep out the bright light of morning. We had not moved during the night. His hip next to mine warmed and soothed me.

Drawn by the flavors of yesterday's food, I decided to surprise Adam. I eased my body away from his and stood, stretching. I walked to the trees, searching for the foods I enjoyed the day before. I worked to remember the name of the big purple fruit. Oh, yes. Adam called them figs. After several tries, I managed to jump and pull two from the tree. Other fruit, identified earlier by Adam, grew close by, tantalizing my senses. I added bright red strawberries and oranges, bigger than both my fists together to my cache. Animals joined me. Some plucked fruits from the trees while others grazed on the green grass. Thinking of Adam's love for flowers, I tucked an orange blossom behind my ear. Its sweet aroma moved with me as I adjusted the fruit in my arms and toted it back to where Adam lay.

"Food?"

Busy balancing the different sizes of round fruits in my arms, Adam's voice startled me. I looked toward him to see his blue eyes sparkling with laughter.

"Yes. Food," I frowned as fruits tumbled from my arms into a jumble on the ground. "I thought you would like some."

"I would. Thank you." Adam pushed himself to stand. "That looks tasty. Be right back."

He smiled and slipped between the trees as I found a large leaf and busied myself peeling oranges and dividing everything on either side of the leaf.

dam returned with two long, yellow fruit.

"Bananas," he explained.

I accepted the banana he handed me, watched him strip back the peel, and imitated his moves. Though not as juicy as the others, this fruit perfectly complemented them.

"Good," I said between bites.

Adam swallowed. "You did not need to gather food for me."

With my banana gone, I reached for a fig. "I wanted to surprise you. Did I?"

He nodded and reached for a strawberry, and then leaned back on his arm, satisfaction glowing on his face. We continued to dine to the songs of birds and distant animal sounds.

When we ate everything, Adam scrubbed juice from his face with his hands and grinned. "I think we need to wash. Race you to the river?"

Without waiting for my reply, he leapt up and ran toward the quiet bend in the river. I bounced up and chased after him. Laughing, we jumped into the deep water.

I surged out with a gasp, struggling to regain my breath, taken from me by the coldness, colder than I expected. I soon forgot the chill as we played.

A splash hit my face. I stood, shook my head, and began to brush the moisture from my eyes. Another splash covered me.

Adam.

"You asked for it!" I squealed as I turned and splashed at him, laughing.

I soon learned to create a bigger wave. We enjoyed our pleasant game until he pulled me under the waves.

I struggled up, spluttering.

"How could you do such a thing to me?" I shouted as I scrubbed the wet from my face. "Why would you drag me under the water?"

"Sorry. I thought it would be fun."

"It was not fun." I shook my fist at him.

Adam's hands slid into the river without a ripple, and his laughter became a pout, his teeth held his lower lip.

My anger shed almost as fast as it grew. I dropped my hands into the water and splashed him. He reached out his arms and pulled me almost under the surface in a tight embrace. I gazed into his face and smiled. We played a while longer, careful not to pull the other beneath the surface.

I scrubbed the last of the stickiness from my face and body and began to squeeze water through my hair when Adam handed me a plant.

"Rub this into your hair. It will clean it."

Bubbles and tingling covered my head as I scrubbed and rinsed my hair. I flopped onto my stomach on the bank and lay in the heat of the sun. Adam dropped beside me, his hand comfortably resting on my back.

I turned on my side and draped my arm across his body. He slid his arm around my waist, turned, and drew me close. Slowly and gently our lips met in a kiss.

We separated and I giggled at his grin. Adam stroked his fingers through my hair, loosening the tangles. He searched for something under a nearby tree until he found a small branch with several thicker twigs. He stripped the leaves from it and ran it through my hair.

"Better," he said, "smooth and shiny. I love your long, red-brown hair. But your flower is gone." He reached out and picked a bloom from a nearby lilac bush. "Try this." He tucked the flower behind my ear. Its sweet bouquet filled the air.

I smiled up at him and kissed him soft on the lips, taking pleasure in his touch.

Over the next days, we explored, we ate, and we danced in the rains watering Eden. We saw different animals and discovered many new things. I exclaimed at the tall giraffes. The lions and bears allowed me to run my hands through their soft fur.

One day we passed through thick grass until we came to a wide river inhabited by new and interesting animals, long nosed alligators and fat, round hippos. We slipped in the mud along the banks. It covered our bodies. The drying mud itched.

The afternoon rains fell and washed some of the mud from our bodies, leaving them striped like zebras. We pointed and laughed at each other. Before we were entirely clean, the rain stopped. We found a pool of clear water, stepped into it, and scrubbed off the remnants of thick, dry mud.

As we washed, round little animals bumped into our legs.

"How cute. Are they turtles?" I asked.

"Yes."

I searched around and found the water plants the turtles were eating. I stripped off a leaf and offered it to them. One hesitantly nibbled.

"Do you like these plants?" I asked. "Oh. Ouch! He bit my finger." I bounced back and pulled my hand up out of the pool. The turtle clung to my finger. I shook my hand until the turtle let go and fell off. I stared into the depths around my knees where the turtle now swam.

"I am getting out now before another turtle decides I am dinner." I climbed out of the water.

"Poor turtle," Adam laughed as he followed me to dry ground. "You startled him."

"I did." I joined in the laughter. "I am happy he is not hurt, but I do not want to be his food."

In our daily strolls through the garden, Adam found a fresh blossom to tuck behind my ear. Each became a fragrant reminder of our growing love.

On one of these days, we examined the many different trees in our Garden. I ran my hands across their trunks, admiring the different textures. Some barks were smooth, while others were rough. A hawk floated in the air above us while small sparrows chittered and chirped in an attempt to attract our attention.

A tiny bird dipped his long beak into a blossom, hovering in place as it ate.

"I have never seen that bird. What is it called?" I asked, wonder filling my voice.

"A hummingbird. Listen. You can hear it hum," Adam set his finger across his lips.

The red-throated little bird flew close to my hair, tasting the nectar in the red trumpet vine bloom behind my ear. Its little green wings brushed my face, tickling. I laughed softly at its gentle touch.

The variety and number of tastes, smells, sights, sounds, and textures that day almost overwhelmed my senses. Finding a need to retreat, I closed my eyes and breathed deep and slow, returning in my mind to the quiet moment when Father and Jehovah left us. We sat together and spoke of our Gods.

"Father asked us to obey and we have." I remembered the commands given to us. "We have been good to each other and the animals."

"We have explored." Adam gestured about us. "We named our garden, this beautiful Garden of Eden."

"We have obeyed all the commandments Father and Jehovah gave us."

"All except the first commandment. We have yet to multiply and replenish the earth." Adam plucked a blade of grass and began to shred it.

"What is multiply? How do we replenish the earth?"

"Children, little ones like us." He looked up from his shredded blade of grass and stared into my eyes.

"Nothing changes here." I gazed at the trees, the animals around us, all were the same. No little ones—all adults like us. "What do we do to have children? How do we obey this command?"

Adam shrugged. Though we returned to this question often, the answer never presented itself.

Each night we slept under a tree wherever we found ourselves. In the morning when we woke we were still touching the other, still warm. Over time, I learned to love Adam: his touch, his scent, and his beauty, happy to be in this paradise with him. Almost content.

CHAPTER TWO

Tempted

S ome days we spent every waking moment together. Others, we went our separate ways, to wander, to contemplate, or to gather a favored food. One morning I went to the center of the garden to pick vegetables. I pulled one last carrot, brushed off the dirt, and stood to find Adam.

"Can you eat all the fruit in the garden?" a serpent asked, twisting and turning in front of me.

The large serpent with bright green and black diamond-shaped patterns slid down a tree and opened its mouth to speak, once more. Why would it speak our language? Why would it not hiss as serpents did? My mouth opened to speak, though no sound came out. I blew out a big breath and tried again.

"Why do you care? We are given everything we desire." My eyes were drawn to its moving coils. "Why do you speak?"

"I speak so you may grow and learn."

"Why should I grow? Our life is good here. If we need to learn, Father and Jehovah will teach us. We love our life." I turned to walk away, but the serpent hung from a tree in front of me."

How did he do that?

"You must eat the fruit." Its coils twisted and turned, making me dizzy.

My eyes flicked from the serpent to the tree and back. The tree stood there as ever, filled with small purple fruit.

"The fruit Father told us we must not touch or eat or we will die?" My eyes jumped back to the forbidden tree, drawn to its suddenly enticing fruit.

"You shall not die," it whispered. "The fruit will give you knowledge. You will learn things you never expected. You will know about good and evil."

Good? Evil? What were these words? They held no meaning for me. I could not desire something I did not understand.

"We do not need to know. We are happy here the way we are."

"This fruit tastes superior to any in Eden. It will make you wise." The serpent rumbled strangely like the cats. My eyes focused on the tree.

Persistent serpent.

"No!" I dragged my eyes from the tree. "We eat many delicious fruits and vegetables. We do not need this one." I started to walk away.

23

"You cannot know good without bad. With sorrow, you can understand happiness. Sickness allows you to appreciate health. Light defeats dark."

Pushy creature. Why did it care?

"I understand dark and light, day and night. Those others are not important. Father provides all we need. Why should I disobey Father for those reasons?"

The serpent moved its head closer to mine, staring into my eyes. "You must eat this fruit or you will never have children. You cannot obey the commandment to multiply."

No children? How could I eat the proscribed fruit? I would not. I would obey. We had been told specifically not to touch or eat it. Yet, we were also commanded to multiply and replenish the earth. No young lived here. How could I obey both commandments? Was the serpent right? Would eating this prohibited fruit make a difference? Would it help us have children?

The tree stood near with its purple fruit dripping enticement.

The tree stood in the center of Eden and never entered my consciousness in all the time since Father commanded us not to touch or eat from it. Why now? I ran my hand through my hair.

"Why do you hesitate?" the serpent said, its voice alluring. "You must eat this fruit to be like the Gods, to have children." Somehow a fruit now balanced within its coils.

Thoughts raced through my mind, my chest tightened, and my stomach seethed. I looked from the serpent with the fruit balanced in its coils to the tree and back several times. We could have children if we ate the forbidden fruit? Could we find another way? Did the serpent speak the truth? Could this be the reason we had no children? Children! How could I obey both commandments? Could I take a chance the serpent spoke lies? Was there another way?

Tears of frustration ran down my face. I did not want to believe.

"How can this be?" I whispered. "Is there another way?" Would we ever have children if we did not eat the banned fruit? How could knowledge be worth disobeying Father? I shook my head. No, knowledge could not be. But, children?

"This is the only choice," the serpent persisted.

"To have children?" I said through my tears, lifting my chin.

"Here. Eat," it urged.

I took the fruit from its coils and stared at it a long moment, wondering if I could do this. I moved to return the fruit to the serpent, but it moved away in refusal.

"Eat."

I surrendered and took a bite. Warmth rushed from the center of my chest, coursing up into my head, burning and ripping back to the center and down to the ends of my fingers and toes. Other sensations fought for my attention, an urging in my groin, a pounding in my head. What did it mean? I moved to throw the fruit to the ground. No more!

The serpent's attitude changed, becoming demanding, "No! Adam must eat the fruit, as well. Take it to him."

Adam? Oh, Adam. What would he say? I would die! But what about Adam? Would he eat? Would he die? How could we have children if we died? What had I done?

I stumbled through the trees, searching for him, carrying the fruit out in front of me. At last, I found him picking apples. My beautiful man, so obedient, and so innocent. Would he do this? I took a deep breath and hurried to him.

With a voice filled with emotion, I choked out his name. "Adam?"

He looked up, joy filling his face, until he saw the fruit in my hand. His joy collapsed.

"What have you done?" He stepped back from me and breathed in deeply. He licked his lips once, twice, before he managed to rasp out, "You did not eat *the forbidden fruit?*" *His eyes* fastened on my hand, his face lost all color.

"Yes," I spoke in a low voice, my eyes focused on his. "Try it." I stepped closer to him.

"I eat every fruit except *that* particular fruit. You know we will die if we eat it." He lifted his chin and stared into my eyes, breathing rapidly.

"How can you obey all of Father's commands?" My voice quivered.

"I will."

"Do you remember the commandment to multiply and replenish the earth? How can we obey it? I do not know how to obey, except by eating this." I held the fruit out to him.

Adam stretched out his hand toward mine, pulled it back, and reached out again. I held my breath, willing him to take it. Again, he jerked his hand back.

"I have eaten this fruit. I will die." My voice dropped. My hand quivered along with my voice. "You will be alone once more."

He gazed at me with longing, before focusing on his hands. He caught his lower lip in his teeth. My jaw clenched, I fought to slow my breathing. Would I be alone? Would I die soon? I remembered our love and a small hope filled me.

"I will taste it." Tears welled, balancing on the edge of his eyes.

Adam took the fruit from my hand, slowly brought it to his mouth, and took a bite. I watched as the heat spread through his body, and he experienced the other changes I experienced earlier. The tightness inside me relaxed, my head felt light, and I wanted to laugh. We fell into each other's arms.

What had we done? Would this be the end? As we parted, we looked down at ourselves. We were naked. Embarrassment warmed our ears and faces.

How did we not know? Were we that innocent? Were we aware now because we now had knowledge? Or, did we know now because we were disobedient? Did it matter?

"We should cover our bodies," Adam suggested.

"Yes, but how?"

We glanced around the glen in which we stood, searching for something, anything large enough to provide covering. A fig tree stood near with its large leaves. No other tree growing near us grew larger leaves. One would not be enough. Adam plucked several and found a thin vine. We twisted the vine around the stems, forming a covering, which we strung around our waists and tied.

We heard Jehovah and Father enter Eden. Their voices rang through the glade as the moved toward us.

"What shall we do?" I asked. "They will know!"

Adam started forward, ready to rush to meet our Gods, and then he looked down. His face fell and he glanced about us.

"Hide!" he whispered.

We slipped into the center of some nearby bushes. *How did I not feel the bushes scratch me before?* Maybe they would not see us or look for us this time.

~

"Adam. Eve. Adam." Jehovah's loving voice called.

Adam glanced into my eyes and shook his head.

"We are here to visit you. Where are you?" Jehovah's voice called louder.

I shared Adam's trepidation as he disentangled himself from my arms. With slow steps, we entered the clearing.

"Here," Adam said.

"Why did you not come sooner when I called?"

"I was afraid," Adam replied, dropping his head and looking at his feet.

I reached out and tucked my hand into the crook of his arm. He glanced at my hand and returned his eyes to his feet.

"What have you done?" Father's voice was harsh. He raised his hand almost closed in a fist. "Did you eat the fruit of the tree you were commanded not to touch or eat? Were you not warned it would cause your death?"

Adam shuffled his feet and glanced at me before he lifted his head to answer, "Eve gave me the fruit. And I ate it."

Amazement filled me. Adam had the courage to look into Father's face.

Father turned to me, "What did you do?"

I swallowed the lump in my throat. Would I die now? I thought about lying, but decided to tell the truth. I followed Adam's example and lifted my head, though I did not quite look into Father's face. "A serpent enticed me and told me we could not multiply nor grow and learn unless we ate the fruit. So, I ate some of it."

My eyes darted once between Father and Jehovah. Then, like Adam, I stared at my feet, waiting to learn when we would die.

"Lucifer," Father called. Though He did not raise His voice, the intensity of the demand rippled through our bodies, as it flowed through the garden.

I wondered why He would call this Lucifer. A serpent beguiled me. I jerked my head up in time to observe a man much like Jehovah, though shorter, stride from behind a tree. Smugness filled his ruddy face. Ornate green and black patterned clothing covered his body and his cloak flowed freely behind him. The gold cane he carried echoed the black and green design of the serpent and writhed along its length.

Father and Jehovah turned toward him. "Why are you here? I see what you have been up to."

Lucifer straightened, holding his blond head high. "Your plan is ruined! You will never bring children back to you, these two or their posterity." Lucifer thrust his cane into the soil. I watched the serpent along its length twist and turn.

He turned toward us, scorn filled his face as he pointed toward Adam and me. "I have won. If you send them children, I will control them and teach them to honor me, not you." He turned back to Jehovah and pointed to him. "They will be mine. I will have glory and honor from these people. My followers and I will take the bodies you give to the children of Adam and Eve."

Lucifer swept his eyes across us and back to Father and Jehovah, hard and insistent. His voice mocked our Gods. "I tempted the woman. She ate the forbidden fruit against your command."

The serpent design along his cane appeared to stop moving for a moment. It glared in my direction.

Father spoke to Lucifer, his voice harder than I ever heard it before, "Because you did this, you, and your serpent, are cursed greater than any animal. You have not won the war, not even this little battle. There shall be hatred between you and this woman and her children. You may win some of the people of this earth, some may forget, but *I will win* the war."

Hatred between my children and Lucifer? Will I not die now?

Lucifer continued to stand defiantly glaring at Father.

"Go away," Father demanded.

"This has not ended." Lucifer shouted his in his rage, his voice rose higher and tighter. He stomped his foot and pounded his cane into the ground. A crack started to run away from the cane point before closing. "I will win this war. I will win the hearts of the children of these people. Your plan will be destroyed!"

He gathered his cloak tightly about him and turned. Lightning from a black cloud struck nearby, followed by a crash of thunder. He stomped away inside a great storm.

I looked into Adam's pale face. He trembled as much as me while we listened to the interchange between Father and Lucifer. I worried that Lucifer would cause us more trouble. Although, how much worse could it be? We faced Father as he returned to us.

Father's shoulders drooped, if only a bit, and He stared at me, His face immobile. "Eve."

I sucked in a deep breath and held it as I waited to find how I would pay for my transgression. I stood tall, with my arms clamped to the side of my body and lifted my head.

"Pain and sorrow shall accompany your life, especially when you bring children into this world." His arm lifted in my direction. I felt His sorrow for our actions. He closed His hand into a fist. "Your life will be difficult. Listen to your husband, as he listens to me. The time will come when you will appreciate his directions." His hand opened again as he dropped it to his side.

My mind latched onto the word children. What joy! I could now obey the first commandment. Joy and sorrow battled within me. Although I felt guilt for my actions and this punishment, hope rose as I thought about children.

Father turned to my sweet husband. "Adam. Because you listened to the voice of your wife, eating the fruit I commanded you not to eat, the soil of the earth shall be cursed, allowing you to learn." Father gestured to the plants growing near us. "Thorns and weeds will grow. You must work to feed yourself and your family by the sweat of your brow, until you return to your Heavenly home for you will die. In sorrow you shall live all the days of your life."

Death would come, later. We would have children. We would have to work hard to eat and to live. But I knew it would be worth it.

Father's voice pierced my reflections. "It was your choice to eat. You will now continue to choose. As you consider the alternatives, choose good over evil, obey our commands. Remember the commands you received and all those you will receive. Jehovah will give you further commandments, listen and obey."

Father withdrew. We were left with Jehovah who gave us commandments to help us live in their love and protection.

"Adam, you have the privilege and responsibility of acting in my name." Jehovah lifted His hands. "This responsibility is called the Priesthood. You can only use it to help others in love. As we love you, love Eve and your children. Bless them with my Priesthood." He allowed His hands to fall to His side.

Adam squared his shoulders and stood taller. Without looking, he stretched his arm to hold my hand and squeezed it.

"You may no longer live in this Garden of Eden," Jehovah continued.

I twitched and looked into Adam's eyes. After all we heard, we did not expect to be ejected from Eden. My concerns reflected in his eyes. Where would we go? What would we eat? How would we—?

"You will be given coats of skins and sent away."

"Watch, Adam. You will sacrifice later as I do now, as I will be in the future. I mediate for you with Father that justice and mercy may both be satisfied."

We held hands and watched silently as Jehovah called for a mammoth. One came to his call, studied Jehovah's loving eyes, and lay at His feet. Jehovah drew a sharp object from within his belt and cut its throat.

Horrified, I brought my hand to my mouth to prevent gasps from escaping. I forced myself to watch as he carefully cut off the skin, waved a hand over it, softening it, and then formed robes, cloaks, and foot coverings for Adam and me.

Jehovah cut meat from the mammoth, commanding us to eat. We hesitated. I had brought death to this creature. Adam took my hand and helped me reach to receive my portion. I bit off a bite and chewed. It filled my mouth with unfamiliar stringiness. I choked, cleared my throat, and managed to swallow. The following bites went down my throat no easier.

As we ate the flesh, something we did not eat in Eden, Jehovah caused a fire to consume the remainder of the animal. The fire cleansed the garden of the remnants of the mammoth.

As we remembered our first home, this sacrifice would always be connected to those memories.

"In the same way, Adam, you will sacrifice to me." Jehovah gestured toward the place where the animal once lay. "You are to sacrifice only the first born, unblemished of your flocks, when your flocks grow large enough. Until then, you may call on the beasts of the forest." He motioned toward the trees.

Adam nodded, unmoving, his head and spine bowed.

"You may not eat fruit from the Tree of Life. To do so would cause you to live in your sins forever. To protect and prevent you from eating, Cherubim will protect Eden."

Cherubim and their flaming swords turned every way, protecting the Tree of Life and the entrance to Eden.

"The two of you must now leave Eden, never to return." Jehovah's sorrow tinged his voice. "Your lives are forever changed. Pray to Father. I will send messengers to give you further light and knowledge."

Adam put his arm around me and we walked past the Cherubim, flinching away from their swords, and passed through the archway into the world. The sun stood near the tops of the trees. We stumbled across the rough land. Wind slammed us, pushing us back, and making it difficult to walk. Until that moment, I did not know how protected we had been in Eden.

Trees laid in ragged piles. Great gashes cut the earth where others had been torn from their roots. Broken branches and leaves littered the ground. The odor of burning wood filled the air. Would we face this harsh weather often in this new world? I hoped not.

Wonder and confusion filled Adam's eyes and his smile wavered. This morning we were innocent. Now what?

"This will be worth it." I touched his arm with my free hand.

He covered my hand with his. "It will. It is too late to look back now." Yet, he stopped to take a long, last glimpse of our paradise home. For a long moment, he avoided my gaze, and then he shrugged and smiled at me. Resolutely, we faced forward and continued on, his arm tight around my waist, face into the wind.

CHAPTER THREE

Ejected

Away from Eden, we crossed a meadow and trudged up a small hill. Adam reached out to steady me when I stumbled. The hill felt as though it was a mountain, until I glanced up once more to see we were near the top.

As we reached the highest point, I turned to Adam. "Now what?"

"I have no idea. We cannot sleep in the open in this wind. Watch for shelter."

We searched for a place out of the intense wind tearing at our clothing, pulling it apart and chilling us. The difficulty of the uneven ground slowed our travel. Dust blew in my face, hiding the world in front of me.

I kicked through the leaves and broken branches at my feet and caught one on my foot. Adam steadied me before I fell.

Three large, green peppers clung to a small bush bent against the wind. I stopped to pluck them, almost out of habit.

Adam helped me stand. I nodded my thanks to him and folded over the edge of my cloak, making a small pocket to carry the peppers in. We faced into the gale and struggled on.

The sun dipped behind the trees and the light faded. Adam pointed to a thick stand of trees, somehow still erect in the force of the tempest. He leaned close to my ear and shouted, "Perhaps we can find safety in there."

He helped me across fallen trees into the shadows of the glade. The wind dropped, suddenly barely noticeable in the midst of the ancient, tall trees. One giant tree had fallen sometime in the past with such violence it was now driven deep into the earth and was now covered with forest litter. An enormous overhanging limb stretched out and formed a cozy cave. Overhead, birds chirped and settled into nests for the night, waiting out the storm. A bobcat snarled and hissed as it leapt from beneath the tree limb and ran from the glade. I jumped and grabbed Adam's arm, clinging to him.

"We encroached on his shelter," Adam sighed. "He could have fought us for it."

"Will he return? The wind is cold." I knew the bobcat's fur prepared him to face the cold better than us, even as I worried about his return.

A rumbling startled me. I felt my chin tremble. "What was that?"

"My stomach," Adam mumbled. As he put his hand over his stomach, his ears reddened. He caught his lower lip between his teeth.

"Your stomach? Why would your stomach make a rumbling noise?"

He shrugged his shoulders and grimaced.

"My stomach feels strange, as well, with a small pain. Are we … hungry?" I asked.

"Hungry? The word is strange, yet it expresses the need in my stomach. Do we have food? Is there any near here?" Adam stared around the glade.

"I do not know about food in this glade, but I picked green peppers earlier. Will they help?" I opened the little pocket I had formed earlier and drew out the peppers.

They were crushed, but still crunchy. A fresh fragrance escaped. Adam took one, broke it in half, and scraped out the seeds.

"Is this all you have?" He looked for more, then shrugged. "I should not ask. I did not think to pick any food. Perhaps we should eat only one tonight and save the others for tomorrow." He handed me half of the pepper.

I looked at the half pepper in my hands. It did not look like much to eat. I took a small bite. Its pungent fragrance filled my nose. It tasted better than I remembered. I relished the unexpected moisture. This small piece of a green vegetable quenched my unrecognized thirst.

"Save the seeds."

Adam scraped the tiny seeds from the soil between us. "Why?"

"I believe we will need them later. I do not know why, only that we need them."

Adam considered this as he munched on his last bite. "You are probably right, if we can learn how to make them grow."

"Did it quench your thirst?"

He nodded and ate his last bite. We sat together in silence. My thoughts turned to the events of the day, and I began to fear what would happen next. Guilt filled me. Why had I listened to the serpent? Everything we now faced was my fault. What would happen to us now? What could Lucifer do to us? The ferocity of the world frightened me.

Shivers filled me and my throat closed as I contemplated our situation. I did not want to break into Adam's reflections and stared at my hands in my lap. At last, I glanced up to see him inspecting me with his clear blue eyes. He reached over and touched my arm.

"Eve, I am happy to be with you."

"Oh, Adam." Despair filled my voice. "I am sorry I changed our lives. I should have been stronger."

He reached out and held my hand. "No. It was necessary. This is the right thing to do."

I sniffed. "Are you sure? Why am I so weak?"

"Lucifer tempted me, too. He came to me twice, pushing me to eat that fruit. But I refused. He must have influenced the serpent to tempt you." He reached up to stroke my cheek with his other hand.

I stared at him. "He tempted you? Why did you not tell me?"

Adam shrugged.

Adam resisted twice, but I gave in the first time. How weak of me! The knowledge caused my throat to tighten even more. I sighed deeply and coughed, trying to break through the tightness. "Why did I listen?"

"Eve, we changed. Father told us we would have children. Maybe this curse holds a hidden blessing."

I managed a shaky smile, and my love for him grew in that instant.

After a moment of silence, I opened Adam's hand to look at the tiny pepper seeds it held. "How will we take these with us until we are ready to try to grow them?"

"Can you carry them in the pocket in your robe, the one you used for the peppers?"

"Seeds this small? I will lose them if I carry them either in the pocket or in my hands. We need something to keep them together."

His eyes searched the area. "Would it help to fold them into a leaf?"

"Perhaps."

I searched among the leaf litter and on the nearby trees. At last, I found a green leaf the right size. I folded the small white seeds within it. Now, where could I put it to keep the seeds safe and find them in the morning? I tucked the packet near the fallen tree, along with the uneaten peppers, where we could find them.

The sun fell behind the trees and the darkness deepened. We knelt outside the sheltering space under the tree and thanked Jehovah for the food and clothing, and then crawled beneath the overhang and lay on the soft leaf litter. I felt safe in our little cave, grateful for the protection our cloaks provided from the sharpness of the leaves poking into our skin.

I could not remember leaves poking us in Eden. Why did they now? Another mystery I had no way of knowing, or finding, the answer.

I lay in Adam's arms where he pulled me close. We kissed, aware of the newness of our bodies, sharing love in a way we had never considered in Eden. He explored my body and I explored his, learning to enjoy the love we shared in entirely new ways.

Later, I lay with my head cradled on his chest. I wondered at the unfamiliar thumping there. What else would we find new and different?

~

I awoke cold. My cloak had slipped off me sometime during the night. I pulled it up and snuggled closer to Adam's back hoping to share his heat. Between Adam and the cloak, warmth soon filled me, but I felt a need to rise. I moved away from him, bit by bit, trying to let him sleep. As I lifted to my knees, he rolled over and opened his eyes.

"You are awake," he said, as he flipped the covering cloak back and slid toward the front of the hollow. I followed until he took my hand and helped me out. Adam pulled me to my knees. "We must pray." With praise and gratitude, he offered a simple prayer.

A golden songbird we had not seen before lit on a limb near our faces and trilled a song full of gladness. It filled me with hope. Its sweet song filled the air for a long time. When it left, I shook my head to clear it and tried to remember what I needed to do. Yes. Peppers. I bent to retrieve the remaining peppers and the packet of seeds, finding them by the fallen log where I left them.

"We do not want to lose any seeds." I sat and broke a pepper open over my robe. Several seeds fell into it. I scraped those that clung to the inside and those on my robe into my hand before handing the larger half to Adam.

I opened the leaf folded from the night before and dropped the tiny seeds on it, before folding it once around them. I looked for a place to carry them in a way they would not be lost.

"You need to keep your hands free," Adam reminded me as he took a bite of his half of pepper.

His grip on my arm had kept me from being blown over on the unfamiliar, rough terrain more than once during our trek from Eden. After a moment of consideration, I tucked the leaf packet between my robe and tie. I ate my share of the pepper and considered the last one.

I shrugged. "I will carry the last pepper in my robe pocket for now. It will help quench our thirst, but we will need water soon."

Adam agreed and stood, offering me his hand. I joined him, checking my packet of seeds. I shadowed him as he led us out of the safety of the glade, holding together the pocket with the pepper in it.

As we moved forward, I wondered what we would find in this new world. I hoped there would be water. Jehovah would not send us away without water and a way to find food. What else would we find?

The wind blew my hair into my face, though with less sting than the day before. The grass and bushes swayed, no longer flattened against the ground. Still, Adam held onto my arm to help me balance.

The land varied as we walked through it. We trekked through a shallow valley, surrounded by low hills. In the distance, we saw tall mountains, purple colors blending together against the sky. Trees and bushes scattered through the rough and broken valley floor. Eden was different from this place. Its soil lay smooth, the breezes soft. How could we survive this wild and dangerous place?

As we pushed through the bushes, I followed directly behind Adam. I bent to pick a handful of the dark purple, sweet smelling black berries and pulled back from the sharp thorns. I tucked them into my pocket, before realizing I felt pain.

The thorns hurt. They left white lines and red drops. I brushed the red drops from my arms and enlarged my pocket for the plums Adam handed me, picked from one of the scattered trees. We each ate one, filling a spot in our hunger and somewhat slaking our thirst.

We stopped occasionally to harvest the few remaining pecans and dug a few carrots we discovered along the way. These, and other bits of food, found their way into my enlarging and heavier, make-do pocket.

At last, the sweet melody and fragrance of rushing water reached us. We followed the sound until we stood on the edge of a cliff. A large river roared far below. Water teased us in the distance. Our thirst worsened by the nearness, yet impossibility of reaching the water. We needed it.

Focusing on the river as we struggled through the bushes and grass, I stumbled, landing on my hands. I cried out as I fell. My robe pocket flew apart, flinging away all the food we had collected. As I gathered it into my lap, my hands began to hurt and burn in a new way. Falling had never caused this pain before.

I peered at the jagged flesh and the red fluid flowing down my arm. I lifted my hands to my face and inhaled the coppery scent. I tasted some of the liquid. Though not horrible, it did not entice me. It would not solve my hunger.

Adam heard my cry and returned to find me on the ground. He stooped to help retrieve the scattered food.

"What is wrong?"

"My hands. They burn and sting. And there is red liquid oozing from them. Look." I held my hands out to him.

He set down the plums he had recaptured and took my hands in his. "Strange. You fell before without this happening …

In Eden. And Adam had, too.

"Is it because of the alterations in our bodies?" he wondered. "I heard a thumping last night as you lay your head on my chest."

I experienced many new things the night before. A small smile crossed my face. "I, too, heard a pounding in your chest. My hand has a small throb. What is it?"

"It must be blood, one of the transformations caused by our ejection from Eden."

"Are you sure?" I asked, my chest growing tight and heavy from the knowledge that the differences were caused by my disobedience. "How do you know?"

"Jehovah warned us there would be modifications to our bodies. Do you not remember?" Adam pulled some grass and pushed it against the oozing blood.

"This is my fault. We would not be able to be hurt or bleed if I had not listened to that snake," I whispered, sorrow breaking my voice.

"It is for the best. Remember." He reached up and touched my face. "Without this, we would never learn and grow, never have children."

I watched him tie the clump of grass around my hand. His words made sense, but inside my head I continued to insist on my guilt, until the word 'children' penetrated the confusion.

"Yes, children. For children, the changes are good," I breathed.

I helped search for the pecans that had bounced away and placed everything back into the reformed pocket of my robe.

"We need a better way to carry this."

Adam agreed as he placed the last nut in the pocket.

I moved with care, watching the path ahead. Our progress was barred. Thick, spiked bushes embraced the path. We could not pass through them. Adam ranged back and forth until he found a space between them. We turned sideways and stepped slowly through. I covered my hands with my cloak to avoid scratches.

On the other side of the patch of spiked bushes, a steep ravine crossed in front of us. As far as we could see, the ravine ran wide and deep.

Adam shrugged. "Through it, then."

I nodded and followed him down. I hung on to bushes to keep from sliding down the side. We moved across the steepness, always angling down, until we reached the bottom. We paced along the bottom a distance until I found the courage to climb up the other side. Between Adam and deep-rooted bushes, I managed to pull myself up the steep sides and out of the ravine.

We stopped to pant and eat some of the fruit and nuts we had gathered. After a short rest, we pushed on toward the beckoning water.

We were surprised by a stream, small in comparison to the river, but too wide to step across. We stooped to drink of its clean, refreshing sweetness. I untied the grass around my hurt hands and swished them in the water.

"Ah!" I sighed. "That is better."

"Feel good?" Adam asked, lifting his head from the water.

"Soothing." The bleeding had stopped, though torn and ragged flesh covered my hands.

After another long drink, we jumped across the water, stepping on rocks dividing the stream in small swirling eddies and trailed beside it toward the river. As we came closer, it spread wide, becoming slow and shallow, before joining the rushing river.

We left our precious food wrapped in our clothing on the bank and waded into the river for a bath. A bear stood in the middle of the river down from us. Fish swam around his feet. We watched the bear, wondering what he would do. He reached in and snagged a fish with his great paw. He shoved it into his mouth and ambled out of the river. He dropped the fish on the bank, held it with his paw, and began to rip it apart. He devoured it!

I stood with my hand in my mouth, horrified. No animals preyed on others in Eden. The differences of this world continued to surprise us.

"Will he eat us?" I whispered with a shiver.

Adam shook his head and released his lower lip from between his teeth. "He has his fish."

"Will we need to catch fish?" I asked, a tremor filling my voice.

Adam blanched. "Not while other food is available."

The tightness in my chest that had grown while watching the bear loosened. "Good."

After we dressed and tucked the seeds and fruit away for safekeeping, we drank deeply from the clear stream before striding away. The need to discover more food drove us from its secure banks. We forged on, knowing we could return for water, if we did not find more.

.

CHAPTER FOUR

Earth

The plant life changed as we pressed on. Rough brush became tall grass with golden kernels growing at the tips. Morsels of these dropped into my hands as I brushed through them. They had a warm, earthy fragrance.

Adam wondered about their safety as food and, after smelling them, bit one in half. He chewed for a long time, especially for such a small morsel.

"Not much to it. No bitterness. Nothing to harm us. Perhaps more would make enough to enjoy." He tossed more into his mouth and chewed for a longer time.

I stood watching, amazed he would try it, and hoping it would be good. At last, he smiled.

"You should try some. This is delicious."

He was right, they did taste good. It surprised me to find something so small sated my growling stomach. Something else to eat. I added a couple handfuls to the load in my robe pocket.

As we continued to explore, Adam tucked a daisy behind my ear, as he had in Eden. I could not resist reflecting his smile as I reached up to settle the flower. We crossed through other grains; some were safe, while others were bitter and inedible.

We arrived at the edge of the plain and began to climb the low rising hill. Though not steep, the varied terrain, so different from Eden, we crossed already that day tired my legs and other parts of my body. I panted and felt my cheeks grow hot well ahead of reaching the apex. Adam's face, too, glowed a bright red when I glanced toward him. He breathed deep, with difficulty, as I did.

Another stream flowed downhill. We stopped to drink and rest, and then trudge upward beside it. When at last we arrived at the top of the hill, we threw ourselves onto the ground to rest and to allow our ragged breathing to ease.

Adam regained his strength long before I did. I watched as he searched for large stones. He piled these near the rise.

"What are you doing?" I asked.

"Building an altar."

"An altar? I do not understand."

"We must give thanks to Father for this new home, and for the food and water we have found. We were commanded to pray."

I joined him placing stones on the pile. After much work and much more sweat, an altar stood near to Father. We knelt beside it, and Adam raised his hands.

"Oh Father, hear my prayer," he prayed.

We heard a high-pitched, smooth voice, "What do you desire?" A man stepped from behind a tree.

We stood and stepped away from our altar.

"Why do you interrupt our prayers to Father? Who are you?" Adam demanded. His fists were clenched at his sides.

I recognized the intruder—Lucifer, he who beguiled me. I glanced up at Adam, who regarded me from the corner of his eye. He saw my recognition and the slight shake of my head.

"I am your god. What is your desire?" Lucifer demanded.

"We call upon Father. You are not our God," Adam said.

We turned on our heels and walked away, offended at the interruption. Lucifer raged at our backs.

"I am not finished with you," he yelled. "You will give me obeisance. I am your god."

"That creature is not our God," I fumed. "He tried to supplant our love and obedience to Father with his lies. Never again." As we walked in the direction of the valley, I found myself stomping in frustration.

Adam reached out and put his arm about me, "We will return later."

His words calmed me.

The sun had moved across the heavens and now set just above the distant mountains. This day was nearly gone. Dark clouds crowded the sky. We needed a place of protection for the night. We drank again from the trickling creek before searching for safety. Thunder rumbled near. Tall pines rose close, inviting us. We made our way toward them.

I felt a sizzle and heard thunder rock the earth around us as the heavens opened and a deluge poured on us. Adam grabbed my arm and helped me run to the shelter of dark, green pines, still clutching the contents of my folded over pocket in my robe.

Sheets of rain pelted the ground beyond the trees. We were grateful for the thick needles over us. They kept much of the moisture from soaking us. A few drops hit us when the wind blew a mist in our direction. We sat on a comfortable, thick mat of leaf and pine litter under the tree, watching as glowing flashes lit the firmament, followed by great crashes of thunder. A sulfur odor filled the air.

I opened the pocket and retrieved fruit and nuts from within. As we ate, the precipitation subsided and the sun set behind the mountain. Clouds reflected pink, purple, orange, and gold. We beheld no magnificent sights like this in Eden. Perhaps there would be other wondrous scenes of beauty to make up for being required to leave Eden. Adam's hand stretched out and found mine. I clasped his hand, turned to face him, and smiled. He leaned in and kissed me on the cheek.

"Looks like we are sleeping here," Adam said.

He pushed the thick needles together into a large pile and placed his cloak over it. I lay down and he joined me. I pulled my cloak over us and snuggled close to him. We listened to the song of the wind in the trees overhead.

As the vault darkened, the moon rose, big and round. The familiar brightness comforted us, until it soared out of sight above the trees.

~

Exploring this land became important to us. We needed to know where to find things to eat and safe places to hide from the weather. Trees, plants, and bushes blossomed with promise. Fruits, vegetables, nuts, and grains we discovered in those early days did not last long. It was eaten and gone. We could no longer find anything available to eat. The food we gathered as we explored had dried and blown away or rotted into the soil.

We walked past the fields where grains grew when we arrived. Tiny, new green growth grew at the base of old grains. Some lay dormant, while others began to bulge with hope, pushing into the soil. We observed them, hoping to learn how to grow.

We planted some of the tiny pepper seeds I saved earlier. The little greenery began to grow, and then wilted when the rains stopped falling. We had no way to bring water to them, and they dried up and blew away.

Above all, feeding ourselves became the center of our thoughts

At night, we often found ourselves in the rain in the mountains. The high forests filled with flat leaves, some wide, others narrow and small, did not protect us from the rain as the pines did in the first valley we entered. Some nights we sat and slept together under our cloaks, others we located a cave in the hillside where we waited out the storm. Once, we saw a strange mountain in the distance with smoke spewing from its summit.

One day as we returned to our original valley, thunder echoed across the ridges behind us. Lightning sizzled, causing the hair to stand up on my arms, followed immediately by thunder. We hurried, running around gray boulders and fallen timber. Deer and elk raced by us. Adam turned to see what chased them and grabbed me by the arm.

"Run!" he shouted.

As I ran, I glanced back to see the tall forest crackling with flames. Small animals raced past us. We raced the blaze until we reached a river. Adam leaped in, pulling me in with him. We watched the red, orange, and yellow blast race with the wind, blackening everything we just crossed. The unbearable heat, forced us to duck below the surface and fight our way across the river. On the other side, we regarded the inferno as it licked the water and sizzled into nothingness.

Many days later, we walked up the same mountain once more. Black charred bits of wood littered the ground where tall trees had stood. Others showed the blackness of fire that touched them, though they continued to lift their branches to the sun. Burnt animals, too slow to escape, lay blackened across the land. Adam used his walking stick to stir in the ashes. An ember glowed and jumped to life along it. He dragged his branch through the dirt, quenching the blaze. Among the black dust, new growth sprouted.

Not long after, as I squatted to relieve myself, blood flowed from within me. By the end of the day, I still bled. "I will die!" I cried. "I should not bleed like this. I have not been injured. This does not end."

Cramps, deep and intense, joined the flow. Adam made me a bed and soothed me as I moaned. He brought dry moss to soak up the mess.

On the second day, the cramps lessened. I fashioned a woven pocket and tied it about my waist. I filled it with moss to absorb the fluid. It was not comfortable, but I remembered Jehovah's warning that I would have pain and sorrow.

After five days of bleeding, it ended. I silently cheered and burned   the   woven   pocket.

~

Not long after then, Adam looked to me with sad eyes and a growling stomach.

"Is there anything to eat? My stomach hurts." His arms cradled it beneath clasped fists. His teeth held his lower lip.

"We ate the last of the grain we gathered at first. We have not identified anything else ripe enough for many days." Mine hurt, too. I made a suggestion I had avoided. "Do you remember the bear catching fish?"

I did not want to follow the bear's example, but we had no choice.

Adam's eyes lit up with hope. "I forgot about him."

"Can we catch them? Can we eat them?"

55

He thought about if for a long moment, rubbing across the ache in his body. "Yes. If the bear can eat swimming flesh, we can. I have not desired to try flesh, but the time has come."

He caught me by the hand, and we hurried to the stream. The silver, gold, and red of the swimming animals tantalized us. We removed our foot coverings and I braided my hair to keep it out of the way. We waded in and stared into the water. All the fish had fled.

Adam looked up at me. Bewildered surprise filled his face. I tried to hide my laugh, but he saw it and joined in. Our hunger soon quieted us and we stood still, waiting. The fish grew accustomed to us and swished out of their hiding places, swimming around our feet.

Adam bent low, watching them. He struck out to capture one, but it twitched its tail and darted away. I concentrated on one swimming around my feet. I reached for it and felt the softness of its belly, but it flashed away before I could clutch it. Over and over, I stretched to grasp one, and over and over, missed.

I stood with my hands on my knees laughing at the absurdity of our efforts, as Adam once again fell in. He stared at me with a frown. Frustration flitted through his eyes before he laughed, too.

I wanted to quit. The difficulty of the task frustrated me, but we needed sustenance. I returned to my struggle.

Eventually, Adam stood with a shout. He had a fish! He carried it to the shore and tossed it far up on the bank.

"How did you do that?" I asked my mouth agape.

"Slow and careful."

I followed his instructions, letting my hand dangle. The fish I tried to catch slipped away at the last moment, but I understood better. I let my hand float in the current. One moved toward my floating fingers. I wanted to grab it but knew it would twitch its tail and escape. I waited until it swam into my curled fingers. Slowly, I brought them together and snatched at its head. With a slippery trout in my hands, I straightened and cheered. I threw it on the bank.

Adam caught another in the time I caught mine. We had three big, fat trout, but we still were not sure if we could eat them.

Adam bashed their heads against a rock and sliced them open with a sharp stick. He scraped the insides out and dropped them beside the bushes. The heat of the sun increased the odor of the entrails.

"It stinks," I said. "How did you know to remove the smelly parts?"

He shrugged.

Cats slunk through the tall grass and pounced on the stinking innards, dragging them away. Adam silently gave me one, taking one for himself. We offered a prayer of gratitude to Father, and then took a bite. It did not taste sweet like fruit, but it was food.

As we ate, goats joined us, scarfing the skin, bones, and heads we discarded. We would not starve. We ate all three and caught more when we were hungry. We continued to explore other parts of the earth, always aware of finding food.

Adam uncovered a black rock which broke off into long sharp slivers. He took home a chunk of it for later use. He called the splinters knives and used them to cut items. Most importantly, it allowed us to consider sacrifices.

In our need to find a better way to tote the objects we encountered, I sat down one day until I taught myself to weave grass and leaves into round baskets for carrying things with us. As I worked, two small cats peeked from a bush close to me. I wished I had a bit of fish to entice them, but I did not, so I bent back to my weaving.

When I peered in their direction once more, the black cat had moved nearer. I spoke softly to it while I wove. As I reached out for more materials, my fingers brushed through its thick fur. It rumbled to my touch. Occasionally, I reached out to stroke her fur. She became my friend, Black Cat. She and her mate visited us when they felt like joining us.

Adam attempted to create a basket like mine, while I wove another. His had widely spaced openings at the bottom while the weaving became closer together near the top. We saw no use for it. It seemed to be a loss. We set it aside and wove more.

Over the next days, we managed to make baskets of all sizes, including some woven tightly enough to carry water. After then, we carried them with us in our explorations. We used large ones for carrying food and other interesting things we found. Small, watertight containers, wide at the bottom and narrow at the top to prevent spills, and with long braided handles were slung across our shoulders. We dipped them into streams and transported water. This made it possible for us to travel farther away from the streams.

Along with these, I was forced to make another pocket to hold dry moss to catch my bleeding. It did not frighten me this time, though it continued to be uncomfortable.

That night the moon rose, full and round.

"Now I know," I whispered.

"Know what?" Adam asked.

"The moon is full when I bleed. I understand when to expect it next."

We called it my moon time.

CHAPTER FIVE

Fire

Adam did not forget his obligation. He left me behind and went into the forest to find an animal that would agree to be offered as our sacrifice. I do not know how he did it, he never told me. I suspect he spoke to the animals and waited for one to step forward.

We trekked to the altar. Adam followed the required actions and killed the animal. He cut off the skin and a portion of the meat. These, he wrapped together, and knelt to pray.

We had no means to start a fire, yet. As we prayed, a flash of lightning struck the altar. It burned the remains of the carcass and cleansed it of all animal remnants. Father provided for us.

We cut the meat into thin strips and set them to dry. We tried to dry the skin as well, but it did not soften. It was not practical to use. The first ones dried hard and useless, to our regret. After each sacrifice, we experimented and practiced until we learned to scrape and roll the skins with ashes, which softened them, finally making them usable.

In our explorations, we discovered a danger we had not expected. The goats followed us wherever we went. The leader often leaped ahead, fell behind to check on slower members, and then bounced along beside us. He butted his head into our hands seeking attention. We named him Pasha.

We learned to trust their instincts. They disappeared moments before animals clashed across path in the midst of a mating battle or another fight. We followed them when they slipped into the bushes.

One day, the goats disappeared as we heard a snarling and crashing coming through the trees toward us. We had no time to hide. Adam dropped his basket and stepped in front of me, bringing up his walking stick. Three huge wolves broke from the brush, growling. Spittle dripped from their open maws onto dirty gray fur. Their stench almost overwhelmed me.

Adam spun his club, cracking the lead wolf on the head. I shivered as it fell with a whimper, unmoving. Adam could not rest. A second wolf surged toward him, snarling and growling. The third filthy animal ducked around Adam after me.

My heart hammered. I flung my basket toward it. I held my walking stick before of me with both hands. I stabbed at it, pushing it back. It growled and leaped at me again. I had no time to think. I spun the pole and hit it. My steadiness surprised me. My heart raced.

The wolf jumped back and shook its maw. It leaped at me once more. Its teeth scratched my arm. A scream of pain and rage tore from within me.

Clenching my jaws, I stabbed and whirled my rod again and again, keeping the sharp teeth away. My hands grew slippery with sweat and spittle. How much longer could I do this? I had no choice—fight or die.

The one attacking Adam must have been strong and wily, for it seemed to take forever until Adam turned to help me. His stick cracked the wolf attacking me across the back of its head. I heard a loud crack and it fell to the earth. I bent to rest with one end of my stick in the dirt, my hands grasping it tightly as I stared at the dead wolves. I allowed my body to quiver in shock and fear.

"Why did they attack us?" I gasped through heaving breaths.

Before Adam could respond, the Destroyer stepped from among the bushes. An odor of sulfur clung to his rich red and black clothing.

"You were fortunate, this time. Bow and worship me, or you will encounter others, more difficult to fight off."

"We are protected by Father." Adam lifted his head high. "You can try to strike us, but you will not win. We will never bow down and worship you."

"You think?" he sneered with a half laugh.

The Destroyer's face reddened

and his eyes narrowed. The cords on his neck stood out as he clenched and unclenched his cane. The green and black serpent along the length of gold writhed and hissed during the long moment he stared at us.

Adam faced him and squared his shoulders and raised an arm. "In the Name of Jehovah, be gone."

With a wolf-like growl, the Destroyer spun and pounded away. We watched him go, glad of Adam's Priesthood.

He had attempted to disrupt our prayers and activities earlier, although he had not attacked us in this way before. What next? Adam held me close while my shaking ebbed.

The pelts would be warm. Adam sat me down on a nearby log. He pulled out his knife and cut the pelts from them. Pasha and the goats returned, butting into my hands, and seeking attention. Adam rolled the skins together and tucked them in a basket. When we reached our home camp, we washed them several times and scraped away all the fat to remove the stink.

The full moon came and went without my bleeding. Relief filled me as I realized I did not need the moss pocket.

After many seven-days of near starvation, we were determined to save as much food as possible from our harvests to prevent our starvation. We did not know the time we would wait between harvests. We cut the ripened grains with long knives and, with great effort, winnowed them. This we put in large baskets with lids. We dried our portions of meat from the sacrifices, harvested fruits and vegetables during our travels, and dried and stored them for later use. We inspected each fruit, vegetable, and grain and watched for them to ripen.

Another day, I looked at Adam's loosely woven basket and thought about it. I lugged it with me as I walked toward the stream. What would the fish do if I set it in the water? I slipped it beneath the surface and waited.

They swam in! I jerked the container out of the water with five nice fat trout in it. We no longer needed to get wet to catch them. I dried those left from our meal.

Several evenings later, Adam sat striking a hard stone against his knife to sharpen it. As he often did when thinking, he caught his lower lip between his teeth.

I wove a basket nearby. The tapping paused when he stopped to check the sharpness or turn the blade. The sound soothed me, helping me concentrate on the creation of my pattern.

"Ouch!" Adam cried, surprising me from my reverie.

"What? Did you cut yourself?" I looked up ready to reach for moss to stop the blood.

"Hit my finger." He shook his hand. "The stone slipped." He returned to chipping his knife and I continued musing as I wove.

"Oh. No!"

I glanced over, wondering what his problem was now, and jumped to my feet. "Oh, no!"

I began to stomp on the spark which had leapt from the blackness of his knife into a nearby pile of dry leaves and twigs.

"Help me put it out!"

"No." He pulled me back from the small flame. "Let it burn."

"Let it burn?" My voice climbed two octaves as I tried to pull away from his grasp.

"Yes." He blocked me from the blaze.

"Did you not witness the scorched forest after the lightning strike on the mountain?" I cried, still struggling against him. "Do you not remember the blackened trees, the scorched animals."

"I do. But since then, I considered the effects of fire. It warms."

"It warms?" He may be right, but warmth was not enough reason to give in yet. "It incinerated most of a mountain."

"There is nothing to burn, here. The dirt will not light. We can stop it if it gets out of control."

"There is plenty to ignite here. Look."

"There is nothing by the fire except dirt. Dirt will not flare," he repeated.

"It will not burn the soil?" I quit struggling, beginning to listen to Adam.

"No. Remember?"

I remembered the unburned earth beneath the ash. He could be right.

He stooped to feed a small dry branch into the flame. "Keeping warm may be necessary."

My curiosity got the best of me. "Our robes will not provide enough warmth?" I squatted to watch his efforts. "Can we control it?" I searched his eyes; trusting the surety I found there.

"Fire does not char rocks, either. Help me surround it." He reached for a large one.

We encircled the fire and kept it burning. Neither the soil nor the rocks lit on fire, though they grew hot as we added bigger branches, building it ever higher within the circle. Hot weather warmed us. We stood back from the additional heat and let it flicker low. When the sun set and the daytime weather cooled, we drew closer, building it up again, allowing its heat to cover us.

I woke the next morning to find Adam stooped over the darkened embers, blowing gently.

"Why are you breathing on the ashes?" Sleep urged me back, but curiosity kept me awake.

"Wind stirred the lightning fires back to life. Do you remember?" He took another big breath. He blew twice more, and continued, "I decided to try to bring this one back to life."

"Any success?"

"Yes. It glows hot." He pushed small twigs atop the glowing embers. It soon blazed.

"You did it! But, why on a hot day?"

"I needed to be sure I could return the fire. Now I can burn my sacrifices."

Understanding dawned. "When will we need to sacrifice."

"Soon."

We sacrificed several days later. I worked to learn to cook meat and other foods. It was not easy but with trial and practice, fire changed the way we ate.

~

Now we had baskets to carry water we tried planting the pepper seeds one more time. They grew in the warmth of the sun, especially now we could be sure they were watered. I bent over the plants, urging the little peppers to grow, waiting to taste their sweet crunchiness, with a hint of succulent tartness.

We discovered we loved that first valley we visited after leaving Eden. Other valleys were beautiful. Others were wide and green. But only this original valley held an altar on a hill nearby. We found ourselves returning there, and at last, we decided to settle there. We called it Home Valley.

Days stretched ahead of us with nothing to harvest. With food enough to eat, we chose to leave the heat of the valley for the coolness of the hills. We put out the fire and gathered provisions for a journey.

We followed the river out of our valley, traveling in the course toward Eden, in the opposite direction than usual. Adam wanted a glimpse of past our garden home.

Animals and birds crossed our path along the way. Most were shy, staying within the depths of the forest as we passed. Great, gray mammoths marched across the valley in gigantic herds. Although they had little to fear from big cats or other predators, they kept their frisky young in the center of the herd. Other herds of grazing animals similarly protected their little ones from lions, wolves, and other beasts of prey.

Colorful flowers bloomed in carpets beneath tall green trees. Jeweled hummingbirds flitted among them, pausing occasionally to sip. Music of larger birds rang above us. Iridescent insects buzzed in lazy circles. Splashes sounded from the river, signaling fish feeding and other water animals sliding into it. We thrilled in the moment, basking in its beauty.

We moved away from the river and stepped onto an open plain. A herd of gazelles, dressed in shades of burly wood and white with a slash of dark along their sides, grazed on the tall growth of greenery. I saw movement near them and pointed. Adam motioned me to bend low. I squatted in the tall grass where we were able to espy the tawny fur of a lioness following behind the gazelles.

My heart beat frantically as she surged forward, bounding toward a young gazelle that strayed from the crowd. It saw her and startled into a run. My hands flew to my mouth, covering a cry as the lioness raced behind and leapt on its back. She sunk her teeth into its neck. The animal slowed. The weight of the lioness wore it down. The stench of fear and blood filled the air. At last, it fell to the ground. I shuddered at the violence, though I could not look elsewhere.

The lioness emitted a low growl and two tiny cubs stumbled out from a nearby bush. They joined her in gorging on what had been a live, beautiful gazelle, their maws covered with blood. Adam tensed with a new wariness. The color drained from his face, and he clenched his jaw. Gripping my elbow, he signaled for us to leave. On hands and knees, we crept away.

"I knew things would change," he mumbled. "But, I did not realize it would be like this." He grabbed my arm and held it tight until we were far from the lions and safe again.

After this, we were on constant alert for dangerous creatures.

The sun stood at the edge of the mountain, near setting, when we found the same grove of trees we slept in the first night out of Eden. Adam scouted around, checking to be certain the bobcat, or other unwelcoming creatures, no longer claimed the warm cave, before we crawled into the cavity beneath the fallen trunk.

We woke to the songs of birds. Once more, we hiked toward the garden, planning to explore beyond it. After traveling a long distance over rough earth, Adam paused and stared. The calm day was opposite to the day we left those months ago, lending an air of novelty to our pilgrimage.

"Where is it? We should have reached it by now." Frustration consumed Adam's voice.

"Did we travel the wrong way?" I looked about us, searching for anything familiar.

"No." He spoke sharper than usual, then softened his tone. "At least I do not think we did."

We turned and trekked in another angle. Three times we changed our line of travel without finding any suggestion of Eden. At last Adam stopped and dropped to his knees, his chin rested on his chest, his lip caught firmly between his teeth.

"It is gone," he whispered. "I cannot find it."

"Perhaps we searched in the wrong place. I do not recognize this area."

"No, we traveled in the right direction. Eden is gone." He sat on the ground with his head in his hands.

I stared around and then squatted beside him. I put my hand on his arm, hoping my touch would comfort him now as his touch had comforted me before. Eventually, he lifted his head and kissed me on the forehead.

"We could never go back. I knew we could not. I wanted one more glimpse. Father must have known and taken it."

Adam stood and helped me rise. He embraced me tightly, holding on longer than usual. Then we turned and marched resolutely back to Home Valley.

CHAPTER SIX

Sabbath

While I used the sinew saved from a recent sacrifice and sat stitching new foot coverings, one evening during the next full moon, Adam gouged another mark on his pointed walking stick.

"Why do you make those marks?" I asked.

"I am marking the number of full moons since leaving Eden."

I lifted an eyebrow.

"It has been six."

"Six full moons since we left Eden? That long?" I stared at the marks on the pole.

"We should call the time between the moons a month." He gave me a little grin.

I nodded in agreement. The name fit. I thought of the changes in the weather in those six months. The early cold, windy days had warmed to heat. Food continued to grow, others were already harvested and stored for later use. The peppers were finally big enough to pick. Those we did not eat were dried and put in baskets. Other grains, fruits, and vegetables were ripening. The weather and temperature changed each day.

Adam astonished me with another, unusual question. "Has it not passed your moon time?"

"It has. I am surprised you noticed." I leaned back to look at him.

"I did. And are you not growing here?" He touched my slightly thickening stomach.

"I am. I do not know why, but my nipples are tender, and I have trouble with an uneasy stomach." I had missed one moon time, now a second.

"You must be careful." He put his arms around me. The usual thrill skipped through me.

"I am always careful." I frowned. I paid more attention to my surroundings and fell infrequently, not liking the scrapes, scratches, and cuts resulting from falls.

"Be extra careful, please." He pushed me onto the live oak branch and sat next to me. Green leaves brushed against my cheek from the smaller branches above us.

"Because?"

"Something special is happening. I dreamed you carried a small child. This may be the beginning."

Dreams from recent nights pushed to the surface of my memories. "I, too, dreamed of a child. I will be careful."

Adam's embrace was tender. I leaned into his strong arms contemplating all the differences my body experienced. Mine had changed so much since we left Eden. As I became comfortable with it, more shifts loomed in my future.

Black Cat joined us, carrying a small black and white spotted kitten by the scruff of its neck. Her body grew over the time her little ones grew within her. She set the one she toted in my lap. Her mate followed, bearing another tiny kitten, this one mostly black with white around its nose. He dropped it into my lap beside the first. Black Cat and her mate jumped off my lap and scampered back into the brush. I stared after them, amazed.

They returned twice more, dropping kittens of varying mixtures of white and black into my lap. Six kittens lay there, huddled together. Their parents allowed us to stroke and pet them. This is what I dreamed of, not kittens, but babies in my lap. I glanced up to see Adam's tender gaze and knew he wanted the same thing.

Our subsequent prayers included gratitude to Jehovah for the hope of a child. We were thrilled to be able to obey the command to multiply.

We watched other female animals give birth. She-goats and ewes began to be trailed by baby goats and lambs. Cows had calves, baby birds hatched in their nests. Even female antelopes, wolves, and bears had young following behind them in the mountains and plains. Joy filled me as I watched them, waiting for my own little one to come.

A few days later, we hiked to the altar on the hill with a bull elk that agreed to be our sacrifice.

Adam completed the rite, careful to comply with each step as Jehovah had commanded. After he burned the body, we knelt in prayer. Adam shared our gratitude for the blessings of life, especially for the hope of a child. As he prayed, we heard the familiar voice of Jehovah.

"Adam, you have done well in your stewardship. You begin to comprehend the earth, laboring hard for your food. In this, I am happy."

Adam bowed his head.

"However," Jehovah continued, "you have not kept my Sabbath."

"Sabbath, Lord? What is your Sabbath? If I had known, I would have kept it." Adam bent low, the tendons in his neck bulging. "I covenanted to obey you. I do all you ask. I do not know of the Sabbath."

"The Sabbath is the seventh and holy day, the day we rested after creating this world. I will tell you of the creation, to help you understand."

We listened in awe as Jehovah spoke. A vision filled my mind with his words.

Jehovah told of the events of each of seven days. He and others gathered the elements to create the earth. They divided it from the water and the light from the dark. They planted every variety of plant and established every species of animal, fish, and bird on it. These were commanded to reproduce after their own sort and find joy. After each addition, they came back to report to Father.

One last time, Father called on Jehovah. Man was needed to tend the earth, to care for it as steward and lord. They placed Adam here and brought me to keep him company.

"On the seventh day, we rested," Jehovah ended the story.

The vision dissipated and my mind returned to the present. Sounds of birds and animals again filtered into my ears. A gentle breeze brushed through my hair. Once more, the fragrance of flowers reached me.

"This is our Sabbath, which you must observe. You must rest, as we rest, doing no work on your seventh day. Tomorrow is your Sabbath. Each seventh day after will be your Sabbath."

As Jehovah ended his account, a tingling filled me, my hand lay on my heart, and I closed my eyes to retain the memory of the vision. I had not known of this. I never wanted to forget this symbol of His amazing love for us. I glanced at Adam who also stood in silent respect.

"We will obey," Adam said. "This remarkable world is wondrous. You have given us all we need. We will gladly observe the Sabbath, as we rest and worship you."

"Excellent," Jehovah replied. "More light and knowledge will be given as you are ready."

He withdrew. We were alone once again.

We prepared for the sacred day, bathing and brushing our clothing and gathering food for the sacred meal. Our first Sabbath was a sweet, special day. We knelt in prayer and spent the day discussing memories of Eden and everything we learned in our time on this earth.

I grieved as I recalled my encounter with Lucifer's slave, the serpent. As a memory of our blessings permeated through me, I said, "It is good we were ejected. Because we were, we gained joy and knowledge."

Adam took my hand in his, softly stroking its back. "You are right, Eve. Our purpose is to learn and to love."

"We now obey the first commandment." The small tremor in my voice betrayed my feelings. "We multiply to replenish the earth. Animals multiply, even Black Cat has kittens. The plants multiply, little seedlings grow to be like the original. I, too, carry a child."

I stared into his loving, bright blue eyes. He embraced me and we fell to our knees to thank Jehovah.

~

About a month later, another day arrived with no crops to harvest or prepare for future use. We savored these rare times, glad of the opportunity to escape the heat of Home Valley. We took our baskets and hiked in a route we had not yet traveled to explore once more. We hoped to find different foods to supplement our diet.

We discovered a tree with tart, green apples, some ripe enough to eat. We made sure we could identify it again, stuffing a basket with them, and ate one each. Adam's sharp eyes found carrots growing in a clump. Here, too, we located identifying landmarks, then dug into the ground surrounding them with our pointed walking sticks before bending to tug them from the ground.

We heard a strange thundering, but when we looked to the sky, no clouds appeared. The noise did not come from impending rain or lightning. Adam stood and searched for the source of the sound. He saw nothing, so he stooped to pull the carrots. We pulled all of them in that patch, filling part of a second basket, and moved on up the hill. Peppers caught my eye. I plucked two. I planned to eat them as we walked.

A flock of birds flew overhead, flying one direction, turning as one, and flying toward another objective. They shifted again to fly past our heads and out of sight. The goats dropped to the ground beside us.

"What was that all about?" I asked.

"I have no idea." Adam shook his head. "Unusual for them."

"Strange. And multiple varieties together."

At this time of day, most birds flew or hopped from branch to ground to branch, seeking tidbits of tasty morsels. I had never seen they fly in a mixed flock.

"Should we worry?" I turned in a circle, searching for the cause of their disturbing flight. I saw no reason. The goats stood and shook their long hair.

I handed Adam a pepper, wiped mine on the hem of my cloak and took a bite. As always, amazement coursed through me when it quenched my thirst. Adam and I continued onward. We still had one empty basket.

Adam pointed to a patch of green plants. "That plant hides something good to eat."

He gazed about and located a distinctive stand of rocks standing up in the soil as a landmark and dug into the earth around the plants. He gently tugged. The plant broke away, with yams clinging to its roots. We dug around, searching for more. We had half-filled the second container when we heard a noise from the same course the birds originally flew. We glanced up in time to see a herd of antelope break through the trees.

"Down!" Adam cried.

I crouched as close to the ground as my growing body allowed and threw my arms on top of my head. Antelope raced toward us and leapt above us. I felt them brush past me. Hundreds of them jumped over us and struck the ground near us. My heart pounded as loud as their pounding hooves.

At last, there were no more. I peered at Adam.

"Is it safe?"

Adam uncurled and removed the arms protecting his head, freeing his lips from his teeth. "I think it is."

I cautiously pulled my hands away from my head.

We gazed into the trees, making sure no other animals were running toward us. Adam stood and turned a complete circle. "They are gone. So are the goats. Are you safe?"

I lifted my head and leaned backward on my heels, touching my spine and neck with probing fingers to check for injuries. The thundering herd missed me.

"I am unhurt. You?"

Adam inspected himself. He found only a small scratch on his left hand.

We had gathered most of the yams. There were others near, suggesting the possibility of overflowing the container. I started to dig around another bush.

"No" Adam set his hand on my shoulder. "Not yet. I need to know what is causing such strange behavior in the creatures. Wait for me."

I stared in the direction the birds disappeared, then toward at the wood. "No, I will go with you." I hefted up my baskets.

Adam frowned at our hoard, and then shrugged. "Leave them. We can get them when we return. Our hands must be free."

I set mine on the ground, took up my walking stick, and joined Adam in the march into the trees. Smaller animals—rabbits, mice, squirrels, even porcupines—raced from the depths, most evading us, but some ran across our feet. Snakes slithered by us, turning and twisting away from us.

With a shudder, I glanced at Adam. "Are you sure this is the right thing to do? The beasts choose to flee."

"We need only go to the other side of the wood." He squared his shoulders, clasped my hand, and tromped past the rushing tide of escaping animals.

The stand of trees was small. We soon approached the edge of a beautiful valley covered with flowers and greenery. We stared in amazement. What caused the frightened creatures to rush away?

An unusually symmetrical mountain stood in the middle. Smoke circled its top, pouring from the center. Flames reflected off the dark clouds of smoke. The breeze carried the scent of sulfur, vaguely like the Destroyer, to us. We stared at the mountain in bewilderment.

The ground shuddered. Adam reached out to steady me, holding onto my arm. It trembled under our feet once more.

"Not good," Adam's eyes darted about us.

Another tremor rattled us. We made a quick study of the area. Cracks ran from the base of the mountain, opening wider as they rushed toward us.

"No wonder they run." I stared at the smoking, burning mountain and the cracking earth.

"They run with reason," Adam answered. "Run!"

I spun around and raced into the trees. The shaking knocked me from my feet. Adam stretched down and helped me up.

"Hurry, Eve! We must get away from here. Fast!"

With his hand steadying me, we pelted through the forest. Each step brought us closer to safety. We broke free of the woods and raced on. Adam gathered our baskets up in one hand without breaking stride.

We careened through the hills. The ground swayed as we ran. We both fell to our knees, and bounced up to our feet, running. We ran almost to our home before we slowed, panting from exertion. We sat on the ground to rest.

One small tremor reached us, momentarily startling us up. Adam searched for cracks. When he saw none, we dropped back to rest. We did not sit long. Our horror of a quaking surface pushed us onward towards Home Valley. The goats joined us as we traveled down the hill.

Though we felt no more movement, we were edgy, fearing the tremors and cracks would reach us. What caused a mountain to smoke and burn? Why did the earth crack open? Dread kept me home for many days. Adam worried that my exertions may have hurt the baby. We harvested and dried the foods when they ripened.

CHAPTER SEVEN

Building

In the ninth month after Eden, my body began to bulge and grow hard like the she-goats and ewe sheep. I sat on the live oak branch, thinking. Earlier, small tickles crossed my stomach, but then I felt a solid thump from the inside. Black Cat's stomach writhed when kittens were about to be born. She-goats bounced with the movement of unborn kids. Now, I felt the movement of my own babe. I waited in awe for the thump to return.

"Adam! Adam!" I called when it did.

He rushed to my side. "You have a strange look. Is all well with you and the child?"

"It is. Here, feel this." I placed his palm on the roundness of my stomach. It thumped me once more, under his hand.

He jerked it back and stared at me. I laughed at his astonishment. He returned his hand, waiting for further movement.

He caught his teeth on his lips and his eyes lost focus. After a long moment, the little one moved, touching Adam.

Adam threw his arms around me. Excitement suffused him.

"It is true," he cried. "We will have a child. We multiply."

"You thought I grow like the she-goats for no reason?" I cried in mock annoyance.

He swallowed once and cleared his throat. The tips of his ears flushed through the brown caused by the sun. He walked to a nearby bush and plucked a beautiful pink rose. He stripped the leaves and thorns from it, and then tucked it behind my ear, stroking my hair.

"We require a shelter — a place to protect us from storms and winds — for the child, ourselves, and our food."

"Shelter? Will we need it?"

"Do you remember the winds and fallen trees?"

"I do." Who could forget the devastation? "Will it get that bad again?" I saw the answer in Adam's face. No question, it would be necessary. "Then we must create a shelter. Safeguard our food? From the weather ... and animals? How nice to stop attempting to stop goats from striving to eat it. What material can we use?" I looked about us.

"Not grass. Animals eat it. It burns and rots. Perhaps wood will work. It works for the beavers." I followed his eyes to the pond filling a part of the valley behind a beaver dam.

"Trees burn."

"We can make a snug home of them, but we will have to do something to keep our fire from burning them."

"How will we prevent flames from burning it?" I adjusted my seat on the branch, seeking greater comfort.

"I do not know, yet. We will think of a way. With Jehovah's support, we can do this."

"How will you hold it together?"

"Vines. I tie better knots than I did in Eden and they shrink as they dry. They will support it." His teeth brushed his lower lip and his eyes glazed as he thought about it.

I lay my head on his chest. "Where will we get the trees? Would you cut them?"

"No! I will collect trees felled in the storms. There are many in the hills, I saw them the last time we sacrificed. Your thickening stomach suggests a demand to build it soon."

The heat of the day began to cool at night. We did not know when the bad weather would come, but we could tell changes were coming. Nothing required harvesting or preserving, so we journeyed into the hills the next morning.

Trees of every size lay in heaps, where they fell in past tempests. Adam chose tall, white ash with trunks a bit wider than the stretch of his hands. Using an adz, a square, sharpened piece of his sharp stone attached to a short branch for a handle, he chopped the larger branches off and bundled them for firewood. He rolled ten trees close to each other and connected them in a raft with braided hemp. He connected a double length of the plaited plant to drag the raft down the mountain.

Adam picked up his end and spread his feet wide. His muscles bulged and sweat poured into his eyes. The imprint of his teeth showed on the outside of his lip. The wood did not budge — too heavy for Adam to drag.

I braided my hair and tied it with a blade of grass. "I can assist,"

"No. I would rather you did not. This weighs too much for both of us. I want the child to be safe." He set his jaw.

I put my hands on the swell of my hips. "I can help. I am strong."

"Yes. You are, but I prefer you do not. I will remove enough to lighten the load so I can pull it by myself."

He untied the length of hemp for pulling and squatted beside the raft to untie the knots. I knelt on it, tugging the ones on my end loose.

Adam sighed. "However, ... you are correct."

I sensed he gave in to easily and raised my eyebrows in question.

"I need you to choose a path and make a way down the hill for me."

Adam could be stubborn.

He took away three and retied the knots. Once again his muscles bulged with the stress. He returned to the raft with a growl and untied the logs. Two more were taken off, and the weight continued to be too great for him to drag alone.

"I cannot move these like this." He sat to rest. "Perhaps ..."

I tugged a knot free and waited for him to decide to allow my assistance. Adam marched along the side of the trees, counting as he scratched his chin. I pulled another knot apart and watched him. At the end, he bent his knees and grasped it. He boosted it from the ground to well up his leg. With a grimace, he dropped it.

"Too heavy," he grumbled.

"If I lift the other end?" I suggested.

"No. I told you, I desire to protect you."

Adam rolled his eyes upward and measured several paces along the length. "Bring me my adz."

I retrieved it and carried it to him. He notched the tree beside him, and then chopped at it until he hacked it in two. Adam bent and hoisted it to his knees, then nodded.

He stepped to the next one and divided it, as well. Each was cut in half. Where we had ten long trees, we now had twenty shorter logs.

Adam checked to be sure he had the strength to raise the combined weight as he added them. He was able to lug five, but not six. To these, we attached the braided cord in preparation to transport them home.

We managed to haul them from the hill, taking much longer than expected. The nubs of branch ends caught on rocks, bushes, and other trees. I aided as I lifted them across and around the hazards and helped direct our path down the difficult trail. Their weight forced us to stop and rest often, particularly on the flat places.

"We will never have what is required at this rate. It took us more than half a day to gather five logs. We need lots more." Adam sighed and collapsed onto them heavily, panting.

"What else can we do?" I sat beside him.

"I do not know. We must get as many as we can today, while we can. At least they are cut into lengths for hauling. With other things to do, we cannot put it off." We regained our breath, ate a little, and were off again.

Over the days Adam towed cut pieces of ash into the valley, with my usual assistance, boosting a tip and directing him. We dropped them close to where we planned to build, not far from a stream and nestled in a grove of trees. We hoped they would defend our new shelter from the forceful winds. We had not gathered nearly enough wood for our shelter, our house. Still, Adam decided to begin to assemble it, to find out how many we needed, or so he insisted.

I helped Adam drag them to the location he marked off. We set them in a six-sided shape, similar to the beaver's home. He cut notches on the ends of the wood to prevent their rolling apart. More logs were placed on top, fitting as tight together as possible.

"Adam, this is wonderful," I stooped to hoist another tree, "but, how will we get in when it is finished?"

"Get in?" He gazed at the building, rubbing his chin. Then he laughed. "Oh! A way in. I guess it may of use."

Such disappointment! Four rows sat on top of each other and most of them had to be removed.

"Now what?" I asked with a deep sigh.

"We will leave an opening near one corner. When the walls are taller, we can use longer pieces to fill the length above." He grimaced as he leaned to take off another tree. I hoped we could lug those longer trees.

"When did you come up with this idea?" I stretched up to help.

"When we took off the last one."

I stifled a giggle. We set it aside and reached for the final one.

"Great plan." I arched my back to rest it.

When we arrived at the bottom level, we reset the base and began reshaping the walls, leaving a space large enough for both of us to walk through side-by-side. Once again, we stacked the logs, building as high as just beyond Adam's waist, and then we ran out of trees.

A tour of the fields revealed late vegetables and beans almost ready to harvest. We hoped to retrieve enough wood and complete the house before time to harvest these last crops. Hard work lay ahead.

That evening as we lay close, enjoying at the stars, Adam leaned over and placed his palm on my growing body.

A jumping bounced his hand.

"Did you feel it?" he asked, wonder filled his voice.

"Yes. Do you think we will ever grow tired of feeling the little one move?"

"I do not see how," he said. "I am right to shield you. We do not understand the dangers of carrying a child. You must be careful."

Dangers? I had not thought there might be a danger for the baby. Of course, Adam would. He had a way of knowing. I stared up, thinking of all we were required do. How was I to be careful and assist in preparation for the coming storms?

"But I must. There is so much to do." I turned to Adam and touched a different finger as I enumerated our challenges. "Food must be harvested and prepared for storage. We need trees from the hills, and our home must be completed."

"I know. There is much to do. I wonder if we can get help." His fingers traced the bulge of my stomach.

"Help? From where? We are the only ones here," I squeaked. "Where will we get help? It must be me."

"No. I do not want you or the little one harmed. I prefer you do not try to drag all those heavy logs," he insisted.

"I can, as I always do —"

"I do not desire for you or the babe to be hurt. We are not alone." He held up his hands to still my arguments. "The goats may assist us. They are with us all the time."

"Goats?" My protests were forgotten. "Are they strong enough? Will they"

"If we tie two together to support each other, they can," he nodded. "We can devise a way for them."

"Ask them in the morning," I said with a yawn.

~

The next morning, four he-goats came when Adam called. He ran his hands through their long hair, pulled out burrs, and patted their heads.

"Hello Pasha. Hello Spot and George. Hello Brownie." He greeted them by name. "We need your assistance, little friends."

They butted their heads into his hand and bleated a friendly greeting.

"We are gathering logs for a home. You followed us to the hills and watched our struggle," he continued. "Will you assist us?"

More head butting and bleating.

"You will? If we work together, two of you in a team can drag one raft, while I tote another. With your support, we can collect enough for our house."

"I am braiding harnesses to help you pull it," I held one up. "They are almost ready."

"Your loads will be no heavier than mine," Adam promised. "We will be grateful for your service."

When we reached the hill where the trees were, Adam cut, collected, and tied three rafts, smaller around than those we toted earlier, making lighter rafts. He was careful to give the goats the same amount he hauled himself. I connected them forming teams. Adam joined a long braided rope from the harness to the wood, They were eager to start.

Over the next days we lugged trees down the hill. The path became smoother and easier to traverse. Adam and I led the way; the goats accompanied us, pulling their burdens with no trouble. We were soon in the valley, untying the logs. We rested a short time and ate. We returned for another load, followed by the cheerful goats.

When we finished, I bent to untie their harnesses and glanced into the trees. "The Destroyer watches, yet again," I whispered.

"He will get nothing from us." Adam shrugged.

His gold cane flashed as Lucifer stepped forward.

"What are you doing with my trees?"

"They are ours, given to us as part of our stewardship. You have no say." Adam's voice hardened.

"I am God of this world. They are mine. You may not use them." He stabbed his cane into the ground.

Adam crossed his arms. "How do you plan to stop us?"

Clouds suddenly gathered overhead, and lightning flared around us. I huddled beneath Adam's cloak, watching.

Adam raised his hands and called, "Be still."

The storm blew away as quickly as it formed.

"You have no control over us or this land." Adam continued to raise his hands. "Be gone."

The Destroyer punched his cane in the dirt, swiveled on his heels, and stomped away. I glanced around, expecting the goats to be missing. Instead, they stood waiting for their harnesses to be removed.

They assisted us as we accumulated enough logs for the rest of our home in only three days. We thanked them each time we took off their harnesses. They bleated and butted us gently, as if to tell us, 'we are here if you need us,' and leapt to join the others.

I helped drag them to the house, pushing them up for Adam to shove into place, grateful they were lighter and easier to move. My stomach protruded, causing problems.

Adam worked to settle everything, filling between the roof trees with smaller branches, tying all the branches and trees tight to prevent them blowing away.

We wanted our home to keep us and our child safe from the storm, especially if the wind-blown trees were any indication of the force of the coming tempest. To fill the area between the logs, we searched for sticky mud. We sampled mud until we found it nearby. We managed to fill the open spaces along one side that afternoon.

After harvesting corn the next day, we trudged to the house to put more mud along the walls.

"What happened?" I yelped.

"No idea," Adam sighed.

Dry mud had fallen. I witnessed a rare frown.

"Why? How did this happen? We do not have time to work this hard for nothing!" I rubbed dried mud off while Adam examined other places, his lip held securely between his teeth.

"Look. Some did not fall out here." He pointed to one area in the middle.

I studied the spot. "What is different about this?"

"I am not sure."

We analyzed the mud.

"Do you see?" He directed my attention to a dark portion still clinging to the logs.

I inspected it. This section contained grass, sticks, and bits of chipped wood.

"Is that what kept it together and on the wall?" I asked.

"It may be. We must try an experiment, make sure we understand. We will get small loads of mud — mix grass, wood chips, and sticks into one and put it here." He indicated to one short section. "And daub clean, mud here." He indicated another location at the opposite end of the wall. "We need to know which one works best, if either one works."

We trekked back to the stream, dug a chunk of light brown, sticky mud from the bank and dropped it into two baskets. Adam lugged them to the house where he mixed wood chips, twigs, and grass into one basket. Meanwhile, I slathered the plain mud on the trees on the end he indicated. He covered the spaces of the other end of the wall with his mixture.

"Bath and food," Adam finished slathering his on the logs on his experimental site. "We can decide if this stays put tomorrow."

Arm in arm we walked to the bend in the stream. Exhausted by the harvesting and experimentation, the quiet, warm pool invited us. I undressed and waded out to sit and rest. We sat in silence, relaxing and pondering. A melody permeated through my mind, then words slipped in. I hummed the tune and sang the words.

"You sound happy." Adam looked up and smiled. "What noise do you make?"

"I am happy. I am singing a song placed in my mind. Do you like it?"

"It is nice. Can you remember it?"

"I can now, but I should write it down so I can remember it later." I stopped humming. How did I know about writing? It must have come from my past.

"I remember writing before — and I … almost … remember reading," Adam paddled close to me.

I thought back and discovered lost memories. "Yes, I did write —and read."

"What can we use to write with?" He rubbed his chin.

I looked at the things around us. Nothing seemed to meet our needs. I shook my head.

I hummed the melody, then sang the words to my song. Adam joined in, following my lead in his lower voice, creating a beautiful harmony.

We returned to our camp in deep contemplation. I hummed my tune as I considered a way to write. One of us would think of an answer, I was certain.

Later in the evening, as we settled in to sleep, I laughed. Our baby reminded me he of his presence, poking and bouncing within me. Adam placed his big hand over the growing child.

"He will be strong and intelligent, like you." A smile filled his voice.

"Um-hmm. And tall and brave, like you." Laying in the safety and comfort of his arms warmed my soul. "Will this little one be a man, like you? It could be a woman, like me."

"It will be a man. I have seen him in my dreams." He chuckled as the babe moved beneath his hand.

CHAPTER EIGHT

Challenges

We completed our next sacrifice and knelt beside the altar to acknowledge everything given to us by Jehovah, including the little one. In my mind, I, too, added gratitude for Adam's Priesthood. The babe joined in, kicking. Adam prayed about writing, asking for confirmation that we should, and, if it was necessary, for help in finding the correct materials.

"You have not spent enough time considering and experimenting." Jehovah's gentle voice swelled within us. "Ponder this challenge, try the unexpected. Keep trying, keep pursuing the solution. An answer will come."

"Thank you, Jehovah. I will." Adam bowed his head.

I felt a thrill as I listened to his hallowed voice.

"Your desire to write is good. Keep a Book of Remembrance. Record the important events of your life. Retain a list of the sacred commandments and instructions you receive.

Address your impressions from the spirit. You will know what is right to write."

"I will." Adam nodded.

We were alone again. I looked at Adam in wonder.

"I heard Him once more," I whispered. "Does this mean Jehovah has forgiven me?"

"I think so," Adam turned and smiled. "How wonderful to hear Him speak to us."

I saw my emotion echoed in Adam's smile. We no longer walked and talked with Jehovah. Even Adam seldom heard His voice. Joy filled me along with His love.

"Do not worry that you ate the fruit, Eve. This earth is beautiful." Adam caressed my face and dropped his hand to my stomach. "And now we are obedient to the first command —"

"— to multiply and replenish the earth. Yes. It is good to be on this earth. I feel his forgiveness, here," I set my hand in the center of my chest, "in my heart."

"Yes. We are forgiven. And we have another commandment."

I let my hand fall to settle on his hand.

As we trekked down the hill with the hide wrapped around our chunk of meat, we shared our joy at being forgiven and our concern about discovering materials for writing.

Adam ran a hand through his dark brown hair, ruffling it like a bird in the wind. "Do not worry. There is an answer. We will uncover it."

"But, how?" I hitched my hip onto the low hanging branch of the live oak. Adam sat beside me, reaching for my hand.

"I do not know, but we will do it. Jehovah knows we can, or He would not expect it of us."

"Any ideas yet?" I focused on his penetrating blue eyes. He returned my gaze. "I have contemplated this since your song graced my soul. We see marks on trees from animals and our knives for many months, but trees fall or burn. They will not work." He bit his lower lip and spit it out again.

Many possibilities suggested themselves to us—rocks, mud, and woven grass mats. Upon further consideration, their challenges made them unusable.

"There is a solution," Adam said at last. "We will encounter an object on which to write our words."

"And a way to place them there? It is a puzzle." I pulled my hair back from my face, separating it for a braid.

Adam took it from my hands and plaited it, "Jehovah instructed us to study the challenge." His voice warmed with the name. "We can solve it. What about berries or fruit juice as an ink?"

"Ink?"

"Yes, ink, a liquid."

I brushed the front of my robe, attempting to brush away the stains left from the mulberries I ate a few Sabbaths ago. "Like mulberry juice? I still have stains from the early mulberries."

"That may work." Adam tied a length of grass around the end of my braid. "We can try it tomorrow. But how do we use it? There must be a carrier, a tool."

"An object to dip in the juice, or to put it in." I saw the need. "Surely we can find one."

Adam picked a dandelion and inserted it into my hair. "A resolution to all these problems can be created."

I thought of using the hollow dandelion stem to write with and discarded the idea. They flopped over not many moments after picking and dried soon after. Perhaps a similar plant.

I pulled our dinner from the fire with a long stick.

"We could use a better object to put the food on. Leaves work, for now, though they are flimsy and do not hold much." I shrugged a shoulder.

Adam flashed a quick smile. He sauntered to the pile of trees and found a thick piece of bark. He split it in two and brought it to me.

"Here are dishes."

"Dishes, huh? Wash them, please. I do not want to eat dirt." While he cleaned them, I withdrew the last of the meal. He handed them to me and I placed the roasted meat onto a dish and sliced it. Breadfruit and two apples followed, divided between the plates.

"See. These do not flop and spill, as leaves do," Adam said as I handed his to him.

"No lost food with these," I laughed. "Improved serving tools would be nice. Can you create them?"

He took a bite. "Yum. Yes, I should be able to devise something better than a stick."

Later the same afternoon, we strolled to the house to check on our experiment. The plain mud had fallen in chunks. Adam touched the hole in the scraps of dusty remnants clinging to the log.

"This is disappointing," he sighed. "I hoped it would stay."

We walked to the section where the grass and twig filled muck had been slathered.

"Look, Adam!" I cried in delight. "This did not fall as it dried. Perhaps this problem is solved."

Adam inspected the wall closely. "It is sticking. We will want to complete this soon. We can apply it to all the cracks to keep the wind out of our home. The sun sets earlier each day and the nights are cooler. It is important we occupy our completed home before the storms arrive — and before the small one arrives." He turned toward me. "Any idea when?"

"None. The child continues to grow." My hand covered my bulging stomach. "When I compare the time it takes for cats to have kittens with the other animals to carry their young, I believe our wait continues. I am stretched larger than the cat. I am almost as big as a she-goat."

"But much prettier. We can move ourselves, food, and our baskets of supplies inside when the mud is on the walls. It should not take long." He contemplated the space, eyes out of focus.

I touched his arm and he jumped.

"Tomorrow will be early enough. Come with me to locate wood to create those spoons you mentioned." I led him toward the log pile.

"Spoons?" he asked.

"Yes, spoons." I smiled and caught hold of his hand. "I decided to call them spoons."

"Sounds right to me. There is much to do. I should have time to make your spoons in the evenings. We still need to find a means to compile our Book of Remembrance."

He hunted through the pile of wood until he located a long slender branch with no knots. He found chunks of wood to use for other tools he planned, as well. These we set inside the house where they would be safe and easy to recover.

Darkness enclosed us as we returned to our little sheltered camp. The small fire within the stones welcomed us. We knelt to pray and lay in our bed of grass. Black Cat and her mate leaped up and curled in a furry ball near our feet. The goats and sheep settled around us. All was peaceful.

"Look!" Adam whispered. "A streaking star."

I squinted into the blackness and observed a light, like a star, streak across the sky.

~

The next morning did not include slopping mud onto the walls of our home. Adam took an early stroll through the trees, searching for something to add to our breakfast. He returned with a container full of red and gold fuzzy peaches, some almost too ripe to eat.

"The trees are loaded. See how soft they are. If we do not pick and dry them now, we will lose them." He set the basket beside me.

"All are ripe?" I chose a round peach and bit into it. Sticky juice dripped off my chin. "Yum. These taste sweet. We cannot lose them."

"We must harvest and store them today or we will." Adam wrinkled his nose and grimaced. "I planned to work on the walls. Maybe later."

The peaches took all day, late into the night, and the next two days to harvest and dry them. No mudding in the late afternoons. We were exhausted. After the peaches, beans, pears, apples, and other crops ripened, requiring our consideration.

We spent the next days harvesting beans and food. We packed everything in storage baskets and set them inside the house.

"Our work is never done. By the sweat of our brow," I said wiping sweat from my forehead, remembering the commandment to work.

"By the sweat of our brow," Adam agreed.

As we turned to retrieve more, a she-goat with a young kid crossed our path.

"Look how sweet they are together." I bent and rubbed her head. The kid bleated and bumped into me, begging for attention.

"Like you will be with ours." Adam stooped to pat the kid's back.

"When he comes," I stood with a sigh and hiked toward the full baskets waiting to be set within our unfinished home. "I long for him to be here with us, where I can hold him in my arms, see his little face, and watch him grow. But I worry. Will I be able to care for him? Will I learn what to do? I do not remember caring for a child."

"You will know what to do," Adam encouraged. "Jehovah will allow the memory to fill you if it is necessary."

"Are you certain? This is all so new and there is no one to teach me."

"I will help you. We will manage."

I trusted his certainty.

We passed beneath the wide mulberry trees.

"Will mulberry juice work for ink? And reeds to carry it?" I glanced at the reeds in the pool.

"I hope so. Jehovah will be patient for a while, but we need to find the answers to writing." Adam slipped his arm around my waist. "We can try today. We must finish our home tomorrow." He sighed.

After lugging the last of the baskets of food to the house, we gathered the red fruit and bright green reeds while the sun shone.

"Will a basket hold the juice?" Adam asked.

"A small watertight one may. It is worth a try."

I found a tiny one, dropped a few red berries in it, and smashed them with a twig to protect my hands from staining. The dark red liquid poured from the berries, but how to get it into the reed?

Adam took the basket and tried to pour the juice directly into the reed. It spilled all over his hand.

I plucked a leaf from a nearby bush and folded it, not aware of my actions, as I watched him.

"Perhaps," Adam said, "if we pour it into a leaf like the one you are folding, I can pour it into a reed."

I looked up in surprise. "This leaf? Oh. Yes, it may work." The mulberry juice poured through the pale leaf and across the top of the reed, spilling onto and staining our hands. I narrowed the opening and tried again. It worked better, but it still splattered. I reduced it one more time, leaving an opening just large enough for the liquid to flow and tried a last time. At last it filled. I passed it to Adam.

He cut a wide angle at the other end of the reed and drew it across the basket of juice. The ink rushed out, smearing and blurring the line. It would not work like this. Pasha pushed his nose in to see, but Adam ignored him, focusing on the mark he made, his lip caught between his teeth.

"Too much, and it needs to be less … less … smeary, less … wet," he sighed.

I stared around the clearing where we sat searching for a solution, wondering what would make the ink smear less. "Will dirt work?"

Adam took a deep breath and let it out. "We can try."

He prepared another reed while I dripped juice into a folded leaf and sprinkled fine dust into it.

"Enough?"

Adam stirred it with a twig and poured the mixture into the reed, spilling less. He cut a steeper, narrower angle in the end, making a smaller opening.

"I hope this works," he said.

Once more he made a mark on the basket.

"This may work. Still messy, but it does not smear as much. I will know better when it dries." He put the reeds in the basket and carried it to the house, out of reach of the goats. "Until then, I believe I will work on a bowl for you."

He retrieved a chunk of light pine and his container of sharp tools. He chose a large broad tool and a smaller, thin one. Although the sun moved toward setting, the light shone onto Adam's lap and the block. We sat near the low fire and he shaped the outside to look much like the ripe peaches. Bits of pine flew into the fire, causing sparks of blue flames to flare.

I observed him chip for a time with interest, and then reaching for a large basket of weaving. I had soaked and pounded dark green palm fronds until they were soft, soaked and pounded them three more times. The color washed away and the light-colored remnants waited, soft, pliant, and ready, I planned to make a mat to cover us at night.

Adam finished forming the outside and started to shape the inside of the bowl. The sun dropped near the tops of the trees. Adam added a length of wood to build up the fire to brighten our area, then picked up his small tool and the bowl. He moved slowly, controlling the tool. Fascinated by his careful efforts, I watched again a short time, before returning to my weaving. We worked in silence. I loved the sound of Adam's chipping.

A loud crack startled me.

"No!" he cried.

I leaped to my feet, my heart racing. Adam held up the two halves of the bowl. "What happened?"

"Too heavy on the chipper, too close to the edge, I suppose." He shook his head. "Back to the log pile."

He stood and brushed the broken bowl and chips into the fire. It flared white hot before settling to red and orange flames.

"I suspect pine is too soft for me. I will find cherry or mahogany. We brought some of those woods with us the last time we harvested wood." He kicked at the shavings under his feet.

I tucked an end into the mat. "Choose three pieces of wood. We need bowls for us and a tiny one for ink."

"I am not ready to try a small bowl." He extended his hand toward me. "Come with me. We can check on the house."

His palpable frustration encouraged me to set my weaving aside and join him. I understood. Our work never ended. I often became frustrated because of my awkwardness, my stomach protruded into everything.

Adam kicked at rocks as we walked to the woodpile together. I sat on a stump to keep Adam company while he searched.

"Here come the cats." Adam smiled.

They jumped into my lap. Black Cat stretched out her paws and clawed at my robe a few times, then curled up and went to sleep. I let my hand drift across her warm stomach.

CHAPTER NINE

Injured

The sun set near to the mountain when Adam climbed onto the log pile. Dim light showed him standing on a large springy limb hanging above the others. He bounced a bit and pushed branches aside. One hand held to the overhanging limb for support.

The thick limb on which he stood bounced as he stretched out for a chunk of dark red mahogany. He stretched farther and it bumped up and down. A loud crack echoed through the valley and Adam disappeared. I scurried to him as fast as I could. I drug broken branches away until I found him, lying on the ground. The limb he recently stood on recoiled above him, still attached to the tree, rebounding. Twigs and other debris covered him.

"What happened? Are you hurt?" I brushed away the dirt and leaves.

"A bit dazed," he mumbled, his voice quivering. "I ... think ... the limb ... flipped me." He paused and took a breath." Ooh," he groaned. "I felt a ... whoosh of air, then I ... hit something ... lots of something. ... It ... hurts."

I leaned over him in the near darkness, touching his back and moving my hand up his neck. "It looked bad. It frightened me."

He tried to sit but slumped down.

I leaned close and lifted his eyelids. "Your eyes are not focusing. They look wrong." I said then tentatively touching the back of his head. "Oh. There are lumps on your head, here, here, and here."

"My head hurts and everything spins." He allowed a moan to escape.

"You must have hit it when you fell. Lie back. Let it settle." I helped him lie down and leaned in to watch his face. His color concerned me, even in the half-light it had never looked it so gray.

While his head stopped spinning, I examined the rest of his body, searched for injuries and felt for bumps. There were red scrapes on his back, sides, and legs. I found nothing else. How would I know? Nothing like this had happened to us.

Sparse, thin clouds reflected golds and oranges as the sun slipped behind the mountain. I marveled at their beauty as I waited. They lost color, darkening to gray.

Finally, Adam sat up. I could see his eyes still out of focus. The light receded, leaving us in shadows. Still, we waited until his eyes looked better.

I helped him stand. "Are you still spinning?"

He put some weight on his hurt leg. "A little. My leg hurts."

"I am sure it does. You fell on your side. Scraped it and your left leg and back as you fell. Lean on me."

He allowed me to carry much of his weight as he took slow, deliberate steps. He groaned occasionally as we moved through the dusk toward home.

"What was I doing? On a limb like that?" he mumbled.

"Nothing there. Beautiful burl. Mahogany. Right size. Do not remember."

His words slurred and my fear increased. I accessed the strength within me to stay calm, although a scream fought to escape.

"We will find a burl for the bowl later. Now we must get you to bed to rest. I will care for your scrapes and fix the lump on your head."

We inched toward the bed. Darkness surrounded us. The fire beckoned us. It felt like forever to reach it. Adam rambled about the log he had tried to reach. I worried about what to do for his injuries and fought to keep my fears hidden.

At last, we arrived at our bed. I helped Adam lie down. While he settled in, I sliced a bit of leather from my robe and poured water from a skin onto it and cleaned his scrapes. He radiated heat. He complained his head hurt. I poured the last of the water on the leather and placed it on his forehead. He grasped his lower lip between his teeth striving to repress his moans.

"I will return soon. I must fill the skin," I whispered into his ear before hurrying to the stream for more. I needed to cool him down. I knew that much. I knew of only water to use to cool him.

Tips of long willow boughs brushed the river. I worried what to do for his head, his growing heat, the bumps, and his foggy eyes. They scared me.

Silently, I prayed. "What can I do to help Adam? How can I stop his pain? What will fix him? Help me, please."

A gentle voice surprised me. "Eve." Jehovah spoke only with Adam since we left Eden. "Take a small branch of the willow tree. Cut the inner and outer bark from it. Place it in hot water and allow it to steep until it is brown. After it cools, give some to Adam. Then cut a leaf from the aloe plant and daub the seeping gel on his scrapes and other injuries. This will heal him."

"Thank you, Jehovah," I prayed. I felt a huge smile crowd my face, in odds with my fear.

As I dipped the skin into the stream, I chanted my joy. "He heard me. He spoke to me! He gave me the way to cure Adam. Me! The one who disobeyed."

I pulled my knife from my waist and cut a willow branch.

"Is this enough?" I speculated. I cut another and hurried back with the willow and cold water. I checked on Adam, who lay sleeping. His knees and arms jerked, and he moaned as he attempted to turn on his side. I shoved a log into the fire and stirred the coals. The fire grew. I poured water into a cooking basket and hung it to boil. While it heated, I stripped the inner and outer bark from one branch.

The water began to bubble. I let it set over the heat until the bubbles roiled. I removed it and added the bark. I set it aside to steep. While it did, I returned Adam's side to check him further. I rinsed the leather and replaced it. I cut another piece of robe, soaked it, and laid it on his neck. He stirred in his sleep at the coolness of the cloth.

"Adam, Adam." I touched his uninjured shoulder. "Jehovah talked to me! He gave me the way to treat you. It is steeping now."

"Uh-huh."

I cut another scrap of leather and gently washed each of his many scrapes. Some were fire red and raw. I found an aloe plant growing nearby. Thick gel oozed from the leaf I cut from it. I daubed the gel onto all his injuries before covering him lightly with a cloak.

"I will go check the drink. It should be ready."

"Un-huh," he mumbled.

The bark had turned the liquid dark brown. This must be the healing drink. I allowed it to set a bit longer, and then pulled the basket away from the fire and poured the liquid into another drinking basket.

I sat beside Adam, who groaned in his sleep, his lip set between his teeth in pain. I trusted Jehovah. This would stop his pain.

"Here, Adam." I gently lifted his head. "This is what Jehovah instructed me to make for you. Sip a little. It will help mend you."

He sipped, made a face, and then sipped some more. I gave him cool water and set the drink aside for later. The leather strips were warm, so I rinsed them and laid them back on his injuries. I felt the lumps on his head; they seemed larger, but Jehovah promised the drink would cure him. I had to believe.

As I tended to his injuries, I thought about hearing the voice of Jehovah. I was grateful, even excited, to hear it. Since Eden, I heard it only twice, once when he told us about the Sabbath, and again when he gave us the command to write a Book of Remembrance. Otherwise, all communication from Him came through Adam. I had been warned before we left. Hearing His loving voice once more left me with a sense of loss. I grieved. Would I hear it again? I hoped so.

~

"Eve. Eve." A voice broke through my sleeping fog. "Eve."

Adam! All the frightening events of the night before rushed back to my memory — Adam's fall, his injuries, his hot body and hurting head. I turned to stare into his azure blue eyes, now clearer. I recognized what was wrong before, for certain. It showed in his eyes. "Adam!" I cried. "Are you healed?"

As he nodded a twinge of pain crossed his face. "Some. The drink you gave me and the cool cloths help. I still hurt but much of the pain is gone. My body and legs are tender, although they hurt much less than last night."

"Thank to Jehovah." I sat up and folded my legs. "I prayed so hard for you last night. And He answered me. Me! Jehovah taught me what to do help you and how to make the healing drink. And you are improving."

I momentarily forgot everything else, grateful for the help I received and Adam's healing body.

"Is there food?" Adam asked, he slipped his teeth over his lip. "I am hungry."

Food? I realized I was hungry, as well. I found soft food from the afternoon before and brought it to him on a bark plate.

"These wonderful plates are useful already."

He nodded, and then grimaced. "May I have another drink of the stuff you made? It helps."

"You still hurt?" I gazed into his eyes, recognizing his pain. "Of course, you may."

I retrieved the basket with the willow drink and gave it to him to drink.

"Thank you, my love."

He returned the drink to me.

I watched him as we ate, seeking a signal of healing. His face relaxed.

"It is helping," he said.

"Lie back and rest. Your head is only one of your injuries. Let me examine the others." I moved the cloak and looked. "Your scrapes are beginning to heal. Turn on you right side while I apply more aloe." He lay back and turned over. He muffled his moans with his arm. I located the aloe leaf and cut it. Fresh gel oozed. I daubed it on each of the scrapes and cuts. Though I attempted to be gentle, I felt him flinch in pain. Pasha bounded to the bed and pushed his nose into Adam's hand, offering support. When I pulled the cloak over him once more, Pasha lay next to the bed as sentinel.

"I am sorry I caused you pain." I set the aloe leaf in a basket next to the bed.

"No, the aloe is soothing. I am hurt more than I want to admit." He showed exhausted from the effort of eating. My ministrations ensured it. By the time I cleaned up, he breathed slow and deep, almost in sleep.

"I wanted to begin work on the walls of the house," he mumbled, his eyes drooping. "We have so little time —"

"I will work on the walls. And, no. I will not carry heavy loads. I will be back soon to check on you." He would worry.

His eyes fluttered open. Argument filled them, but he did not have the energy to voice it. "Do not carry too much. Smaller is safer."

Even half asleep and injured, he worried for me and the little one.

"I know. I will be careful."

I picked up a smaller basket than I planned to use and held it up for him to see. Pasha lay beside Adam, guarding him. I walked toward the place on the stream where we dug the sticky mud. Brownie followed. I loaded the mud into the tightly woven basket. It was difficult to do it alone. I missed Adam and his help. I hoped he would be well enough to join me for the next Sabbath.

I washed my hands and picked up the heavy basket to lug it to the house. Brownie stood in front of me, his nose in the basket.

"Go away, Brownie. This is not good to eat. I have too much to do." I shoved his back with my basket.

Brownie pushed himself under the basket.

I frowned and wrinkled my eyebrows. "Oh, Brownie. You want to carry the basket? I will be happy to let you."

I balanced the basket on his back as we walked back to the house.

On the way, I checked on Adam. He slept. Pain lines in his face smoothed but were not all gone. Pasha continued to stand guard. I felt the back of Adam's head. The lumps were beginning to reduce. Good. He stirred, opened his eyes, and grimaced.

"Is the pain easing?"

"Yes, thank you. I can help you now." He tried to push himself off the bed and fell back with a sigh, too weak to sit. Pasha stood and shoved his face into Adam's.

"Stay here and rest, even Pasha insists you need more sleep. Soon you will be strong enough to help." I did not know how I knew, but I knew. "Brownie is helping me carry the mud."

Adam relaxed back into the bed and slept.

At the house, I added bits of chips, leaves, and grass to the mud. It would not help for the mud to fall off the walls again. The difficult work made me choose to do it the right way.

I stirred everything in with a long, thick stick, and then used it to dip and slather the mud between the logs of the house. I covered part of one log before my basket emptied.

Each time I passed the bed, with Brownie beside me, I stopped to check on Adam. More wakeful each time, he stirred and suggested he should be helping. By the time I stopped for a mid-day meal, Pasha allowed him to sit up. He gave me a small smile when I gave him another dose of the healing drink.

"Soon I will be strong enough to help. The pain is nearly gone, as are the lumps on my head."

I touched his head. "Almost. I am surprised they shrink as quickly as they do. I look forward to you joining me. I can use the help."

"You work too hard. I am sorry."

"Do not worry. You will be well and back with me soon enough. Rest a while longer. Maybe later you can come watch me work."

He tried to stand, but Pasha pushed him back. His strength had not returned. He grumbled and lay back.

Many trips later, he sat on the edge of the bed.

"I can help now," he declared, reaching for my basket of mud.

"No, you are not ready. I do not want you to fall. If you are this much better tomorrow, you can help," I said, half in jest, half as an order. I tapped his chest. "Wait here. I will be right back to help you." His hand brushed against mine when I resettled the basket. I was reminded once more how much I loved his caring ways.

Pasha stood guard in front of him. I lifted the basket and balanced it on Brownie's back, allowing him to tote it to the house, before returning for Adam. He wobbled with weakness, but with Pasha's and my help, he managed to reach the house and sit down against a large oak next to the basket of mud. As he gathered the leaf litter and twigs and dropped them into the basket, his hand brushed against mine. I was reminded once more how much I loved him.

I stirred the concoction, dipped it out, and smoothed it between the trees with the stick. By now, I had managed to daub mud along most of the trees along one wall.

"Nice work. How did you decide to use a stick?" Adam asked.

"I did not want sticky mud on my hands if I needed to help you. It is much easier this way."

"I am happy you thought of me," he said.

"I am glad you are happy I thought of you," I said.

"I am happy you are glad I am happy you thought of me."

I joined his laughter. To have Adam play our little nonsense word game helped us find happiness in the midst of our fear. I glanced at his face in time to see a tightness of pain cloud his face then brighten. I reminded myself to give him more of the willow drink.

We visited and laughed while I daubed the mud onto the house. I caught Adam wincing in pain when he thought I did not see. But he grew stronger and even joined me on my last trek to the creek for mud. He leaned on his walking stick on one side and Pasha on the other. I would not allow him to carry the basket nor would Brownie. It was enough for him to be with me.

We stopped by the fire to give him more of the willow drink and check on dinner. It had been a long day and tiredness overwhelmed me.

I clasped Adam's strong hand in mine and inhaled his fragrance. He smelled of sickness and sweat. We would go bathe after this last load of mud. One side of the house would be completed. Only five more to go.

CHAPTER TEN

Gifts

Each day Adam grew stronger. On the second afternoon after his injury, he joined me. It took only three more days to finish mudding the house, with Adam's help. and Brownie's and Pasha's.

I stepped inside. Baskets of food crowded the room, leaving little space even to walk. I could see no place to put a bed or build a fire.

"Perhaps we should build a house for food? There is still squash and fruit to store," I moaned, thinking of the work required.

"Maybe, but for now, this will have to do. We can be cramped for a time. It will not be long. As we eat the food, more space will open for us to move." Adam brushed his hands against the sides of his robe.

"Will the roof keep out rain?" I asked. "We have not had any for many Sabbaths."

We looked up. Light sparkled and danced through the branches forming the roof.

"No," he groaned. "We need more to keep out the storms."

I sighed. More work and more sweat. Together we walked with Pasha to the diminished log pile.

"There is not enough." I ran my hands through my hair.

Adam stooped to rub Pasha between the ears and talk to him. "We need more. Will you and your brothers help us?"

The goat nodded. I looked at the goat and smiled. They were always ready to help.

"Tomorrow? Early?"

Pasha butted his head into Adam's hands, his way of saying 'yes.'

With the goats' help, we retrieved wood for the roof, firewood, and all the other projects Adam planned.

"Will there be time to do everything before the arrival of the little one?" I asked as we trudged down the mountain.

"We will find time. We must make time. The little one is our future."

"Will there be space inside the house?"

"Even if we have to hang vegetables from the roof." His hands mimicked the actions of his words.

His words calmed my anxious soul. All would be well.

"We must still devise a way to write our Book of Remembrance," Adam said with a sigh.

I knew he had not forgotten.

"We have not been working on it, but we are searching for a solution during our other activities."

"We tried mulberries and reeds. We can try again. It is good different mulberry trees produce fruit for a long time. We can still find berries."

"I saw some this morning."

Adam veered around a large rock in our path. "We still must find something to write on. What can we use? What will last long enough to share with our children and be light enough to carry?"

"We will find a solution." I avoided the branches of a bush.

We hiked down the hill, trying to find a solution. "We could ... No, that will not work," one would say before lapsing back into thought. The other would rouse with a thought, "We could ... No, it will not ..." When we reached the log pile, the goats butted into our legs to remind us to untie them.

We thanked them and watched them bounce back to their growing little herd. Each of the nannies had a kid or two following behind. Most of the ewes had lambs, too.

"Soon it will be your turn." Adam reached out to help me stand from the ground. "Our little one waits for the right time."

"Even the cats have kittens again. This is their second litter since Eden."

"And our little one will be born in his own time. You are not a cat or a sheep. You are a woman, bone of my bone, heart of my heart. Your time will come." He pulled me close. I inhaled his comforting warmth.

"I know. When it is time." I sighed. Always waiting, always working. This earth was more difficult than I expected. I left him to untie and stack the trees. He would be careful. I watched a moment before turning to check on dinner. I did not want to admit my concern for his safety. Relief overflowed my senses when I found him later, petting the goats and sheep.

We worked all day the next day on the roof.

Adam stood inside, examining the roof for flickers of light. "We need a place to build a fire inside. To do that, we need to find a way to keep the wooden walls from burning."

"Burning? All this work burned? Burning will destroy our shelter."

"We need a fire inside. Even now the fire drives away the cold at night." His eyes swept the area, landing on the rocky circle surrounding the fire. "Of course. Rocks. They do not burn."

More work.

The child grew within me, taking space, like the food stacked inside our house, making it harder to breathe. But I did not mind the work to have a warm, safe house. We lugged rocks for many days and stacked them along a wall and encircled the space we planned for our fire. At last the house was finished and all the crops stored inside. We had time, once more, to consider the challenge of writing.

I retrieved the mulberry juice from earlier we stored in a covered basket. It had thickened over time. I added a trickle of water and folded a leaf to help pour the juice into the reed. Dirt gave the liquid the right texture, but it clumped and closed the tip. I looked for something else to use.

Perhaps ash from the fire, but it meant we had to pick more berries. After they were mashed and juice flowed freely in the basket and ash added, Adam poured drops of the liquid into a reed and cut a small triangular hole in the tip. This time he drew a fine line along the bottom of his robe. It did not smear. We had ink.

"We did it! We have ink!" We cheered together. "At last!"

Just then rain began to fall. We ran into the house. Adam set the ink and reeds inside, out of the reach of the goats and weather. We stared up at the roof. No drops dripped through.

"The roof will keep the rain out." I said.

"It will keep the storms away from our little one."

We danced a little dance together in the houe, watching the rain.

"Now we need something to write on. Then, most of our current challenges will be solved." Adam wiped the spray of moisture from his face.

The knowledge tempered our joy in creating the ink. With only half the problem solved, still more needed resolution. We had ink, but nothing yet to write on. The short storm ended and we stepped into the sunshine, talking of finding a solution. I looked about us for an answer.

"Not again," I gasped. "That serpent, Lucifer, is watching us."

He tried to convince us to bow down to him often during the months of growing. Now, once more, he stepped forward, his gold cane stabbing the earth.

"Are you ready for my help? I can give you all the knowledge you need to live in this world. Kneel before me, honor me as God of this world, and I will give you all you need."

"Father gave us the intellect needed to solve all our problems." Adam squared his shoulders. "If not, we would not be here."

"I can give you more —"

"No. You have nothing for us." Adam raised his hand. "In the name of Jehovah, be gone."

The Destroyer stabbed his cane into the dirt, pivoted on it, and disappeared behind a tree.

"He does not show himself as often," Adam said. "He looks less substantial each time he tries to tempt us. His lack of body is showing."

I shivered. I did not like the creature. Adam hugged me close. I stared at the mark he made earlier.

"The mark on your robe."

"My robe? Yes! My robe! We can use animal skins. The bullock hide is ready to use."

"We can use it to dress the little one —"

"— and to write on!" we shouted together.

"I can begin our Book of Remembrance." He took my hand in his and escorted me to examine the hide.

We celebrated the Sabbath with prayers and song. I no longer wasted time feeling guilt for my choice to listen to the serpent and eat the fruit. The child within me bounced and poked at me. I was happy with the results of the decision.

~

The next day Adam sliced a portion of the bullock hide into squares. He discovered layers in the hide, so he split eight thin squares from each original. He then punched three holes along one side and tied it all together with thin strips of hide. All appeared ready for him to write.

He retrieved the ink and reeds from the house.

"The ink looks good." He lifted the lid from the basket holding the reeds. "But the reeds dried." His shoulders slumped. "They are no longer usable. Are there still reeds in the stream?"

"I will gather more," I touched my palm to his cheek.

I walked to the stream bank, scratching between the ears of my usual companion, Pasha. Ducks and geese flew in, landing in the still bend of the stream. A goose paddled over to watch me, swimming between my legs as I cut a handful of fresh reeds.

There were not many green reeds left, most had dried. Some better solution had to be available, but I had no idea what. I waded out of the stream and Pasha and I started back. A goose waddled beside us.

"Hello there, goose. Do you want to see our home? No birds live with us, yet, though cats and sheep do." Pasha butted his head into my hand. "And goats. I would never forget you goats."

Together the three of us walked to our outdoor home. Only the goat walked without a waddle.

"You brought a friend," Adam said. "Hello, Mrs. Goose. How are you today?"

She honked back in a conversational manner.

"Oh. You wanted to see how we are living away from Eden."

Another series of honks.

"We are doing well, thank you. We are making progress, life is good." He spoke to the goose as though she were a visiting friend.

She honked again.

"I am writing a Book of Remembrance." He held up his recently created book.

She honked once more.

"Why, yes. We are struggling with a carrier for the ink. Do you have a suggestion?"

I turned away to cover a laugh, not wanting to hurt the goose's feelings.

"Thank you." Adam said.

I turned to find three goose feathers in his hand. "Look at what Mrs. Goose gave us! Feathers. The center shaft is hollow."

"How will you get the ink in?"

"Dip it in? I do not know, but it will not dry up and blow away like the reeds." He bent low to speak to the goose, "Thank you again. I will use these and remember your gift."

I turned to the goose and nodded my thanks. She honked shortly and turned. I expected her to fly back to the water, but she waddled back, tall and graceful.

"How kind of her," I whispered.

"She told me Jehovah sent her."

"She told you?" My eyebrows flew high.

I did not know why I had not understood the goose. Was I too occupied with myself? Was it the child? It made me wonder. How did Adam understand her? Was that how he convinced the animals to offer themselves as our sacrifices? It puzzled me.

Adam sat against a tree, legs folded one over the other, a goose feather in his hand, ink and the hide book sitting beside him. I mutely observed his slow, deliberate actions. Thinking, he slipped his teeth over his lower lip. He placed the feather on a nearby rock and sliced a thin triangle across the tip. He cut the vane up to make room for his hand to grip the feather without crumpling it.

He studied the feather, dipped it into the ink, and gently wiped the tip on the edge. Pulling the hide book onto his lap, he lettered **BOOK OF REMEMBRANCE** on the front with deliberate care, dipping the feather into the ink several times for each letter, making it bold and beautiful.

I watched him write, surprised I remembered how to read. He turned the page and began to write closely placed, neat words. The book folded and bent. His ink sat on a rock out away from his arm, forcing him to stretch to refill the feather pen. He needed a way to hold the book and ink.

I searched nearby for a thin flat rock, large enough to hold the book and ink. As I ranged farther away, I pried several possibilities up with a long, stout stick, only to be disappointed. My stomach got in the way, but I wanted to do this for Adam. One peeked from the earth that looked right.

"Please be thin and flat on the bottom," I prayed.

I pried it up to find it just as I desired, flat on top and bottom, thin, and not heavy. I knelt beside the rock.

"Thank you, Jehovah. Once more, you helped me."

Only because you were searching.

He spoke to me! Me! Although I did not understand the goose, Jehovah would speak to me. I was not too occupied with myself.

"Thank you. Thank you for helping me."

Tears of gratitude filled my eyes as I lifted the rock into my arms and carried it to Adam. I set it near him and watched him work. He filled the second page near to the end when he stopped, tip of the feather near his mouth, remembering. He printed more neat words. I knelt and leaned back on my feet. After writing more, he moved the pen toward the ink and glanced my way.

"How long have you been there?" A bemused smile filled his face.

"Long enough to see you mark your face with ink." I inclined forward to wipe it away.

He caught my hand and kissed it. "Where have you been?"

"Searching for something to help you with your writing. Jehovah helped me find this, and he spoke to me again."

"Wonderful. I know you miss his voice."

"I do. I realize how much I miss it each time he speaks to me. Each is sacred and special."

Adam reached up and brushed the hair from my face. "I understand. I miss his voice, too."

I leaned close and kissed him.

"Now, what gift did you bring me?"

I showed him the rock. Together we found two others that he placed in the ground the same distance apart as the flat rock was long. He balanced the flat one on the other two, then slid under.

"What will you call this?" I asked.

He considered only a moment and said, "A desk."

He gathered his writing materials onto the desk and continued to write.

After turning the page, he looked up, "Perfect. Much easier to write without the struggle to hold the book flat. You, my dear, are a genius."

"Geniuses together, then." I leaned over to kiss his forehead. "It took both of us to solve this problem."

Over the next seven-days, Adam spent much time writing in the Book of Remembrance. I returned to weaving the softened palm leaves, which had remained forgotten while Adam healed. Happily, I left the fronds in a covered basket and they continued to be soft and pliable. I picked up my weaving where I stopped earlier and completed a covering for our indoor bed. With the weight and bulk of the babe within me, it took longer to weave.

I no longer moved fast and waddled more like Mrs. Goose. We found more feathers along the stream after the geese flew on, another gift. We picked the last of the mulberries and prepared more ink to use later.

"There is still much to do to prepare for a change in the weather." Adam encircled my waist with his arm as we walked to the house.

"What is left to do? The house is built, food is gathered in, and the fire is even laid and ready to light." I pulled away and set my hands on my hips.

He copied my stance. "We need fresh grass for a bed inside, so we can leave the dry grass of our bed out here, along with the mice and bugs it has accumulated. Most of the grass has dried and we will be going in soon."

Adam always knew about the weather. We tramped to the hills to a field of tall, still-green grass. We put together a new bed for us and set some grass aside, waiting for the child.

CHAPTER ELEVEN

Rains

One day was clear and bright. The next, it rained, hard. We rushed into the protection of our house, followed by the cats. There, the food waited, stacked neatly; the fire space sat ready to be lit; and the firewood stood piled outside, near the door.

Adam bent over the twigs and dry leaves in the fire space, his lip caught between his teeth, intent on striking his knife against the heavy rock. The fire would come. I still held my breath, watching as it took several tries before a spark bounced into the twigs. I let my breath out slowly, fearful of losing the small spark.

He bent close to the tiny flame, breathing life to it. I trusted Adam to build the fire and moved to open baskets to find food for our first dinner in our new home. I returned to the fire as Adam added a second small piece of wood. The blaze grew. The tang of burning wood filled my nostrils. Our first fire in our new home!

I prepared a simple meal and the fragrance of cooking food filled the house. Adam pulled the door open, bringing in a blast of rain and an armful of wood for the fire.

"Mmmm, smells good in here." He pulled his cloak over his head and hung it on a peg near the door.

"Thank you. It helped for the fire to be ready to start. What is it like out there?"

Adam shook his head, scattering small droplets of rain from his hair. "Wet. The wind is roaring and the rain is pounding harder than when we came inside."

I worried about the animals who scattered seeking shelter from the rain. Only the goats stayed close. They huddled under the roof overhang beside the house. Adam assured me the animals knew how to find safety and would return to us at the end of the storms.

He added wood to the fire and sat on the floor near it. He held a piece of soft pine in his hand, turning it over, looking at it from all directions.

"What will you do with that?" I laid a hand on his shoulder.

He glanced up. "I wonder what I can carve from this piece of wood. Is there something we need?"

I shrugged. "A bowl? A spoon?"

He nodded and set his knife against the wood. He shaved small splinters from the length. These he brushed from his lap into his hand and threw into the fire.

After eating, I moved around the house, picking things up and finding a place for them. I spread the new mat over the bed, with sleeping robes nearby, all in readiness for the night. I checked our store of food, ensuring I knew where each was, and how much I had. The little one kicked me, a reminder of his coming. It reminded me of my need to weave a bed for him. I pulled my robe over my head and pushed the door open.

"Be careful. Do you need me to come with you?" Adam began to stand.

I waved him down. "No, I can manage."

The force of the winds and rain hit me in the face. I reached behind the door for my walking stick and stabbed it into the mud, hoping it would help to keep me upright. It did, for the most part. I clung to it even near the house. I moved only a short distance before the winds drove me back. Back indoors, I located the lengths of grass and wide leaves to weave into a basket bed for the child.

The rain fell all day and through much of the night. Something roused me from sleep. I wondered what woke me, then pulled the sleeping robes up over us and snuggled closer to Adam. His warmth comforted me. I drifted back to sleep.

The rain returned with the morning, along with a howling wind. The cats slipped out when one of us opened the door. They somehow knew when we returned and came in with us.

That evening the wind and rains slowed before dark. We threw our cloaks over our heads and trekked out into the rain-fresh air.

We lugged our water skins to the stream. Water raced by, swelling over the banks. Torn branches bounced past. We slogged through the mud to a usually quiet bend, hoping to find it a less dangerous place to dip water.

"Stand well back," Adam said. "I will fill the skins."

I wanted to argue, but even here the water roared. Bits of trees and bushes raced by, bumping into the mucky banks. I nodded and reached out for his skins. He knelt down to dip water, just as a large branch bounced toward him.

"Look out!" I screamed.

He jumped back as it bounced off the bank where he knelt.

"Thanks. Keep your eyes open and let me know if others are coming." He glanced up the raging flood and knelt once more to fill the water skin.

Adam managed to fill one more water skin before a tree caught on a rock in the middle of the stream, its branches raking the banks. Another tree bounced against it, dislodged them both and swirled the mass of trees and branches away down the stream. He bent to fill another skin, while I watched for danger, shouting a warning each time something spun and bounced headlong toward us.

Eventually he filled all the skins and slung them over his shoulders, not wanting me to carry even one. The weight of the baby unbalanced my body. I was glad of my walking stick helping me move through the sloppy mud.

We managed to bring the water to the house. We stripped our wet cloaks off beneath the roof overhang and shook them free of the rain. I feared getting fresh water may be a problem during these storms.

Our days found a new rhythm. We rose early, ahead of the storm onslaught, to relieve ourselves We tried getting water once in the evening, but trees, branches, and even huge animals caught in the flood raced passed by us, making it too dangerous. Most of the storm caused debris rushed past by early morning. We reveled in the fresh air during those early morning treks.

Inside, we found things to do during the day and snuggled close at night. We stepped into the rain washed clean air in the evenings on those days the rain subsided enough to allow a short walk. Adam carved long handled spoons to keep my hands far from the heat of the fire and scooped food onto our plates without spilling. He then carved bowls and plates for eating and a small bowl for his ink.

Inside, we found things to do during the day and snuggled close at night. We stepped into the rain washed clean air in the evenings on those days the rain subsided enough to allow a short walk. Adam carved long handled spoons to keep my hands far from the heat of the fire and to scoop food onto our plates without spilling. He then carved bowls and plates for eating and a small bowl for his ink.

On each seventh-day we observed the Sabbath and offered gratitude for our home and its refuge from the storm. We talked about the coming little one, wondering how to feed him and how to help him survive the storms. We looked forward with faith in Jehovah.

~

Adam rushed into the house one morning, dripping wet. "The rain is rising near the house. If we do not fix this now, we will be washed away like the broken trees!"

I threw my robe over my head and we rushed out into the rain. We grabbed long lengths of wood and dragged them through the mud above the house, at the edge of the hill. Over and over, we scratched a path for the water to follow, across beyond the length of the house and down. Finally, we drew a deep course for the water to follow. We hoped it would be enough.

Each evening for days, when the rain ended, we rushed out to scrape the stream path deeper. Then, one night, the house shuddered with the force of an enormous tree falling near us. Adam stepped out and searched in the dark for the tree but could not see it. We hoped we and our house were safe. The force of the flood stayed away from the house and we no longer needed to race out to dig the stream deeper.

The goats deserted us for greater protection. I missed them.

To ward off the frustration of being forced to stay inside all day, Adam turned to whittling and carving. I knew the little one would soon arrive, although I hoped the rains would end before then. I sewed a robe for him and worked on weaving a basket to lay the child in.

The bed was nearly complete when Adam stopped to watch me sitting on the ground near him. His eyes followed me a I struggled to stand.

"What are you thinking?"

Adam smiled. "You look lovely."

"Me? Lovely?" I did not feel lovely. I had grown bigger than I ever thought I would. "The child stretches my body in ways I did not expect. Even watching the animals, I did not suspect I would change this much."

"I, too, am surprised. But you are lovely. You. Our growing child. All beautiful."

He stood and stretched, pulled his cloak over his head, opened the door, and walked out into the rain. I stared at the closed door a moment before shaking my head in wonder and returned to weaving. He returned quickly with several lengths of logs. Perhaps he planned more whittling.

I thought wrong. He found a length of braided hemp and began to bind the logs together. I was intrigued.

"What are you making?"

"A surprise for you."

Nothing I said would get him to tell, so I gave up and watched him work a while before focusing once more on my weaving. He went outside two or three times, seeking the right length of logs, determined to make it perfect.

I completed the basket and was adding a braided vine to the sides as handles when Adam slipped behind me and wrapped his arms about my swollen body.

"I have a gift for you, my love."

I looked up from my work, eyes wide. Absorbed in making the bed, I forgot about his project. He held an odd shaped item: four short lengths of logs, crossed and tied beneath a small raft of logs.

"What is it?" I leaned forward to examine it closer.

"A stool for you to sit on." He patted the raft-seat. "It should make it easier for you to rise. Come, try it."

"Is it strong enough for my bulk to sit on and not break?" I asked, touching my huge stomach.

"I believe it is. Come. Try it."

His urgings were impossible to deny. He helped me rise from the floor and led me to sit on the stool. I gradually allowed my weight to settle onto it. Stronger than I expected, it easily held my weight.

"Ah. Nice," I sighed after waiting for a moment for it to collapse beneath me.

He smiled. "I knew it would help. And you should be able to rise easier from the stool than from the ground."

I stood. He was right. I dropped the basket bed and threw my arms around him.

"Thank you for this gift! It is wonderful."

He hugged me tightly. "Nothing is too good for you, my love."

"Will you make another for you? You should have one, too."

Adam laughed and set his finger to my lips. "Yes, I will make one for me. There are more logs and we have lots of hemp to braid."

I sat on my marvelous stool, standing and sitting several times, enjoying the ability to do this with such ease.

I looked up as Adam left to find logs for his stool. "Be careful, please."

"Of course, my dear."

The rains began to slow, falling with less force and intensity every day. One afternoon when the rain stopped for a time, we donned our cloaks, ready to pull them over our heads should the rain return and surprise us. We toured the valley to discover the effects of the storms on it. We planned to make this a short trip.

In the previous days, we hurried for water and back into the house during the brief intermissions in the rain. Now, we wondered about the tree that fell with such force. We did not have far to go, for the tree lay a short distance away.

"Look, the tree directed water away."

"I wondered how our puny efforts could channel all the torrent away." Adam walked along the newly formed creek, bounded by the massive tree. "Jehovah is merciful. This tree directed the water away."

We slogged on through the mud, pointing out changes to each other. In warm companionship, we explored. My huge body moved slower than ever. We saw fallen trees and huge rocks drug by the water, scoring the earth. Adam looked skyward.

"We will have to investigate later. The rain returns."

We rushed home as fast as my bulk allowed. I slipped in the mud only once. It covered us both in sticky mud. We removed our clothing and let the rain wash us.

"Do you remember —" I said.

"— the first time we did this?"

"In Eden. We wore no clothing then, but the rains washed ..." My voice dropped.

Adam saw the look of sorrow cross my face.

"It is right to be here." He gathered me close as he threw his cloak around me. "We have gained light and knowledge, more comes each day."

"It does. Each day brings new things to learn."

Adam hugged me tight. "Most importantly, the little one will soon come. We are obedient to the first command from Father."

"You are right," I whispered, tears welling in my eyes. "The memories are bittersweet, and —"

"— and you are changing with the little one. Your emotions are close to the surface. You cry for no reason." He opened the door for me.

"I know." I sniffed and wiped my eyes.

"It will not be long now." His arm tightened around me as we walked inside.

"I hope not. It is hard to move."

We knelt together to thank Jehovah for His protection.

In another seven-days, the hard rains stopped, becoming occasional, gentle rains that watered the earth. The sun released the moisture from the mud and soon we went outside again, dry and clean.

The goats returned first. Pasha and Brownie trotted to us, butting their heads into our hands, begging for attention. Then the other goats surrounded us, asking for a share of attention.

The sheep found their way out of the hills, muddy and thin, but healthy. I brushed the mud from all that would stay still long enough. All the animals brought little ones. Our herds were growing.

"It has been thirteen moons since we left Eden," Adam said. "The sun has moved across the sky and back. It has been a year."

We honored Jehovah for the blessings of the first year away from Eden with a special sacrifice. We celebrated one year together, one year of learning.

We searched through our storage baskets of grain and seeds and found some bulging with life. These we separated into smaller baskets and toted them to the fields where we planted each variety in its own field. We planted vegetables in a field near the house.

Flowers began to bloom in the hills. Adam chose a few, dug them up, and planted them near our home. Brightly colored birds flew over the valley, filling our world with color and sound. This was a beautiful time of year, regardless of my discomfort.

CHAPTER TWELVE

Absalom

Shortly after the rains ended, as I waddled from the house to the outside cooking fire, I felt a sharp pain across my stomach where the little one lay. Small pains pricked me earlier, but this cramp grabbed and twisted.

"Oh my," I groaned. "What is this?"

The pain ended and I forgot about it as I considered the chores to be done during the day. The forgetfulness did not last long. I dropped the basket I carried with a cry as another sharp pain stabbed into me, twisting before it released me.

Adam rushed to my side. "What is it? Is the little one well?" He touched my stomach and forehead.

"I do not know. Pain crossed where the child lays, bit deep and twisted. Now it is gone."

"Has this happened before? His eyes drew together, a small frown crossed his face.

"Just once." I tried, unsuccessfully, to hide my agitation.

"Something is happening. I will stay close today and get some willow bark, in case you need it." He kissed me gently.

I nodded. "That may be wise."

He walked toward a nearby willow with a small and worried smile.

I returned to my cooking while Adam gathered willow bark. When he returned, he found a tightly woven basket and examined it for mouse-eaten holes. When he found none, he filled the basket with water and set it on the side of the fire to heat. Another, larger basket was filled and set over the fire to boil.

"Why are you boiling water in two baskets? One is enough for the willow tea."

"I need a second, larger supply of hot water," he shrugged. "I do not know why. Just that it is right."

As the day passed, the pains ripped through me more often, harder each time, squeezing and sharp. Then, warm fluid flowed between my legs.

"Your waters broke," Adam soothed me. "This happens with the sheep and goats. You are near time to give birth to our child."

I remembered the mess when the sheep last delivered lambs. Before pushing the little ones from within, water-like fluid spewed.

"Of course. I forgot the waters broke when babies are born." I shook my head. "You will help me?"

"How can you doubt? We are here to help each other. You helped me when I was hurt. Of course, I will help you now."

The sun hung low in the sky when Adam helped me lie down in the freshly rebuilt outdoor bed close to the blazing fire with hot water and the steeping tea sitting on the edge. He found a thin, strong vine and checked to be certain his knife was clean and sharp. I did not know why he made these preparations. I trusted he knew. He searched for small, soft pieces of leather and told me they were to clean the babe.

I did not watch all his preparations, for the pain increased. It came in sheets and more frequently. Pressure bore down on the bones between my legs. I panted and gritted my teeth as I tried not to cry out. Adam came close and placed his hands on my head.

I could not understand why he would lay his hands on my head, my belly hurt, not my head.

"Eve, I bless you that your pain will be lessened, that your body will expel the child within you in the proper way, and that you will heal quickly. I bless the child that it will be healthy. In the name of Jehovah. Amen."

His words encouraged peacefulness within me. I managed a quick smile before another sharp pain filled me.

My mouth dried. My heart pounded. "I need to push!"

"Then push. I will catch the child."

Adam positioned himself at the foot of the bed. He gently spread my legs. "You cannot expel the child with your legs clamped shut."

His teasing made me smile and I opened my legs. Another crushing pain and an urgent need to push filled me. I pushed hard. The overwhelming need to push returned over and over.

"Soon, Eve. I see curly hair," Adam cried.

The next pain crushed me, and I pushed. Adam lay his hand on my belly and told me to wait. I lay panting from the exertion as I waited.

He moved to the babe, in a way I did not know. Another pain rippled through me.

"Push, now, Eve. Push. Hard."

I pushed and the child slipped out. Adam gathered it in. He lay its stomach across his arm and gently massaged its back. Thick mucus slipped between its lips until it began to cry.

My cheeks hurt from the exertion and smiles. "Is it a man-child or a woman-child?"

He turned the babe over. "A man-child. A beautiful man-child. You are a mama." He patted my leg and lay the baby boy across my belly.

A mama. At last, I became a mama! I had obeyed Father's first and grand commandment. I closed my eyes to offer a silent prayer of gratitude.

"And you are a papa."

He clasped my hand briefly. I saw him pick up the thin vine and heard it swish together in a tie, twice, and a soft thunk as he sliced something. He dipped the soft leather in the warm boiled water and washed the birthing blood and mucus from the child. Warm liquid dripped from the child onto me.

Adam wrapped the babe in another soft, warm piece of leather and laid him beside me. The little one snuggled near, searching. I could not tell for what he searched, until he found my heavy breast and began to suckle, pulling and tugging, causing a tingling within me.

While I fed our son, Adam returned to my needs, massaging my stomach until he expelled the afterbirth. He washed the blood from between my legs and placed soft, dried moss there to absorb the liquid that flowed from within me. He covered us with a cloak and took away the afterbirth to bury it.

When he returned, he washed in the hot water and lay beside us, holding the two of us in his arms. We looked into each other's eyes, awestruck.

"So this is how a child is born," Adam whispered.

"Father warned me. I remember his words. Do you?" I whispered, as I looked across our son.

"Yes, He said you would conceive children in sorrow. The birth was painful, but the joy of birth! You live. And the child lives."

"I accept this sorrow."

I smiled weakly but joyfully. The child glanced up at me and then returned to feeding. Adam and I lay watching him, our love for each other and the child grew. We took turns running our fingers along his little face, holding his little hands and feet. This was our child, a child we created together. Amazement filled us until exhaustion overcame us and we slept.

~

We named him Absalom. The following Sabbath we dressed in sacred robes and hiked to the altar on the hill. A young male antelope followed us, offering himself as sacrifice. Adam completed each step of the sacrifice with care. Absalom lay in my lap without any sound during the sacred rite. Afterward, we knelt together, with Absalom in my arms, to thank Father for the life of our little son. He truly was worth the sorrow and pain necessary to bring him into this world.

Adam held our child in his arms and presented him to Jehovah with a prayer of thanks. He named him Absalom, peace. He asked for Absalom to be blessed with an ability to withstand Lucifer's ploys. With the same agency of choice as all who would live on this earth, Adam prayed for Absalom to choose to follow the light given by Jehovah. During the blessing, Absalom did not sleep but lay quiet in his papa's arms until Adam returned him to mine. Then, he kicked his arms and legs, cooing.

I spent all my time between the next few Sabbaths close to Absalom. I sat with him in my arms as I fed him, watching his little eyes flutter, holding his little hands. His little body amazed me—so much the form of his papa, so much like Father and Jehovah.

In those first few months of his life, he ate, he slept, and he relieved himself of the food. I covered him with a padding of dry moss, held there with a large, soft leaf. As he grew and began to move about more on his own, the leaf tore away, leaving his little bottom bare. I learned to tie the padding on with a covering of soft leather.

Adam asked me to join him in the fields. I strapped Absalom on my back and joined Adam in the fields. We watched the grain, left in the fields from before the rains, put out roots and shoots. The fields were not as green as the year before, perhaps we had harvested too much. Absalom lay quietly on a robe while we worked to plant and grow more.

We scattered some of the seed we had saved to eat among the others. Soft rains helped the seeds sprout and grow, answering our prayers. We cheered when the seeds began to sprout and fill in the empty space green and full of hope.

Absalom began to stay awake longer, kicking and squealing, growing fast. Adam fashioned a pack to carry Absalom on his back. Absalom loved it.

One morning, we hiked into the mountains to escape the heat. Absalom gurgled and squealed behind Adam until he fell asleep. We retraced our steps toward the place we found the black rock we used for knives, seeking berries and other foods to add to our diet, while we enjoyed the beauty of the mountains.

We kicked through a small meadow, filled with plants we had not seen before. I heard a rattling within an object I kicked. I bent to see what it was. Hard, round objects broke away from the dry vines mixed with the growing vines. I picked a small object up and shook it. Absalom laughed and stretched out his hands for it.

"Do you think it is safe?" I asked Adam.

He shrugged and took the rattling object from me. Bringing it to his nose, he sniffed.

"No smell." He stuck out his tongue and touched the object.

"Must you always taste everything?" I said.

"Yes, if I am to know if it is safe for our child. Everything goes into his mouth."

"True." I nodded. "Is it safe for him to eat?"

"I taste nothing, nothing to hurt Absalom." Absalom stretched toward the object, kicking and squealing. "Give it to him, will you?"

I handed the little object to the baby. Absalom grabbed it around the smaller end and shoved it into his mouth.

"Listen, Absalom." I grasped his little hand around the rattling object and shook. His eyes opened wide and he squealed. I shook it again, loving his squeals of joy. He pulled his hand from mine and shook the rattling object.

"Are there more of those?" Adam asked. "Absalom will lose this one."

I knelt to look for more. I was surprised to find others, some small like the one I gave Absalom, others quite large, much larger than I expected to find.

"Is there a use for these, beyond something for Absalom to play with?"

"There is always a use for Father's creations," Adam said. "Bring a few with us."

"What do we call these?"

"Gourds?"

"That works." I picked a large gourd, two medium gourds, and three of the tiny ones small enough to fit into Absalom's hands. I put them into the basket I always carried when exploring. As a last minute thought, I put a tall, narrow gourd into my basket.

Absalom dropped his gourd several times. I bent to retrieve it for him each time until he began to fuss. He was wet and hungry. I changed his bottom and fed him. While Absalom ate, Adam pulled out some dried meat and fruit from his basket for us to eat.

Later, we put Absalom back into his pack and hiked back to our home, stopping only to pick some near-ripe apricots from a tree and sweet red strawberries. We returned to our home as the sun reached the tips of the mountains.

CHAPTER THIRTEEN

Growth

Absalom amazed me. He did something new and grew every day. One day I found him rolling over. Not long after that, he sat on his own. Soon he began to scoot on his belly.

As he grew, our crops ripened. We traveled to the place where the gourds grew three times, taking both Pasha and Brownie. The gourds were tied together with long strands of vine and hung across their backs. In this way, grains and dried foods were protected from the ravages of creatures and moisture.

Baskets and gourds filled with stored grains, fruits, and vegetables were stored with us in the house. Baskets hung from the roof and were stacked as high as possible and as close together as possible. Gourds stood in piles along another wall and others hung, tied by thongs of hide. Storage spread into our space and began to lean against our bed. We were beginning to be crowded out.

"We need another house for all this food." Adam stood staring at the stored containers.

"We are crowded." I snagged Absalom as he crawled into an empty basket. "Do we build another house for storage or a larger house for us?"

"What do you suggest?" Adam took Absalom from me.

"The fire space is in the house already. We should build a house for our food. A storage house will not require a fire, only fresh air to save things from spoiling. Some vegetables and fruits stacked in the center spoiled.

"One more thing to do with our storage. Move it often so none spoils from lack of fresh air." Adam shrugged his shoulders.

I sighed. "Another house for storage and a need to be sure everything gets air. While we move things, perhaps we can control how much the mice eat. We cannot prevent the mice from taking a share, but we must control the amount they take as we avoid spoilage. At least, the gourds we found seal out both moisture and creatures, if the lid is tight. Absalom is beginning to eat many of the same things we do."

"I wonder if the goats will help us collect wood." Adam rubbed his chin. "They helped us gather trees last year. We will have to travel a different direction, though. Most of the fallen trees from the hill we used last year are part of this house, stools, tables, and dishes already."

They agreed. We trudged up a different hill the next day. Absalom laughed in his basket tied to Pasha's black and white spotted back. He often reached out to scratch the goat between the ears. Pasha bleated and Absalom laughed. Others bounced along beside us, ready to be of help once more. Sons joined fathers this year, giving us four pair of helpers to transport trees.

Adam and I joined rafts of trees together. After much work, we had five rafts ready to harness to the helpful animals. I set Absalom in his basket on the ground while I attached harnesses to each of them, connecting father and son. We tied the rafts to the harnesses and prepared to leave. As Adam gathered his ropes, I reached out for Absalom and his safe container. He was gone!

The basket lay overturned. *Where did he go?* I turned to search for him. A figure appeared, filling my soul with dread. The Destroyer lazed against a tree with an ugly leer. With horror, I realized our little boy crawled toward him.

"Absalom!" I screamed running toward the baby.

Adam turned and saw the child laughing as he crawled toward the Destroyer. Adam dropped his load and ran, shouting, "You leave him alone! He is ours! You cannot have him!" He swooped down, gathering our child in his arms.

"Not yet." Lucifer raised his cane, spinning away.

I stood staring in the direction he disappeared until Adam touched my arm. Absalom sat in his arms as though nothing had happened.

"He just now crawled away!" I cried taking Absalom in my arms, tears falling onto his little robe.

"I know. I saw him when I stooped to pick up the ropes, before you screamed."

"He has not crawled like this earlier. I will watch him closer, now."

"Especially when we are away from Home Valley. The Destroyer has not bothered us for some time. We must be alert to protect our son."

Adam put Absalom into his basket and lifted it to my back. Though uneventful, Adam stared behind each tree on our trek home, his lip sliding in and out between his teeth. In the pack on my back, Absalom laughed and kicked, wiggled and played until he fell asleep. I, too, checked the trees and all around. The Destroyer followed us, though not visible to us. It sent shivers down my spine.

From that moment, I determined to protect Absalom, and each of my other children, from the Destroyer. How would I protect them without taking away their right to choose? For now, while Absalom was small, I could. What about later?

The storage house went up quickly. We cleansed the mold and other filth from our baskets and set them in the hot sun to cure. We placed in the now both older and newly harvested crops into the cleaned baskets.

I kept Absalom close, tied to my ankle with a short length of vine. Pasha stayed near while we worked, attentive to Absalom. Our little boy loved his attention. I found him sleeping with Pasha, laying his head on his friend and protector's neck.

If Absalom tried to wander, Pasha moved between the tempta-
tion and him.

Absalom's curiosity demanded extra watchfulness to keep
him safe. He crawled into empty baskets and gourds, and others half full of produce for storage. Every basket and every
gourd required checking and rechecking to ensure our little
boy did not become lost in the midst. In addition to climbing
into containers, he climbed on top of others, causing my heart
to leap into my throat. Sometimes he and the baskets tumbled
to the earth. The child had no fear. Even Pasha struggled to in
his efforts to keep him safe.

Near the end of the harvest season, Absalom's jabber began to make sense. First, he said, "papa," and "mama" not
long after. We spoke to him all the time, and his babbling became easier to decipher. Still, much of it continued to be baby
jabber and babble.

Adam kept track of the moons and the drop in temperature.
We expected heavy rains to fall soon. We were concerned for
our animals. Not all the ewes and nannies appeared with their
expected lambs and kids the year before. Some did not return.
Others returned alone. Once more, the sturdy animals joined
us in gathering trees to help us build a safe place for them to
live out of the storms. This time, they carried heavier loads,
somehow knowing it would be of particular help for them.

Adam completed much of this animal house alone, as it
was vital for me to stay with Absalom to protect him. His desire to climb on the tree pile, hide behind the trees, and crawl
where we worked prevented me from helping with the build-

ing. Even Pasha could not keep him out of trouble. I breathed a sigh of relief each time he napped. Pasha warned me when he woke. I could only help in building while our son slept, and only if Pasha stood guard, warning me when the child awoke. Considerable work lay ahead of us with little time before the expected rains. All this was made more difficult because of the energy and curiosity of our little boy.

Regardless of all the extra challenges caused by his busyness, Absalom brought us great joy. We laughed long and often at some of his actions.

We offered one last sacrifice for the year. As always, we offered prayers of gratitude to Jehovah, with Absalom kneeling beside us.

"Pasha safe," Absalom added.

Adam caught my eye over Absalom's brown curls. Tears filled our eyes. *Were there times we did not see, times Pasha protected our little boy? Things we did not know about?*

~

The rains returned as suddenly as they had the previous year. Adam opened the doors to the animal house and called.

"Ho, goats. Hi, sheep. Here is a place of refuge from the storms. Come chickens, enter cows. Be protected here."

The building welcomed the animals, many had used the it in the drier weather. Now, they hurried out of the pelting storm, each finding and claiming a space within. The chickens settled into the open work under the roof. Each of the others found a place and settled in, enjoying the food Adam gave them.

During the time we were kept inside, Absalom began to pull himself up to stools, the bed, and anything he could. This forced me to be constantly aware of him while he was awake. I feared he would use the hot rocks surrounding the fire to pull himself to stand. I was grateful when he stood on his own, though my concerns for his safety around the fire continued. He careened off beds, stools, and walls at a run, chasing cats, playing with toys, and running for the sheer joy of running.

Absalom begged to join in feeding the animals. He loved to pour grain into the long, deep dishes Adam created for feeding them. He wanted to help gather eggs from the chickens, even when they were too high for him to reach. They were used to his enthusiasm and clucked at him in good nature while his little hand reached beneath a hen for her eggs.

We were careful to collect only those eggs not being sat on by hens. We knew they, too, were required to multiply and replenish the earth.

The cow bellowed sadly as her calf grew, no longer demanding all the milk she provided. I touched her udders and found them full with milk her calf no longer required. I brought my stool and a gourd into the animal house and squeezed the extra milk from her udders. She sighed in relief as her udders emptied. I patted her side and thanked her for the milk. She mooed in content. I picked up the stool and the milk-filled gourd and carried them into our house.

Adam smelled and tasted the white liquid while Absalom begged for a taste and tugged on his robe. After Adam nodded to indicate it was harmless, I poured some for him into his little gourd cup.

"Yum. Good." A milk white swath covered his upper lip.

"You like it, Absalom?" I wiped the milk from his mouth.

He held up his cup for more in answer.

"It does taste good. You should try it, Eve."

I poured some into each of our cups and tasted. It was good.

"Good thing the cow wants me to take her milk."

Adam nodded, set his empty cup on the shelf, and returned to his tasks. Absalom drank his, set the cup on the floor, and wandered away to play.

It stormed for a little longer than two months. As it had the year earlier, it fell with less force in the evenings. The tree that tumbled behind our house a year earlier continued to protect us and our home from the heavy floods of rain rushing down the hill. Winds shrieked, sometimes joined by the howling of wolves. In all this, we were secure in our house.

The animals that accepted our responsibility for them stayed safe, as well. During the wet time, chicks hatched and young were born to both sheep and goats, doubling the size of our herds and flocks.

The storms abated, ending the raining season. Once again we opened the doors to the animal house and allowed them to enter and leave as they chose. Absalom stood at the door as they left, touching each of the older animals and hugging the new babies. As the sun faded each evening, Absalom hurried to the doors of the animal house, welcoming them home.

I gathered eggs and milked the cow and goats. These I had learned to use in cooking. Our diet changed significantly in those first two years. We no longer ate only raw fruits, nuts, and vegetables.

My monthly bleeding stopped shortly after we emerged into the sun. Absalom had lived almost one year, now another child would join our family. This time I kept a record of the time of waiting for this little one. I needed to know.

We were busy that growing season, with grains and vegetables to plant, all while keeping a close watch on Absalom. I reveled in the flowers near our house and the blooms on the trees. I loved the fragrance of the blossoms Adam placed behind my ear each day. My impatience centered on the wait for the fruit to ripen.

Only a few Sabbaths of the usual gentle rain fell, and then it came less often. To protect the vegetables from drying and dying, we were forced to lug water from the stream to them. Little Absalom insisted on toting his small gourd filled with water to the plants, splashing the few drops that reached as far as his favorite vegetables. It was hard work to keep the vegetables growing. Thankfully, the grains and fruit trees grew even in the modest amounts of moisture.

Absalom continued to jabber more than actual speech, though about four months after my bleeding stopped, Absalom said, "Mama fat—like cow," fingering my stomach.

"Is the cow getting fat?" I knew she again carried a calf.

"Papa say calf. Calf?" He pointed at the swell of the growing child.

"No, little one." I gathered him into my arms. "This is a baby. One day another child will join our family."

"Like me?"

"I do not know. Maybe a boy, like you and papa, or a girl like mama."

"Boy." He folded his arms and stuck out his bottom lip.

"A brother would be nice, but this little one will take time to grow before you can play together." I tickled him until his giggles filled the room.

"When?" he demanded.

"Not yet, a few months, still. I do not know. You took your time deciding to be born. This little one will come when he is ready."

Absalom nodded, rubbed my stomach, and wandered off.

Almost every day, Absalom rubbed my stomach and asked, "Boy?"

One day the child moved, bumping his hand. He laughed and kissed my stomach. Each day he felt for the babe to move, jabbered to it, and wandered off to play with Pasha.

He grew tall and stronger every day. His baby roundness began to stretch out. One night as the harvest drew to an end, Adam and I sat together watching the stars.

"Will Absalom like the little one?" Adam's hand sat on mine.

"I think so. He loves the sheep, terrorizes the cats, and chases the goats. They all love him."

"Sometimes I wonder how you manage the little rascal. Did you see him today with the cow?" He rolled his eyes.

"Trying to suckle milk from her? Yes. I saw. It is a wonder she does not kick him. I saw her flip her tail at him." I flipped my wrist mimicking the cow's tail. "I do not blame her. I would do more than flip my tail, if a little rascal like Absalom flipped my tail."

We laughed together. At last Adam shook his head. "How will he treat the babe?"

"He will probably treat it as another animal to pester. We will want to be watchful of him." I closed my eyes thinking of everything our little son could do to pester a newborn.

"We will. I think I will take him on a short walkabout before the baby arrives. How soon will it be here?" He put his hand on the bump where the little one grew.

"We were so ignorant with Absalom. I kept no records. We became aware of my growing body five or six months before his birth." I stopped to count. "It has now been seven months. I believe this child will be born before the raining times. It should not be much longer."

Adam smiled as the child moved under his hand. "We will need to prepare for this one's coming—be sure we have all the necessary items."

"I am sure you will find everything or tell me, so I can find them." I folded my hands behind me and leaned into them to rest my back. "Are you certain Absalom is ready for a walkabout? How long do you plan to be gone?"

"He is a sturdy little boy. I will make it special for him. Stay away one night. I am sure that is all he can manage."

"And all the time you can manage by yourself with a curious little boy."

CHAPTER FOURTEEN

Bilhah

The days grew shorter and cooler. Fruits, vegetables, and grains clogged the storage building. Stacked baskets and gourds crowded the floor; others hung from the roof. Pumpkins, squash, and breadfruit overflowed through the middle.

As there were no symptoms of a forthcoming birth, Adam rolled up two sleeping furs, tucked dried meat, vegetables, and fruit inside and filled two large water bags. Early the next morning, he and Absalom kissed me goodbye and walked away to explore in a direction we had not yet investigated. I waited and watched for them to turn back to wave, but neither Adam nor Absalom did.

I breathed a huge sigh, uncertain if I should be sad or happy they were gone. I had not been alone for long since coming to this world. Now most of two days stretched in front of me to do as I chose.

I waddled to the stream to gather the moss Adam needed to absorb the blood of birth and clean up the child. Then I gathered palm fronds and sat beneath a tree to weave a new basket for the babe.

I leaned on the trunk, as comfortable as possible with my large stomach, concentrating on my weaving. All of a sudden, I became aware of the hair on my arms and neck standing up. I glanced up. The Destroyer lazed against a tree, staring at me. I felt a sharp intake of breath. He sent wolves to attack us earlier, but Adam and his Priesthood had always been there.

"This one will be mine, too," he sneered.

With an open mouth and glazed eyes, I stared at him. Before I thought of anything to say, two black bears, a wolf, and a pair of mountain lions stepped between us, teeth bared and snarling. I stared, unsure of their intent, until I realized the animals faced Lucifer. Standing erect, he riveted his eyes on the animals, then raised his cane and disappeared into the trees.

"Thank you, my friends," I breathed.

Each animal gazed briefly into my eyes and then turning to follow the Destroyer. I slumped and bowed my head in a prayer of thanks.

The next afternoon, Adam and Absalom returned home. Adam dragged; Absalom bounced. Adam slumped to the ground near me, shoulders drooping, head hanging low, his teeth grasping his lower lip.

"I will not go on a walkabout with one so young for a long time," he sighed.

"Mama! Mama! Look. My new puppy!" Absalom pulled a brown ball of fur from his papa's arms.

"A pup?" I raised my eyes and glanced at Adam.

"We found it today, beside his dead mama," Adam shook his head. "She defended him from a serpent, gave her life for him. The pup huddled near their bodies. How could I leave it there, alone?"

He watched the boy and pup for a moment, his exhaustion evident from the droop of his shoulders. "The little thing is too small to be separated from his mama and could not walk even as fast as Absalom. He fell asleep in my arms. Of course, Absalom loves him."

I ran my hand through my hair. "No. You could not leave him behind. Not when his mama gave her life for him." I avoided Adam's eyes as I remembered the protection given to me the day earlier.

"The pup is welcome. I will get some milk from the cow." My voice quivered with the words.

I rose to go find the cow, but Adam stood and gathered me into his arms.

"Is there a problem? You do not cry because we brought home a new animal. That does not cause sadness."

"No." I took a deep breath and exhaled. "A he-wolf defended me yesterday. And now a wolf pup is part of our family." My throat tightened.

"A wolf?" Adam's voice tensed.

"He joined two black bears and a pair of mountain lions. They stood between me and the Destroyer." I struggled to take a breath, though my chest tightened with the memory. "He surprised me, standing there sneering at me. The wolf and other animals appeared and stood there."

"Are you sure he is gone?" Adam glanced into the trees around us.

"They followed him. What if he caused the serpent to kill the pup's mama because his papa guarded me?" I watched the pup follow Absalom toward the animal house. "How sad."

Adam held me close as I allowed my shuddering of fear and sorrow to relax.

The pup promptly became a member of the family. I gave him cow milk. At first, he had no idea how to eat and sat staring at the bowl. I dipped my fingers into the milk and let him lick it off. He soon learned to lap it from the wooden bowl Absalom claimed for him.

Absalom called the pup 'Bark'. It fit, for he yipped and barked, chased the chickens and yapped at the goats and sheep. Only the cow was safe. As the source of his meals, he treated her with kindness, which for a pup meant he did not bark or nip at her heels. Though he watched her tail swish at flies, he never chased it.

Bark snuggled as close to Absalom as possible at night, often pushing his head under the boy's arm. They loved each other and spent all their time together.

I grew heavier and moved slower. I struggled to chase the two little rascals with my heavy body. Pasha ignored Bark's noise and antics and kept them safe and near me.

We savored those sweet, last days betwixt harvest and storms, although we were busy. We cleaned the animal house, spread sweet grass on the floor, and checked on the food stored for them. Our own beds, packed with stale grass, mice and vermin required a change. We refreshed them with fresh, sweet grass.

Adam and the goats hiked to the hills until they brought all the wood required for fires and the projects he planned. Between my heavy body, too slow to join him, and two rascal little ones, I remained home. Pasha stayed behind, as well, claiming responsibility to keep the young ones out of trouble and mischief. They ran and played, but never out of sight. Pasha kept them close.

Eventually, I counted thirty-nine Sabbaths. The baby moved lower in my body and prepared for birth. Late one night, in the fortieth seven-days, I roused from a deep sleep by the forgotten, but suddenly familiar, sharp pains. I woke Adam, who began his arrangements to help me. He boiled water, located dry moss I gathered earlier, and assembled sinew, knife, and robes for the babe.

The pains increased in intensity. I fought to keep my reaction to this pain to moans. I stuffed my fist into my mouth to muffle the shouts and screams of pain. I did not want to wake Absalom or Bark. Somehow, I managed, and they slept through the night.

The rays from the morning sun shone past the edges of the closed door when I pushed the child from within me.

"A girl, Eve. We have a daughter."

Adam lifted her up for me to see. Even wet from her birth, she was beautiful, and ours! I fell back onto the bed, resting from my suffering, while Adam washed and wrapped her in a warm robe. He placed her in my arms and busied himself with the final bits of my necessary care. I wondered, not for the first time, how he knew the right actions to help me give birth. When I had time, I would ask. I never remembered to ask him.

Our little daughter nuzzled my breast, suckling. I lay exhausted and wondered at her tiny beauty. Her small mouth pulled at my breast. A little blond tousle-haired, blue-eyed boy and a dark brown pup popped their heads up at the end of our bed, morning sun shining a halo around their heads.

"Mama? What is that?" Absalom's little eyes opened wide.

"Your little sister," Adam replied, returning from burying the afterbirth.

"Oh, papa! A sister?"

"Yes, son, a sister." I held out my empty hand. "Do you want to see her?"

The little boy nodded soberly. I patted the bed beside me and he climbed up, taking care not to bump me. Bark jumped on the bed beside him. Absalom's sister opened her blue eyes and gazed at her brother.

"She likes me." Awe filled his voice.

Adam slid into the bed on the other side of me and cradled the children and me together. He rose onto one elbow to gaze at us.

"Beautiful. Both children and mama. We are blessed."

"Truly," I murmured. Sleep called me. The efforts of the night caught up with me.

"Sleep, my love. I will care for Absalom."

As I drifted into sleep, Adam slid from the bed. Later, he brought food for me. Sleep helped me, but Adam had been up most of the night and two days. A groan slipped from me as I sat up and lay our daughter in her waiting basket and boosted myself from the bed.

"You rest. I will watch the little ones," I said when Adam tried to push me on the bed.

He did not argue but dropped onto the bed. Absalom sat in the corner, stacking small blocks of wood and knocking them over. Bark lay beside him, watching.

On her eighth day, Adam offered a sacrifice and took the babe into his arms to offer thanks for her safe birth. He named her Bilhah and blessed her much as he had blessed Absalom.

~

The storms appeared almost as we arrived home from the altar after offering of a sacrifice to thank Jehovah for Bilhah. Once more, we settled into our indoor routine of the rain time. Absalom and Bark chased around the room. As always, I watched them play and feared they would fall into the fire.

When Bilhah and I needed a rest, Adam took Absalom and Bark out to care for the animals. Within two seven-days, I regained my strength and resumed the care of my family. Two children were twice as much work. Even with Adam's help, they wore me out. Bark helped, thankfully, as Absalom's playmate.

Sometimes in the afternoons, when I lay to feed Bilhah, Absalom and Adam laid beside me to talk, and then all of us fell asleep. Those were sweet, happy moments.

In the evening after the rains slowed, we left our foot coverings inside and waded through the mud to explore our surroundings. Adam carried Bilhah. Absalom frolicked and slid in the mud with Bark. Somehow, they managed to avoid trees and broken limbs blown down in the strong wind. These walks ended with a bath in water carefully drawn from the flooding stream.

When we fed the animals, Absalom ran to hug Pasha. The goat joyfully bleated, accepting the child's loving attention. We sometimes brought carrots for the multiplying creatures. Ewes and nannies snuggled with one or two little ones, the cow delivered a calf. A big, black bullock had joined the cow in the shelter from the storms. Chicks peeped from the nests near the top of the house.

On those nights when the skies cleared, the stars shone brightly. The moon and stars comforted us in their sameness, reminding us the storms would end.

Seven Sabbaths after Bilhah's birth, we tromped through the mud on our way home from a short exploration. As always, Absalom and Bark stomped in the mud puddles, splashing and laughing. Adam and I stood still when we saw the Destroyer observing our little family, leaning on his golden cane.

"Your pathetic attempts will not be enough to save you," he sneered.

"You want our animals, now?" Adam asked.

"No, of course not. I want your children, and I will have them." He spun his cane, and leisurely returned to the trees.

Adam clenched his fists and shouted back at him, "Never! Not my children."

We heard his eerie laugh echoing through the forest. Shivers danced up my spine.

"Not our children," Adam said again, perhaps to remind himself.

We held our children close that evening as we bowed in prayers of gratitude to Jehovah.

"Protect our children from the guile of the Destroyer," Adam begged.

My heartfelt plea joined his.

We needed the precipitation to swell lakes, streams, and rivers during this time. Still, we grew tired of the forced confinement long before the rains ended. Our house assumed an air of being cramped and tiny, though just the year earlier we considered it adequately large. Two children in a house made a difference, especially when an active and curious child and a growing dog poked their noses into everything.

"We must build a larger house," Adam said one afternoon late in the season as Absalom and Bark chased each other around and around.

"Or make this one bigger"

"I will work on it. We must begin our search for trees to build with earlier this year. We always seem to need more."

Bilhah grew. She woke more often by the time the weather warmed and dried. She watched us with eyes softened from blue to a light brown. She loved her brother and his dog. She brightened when he peeked into her basket or came to talk and play with her when while in my arms.

Bark gave her generous, slurpy kisses with his black tongue. The dog grew faster than either child did. Bark now stood as tall as Absalom. Boy and dog were best friends. The dog helped keep the boy company and out of trouble during the long days—mostly.

The rains ended. We spent more time outside in the sunshine. Though I loved our little home, their noise echoed less in the larger space of the outdoors while Absalom and Bark ran and played noisily.

At last, our herd grew large enough to use for sacrifice. Adam chose a yearling male lamb from our herd to thank Father for a new year. The ram submitted as those he had sacrificed earlier.

The children and I sat in silence as we observed. There were so many ewes and lambs in the herds, we no longer considered them pets or part of the family. This ram had not been petted like the previous young sheep. Absalom sorrowed for it still.

Adam completed the rite and we knelt to pray. A figure appeared above the altar, glowing with light. He identified himself as a messenger, with all the appropriate symbolism to reassure us he came from Father and not as a lying representative of the Destroyer.

He asked why we sacrifice. Adam responded that he sacrificed in obedience to the commandments we were given when we left Eden. I wondered at the question.

The messenger shared the purpose of our sacrifices with quiet authority. "This is a reminder of the way the Only Begotten Son of the Father will come in the meridian of the history of Earth, to offer himself as a sacrifice for the sins of all mankind. His coming sacrifice allows you to return to Father's presence."

The messenger revealed more to us before he withdrew. A glorious light filled my good husband, extending to me and the children. We felt warmth and joy. Exhaustion from the experience overwhelmed Adam afterward. He required help from both Absalom and me to descend the hill. When we arrived home, Adam collapsed on the bed and slept much of the rest of the day.

That night when the children slept, we sat on our favorite limb of a live oak. Adam told me of the future events revealed to him by the messenger, things I had not heard. There would be happy seasons and sorrowful times for us and our children over the years. There would be ages of love and peace followed by occasions and generations of pain and war. Only as our children and grandchildren through the ages remembered Jehovah would they have those moments of love and peace.

We stayed busy as plants grew and matured. We worked hard to produce sufficient to feed ourselves and our growing herds. The children joined the goats and us on several trips to the hills to amass wood to enlarge the house. Later in the year, we returned for more to burn and carve.

Our home expanded as Bilhah and Absalom grew. During that season, Bilhah began to crawl and tagged after her brother and his dog. Pasha stayed busy working to protect them. I tried tying the children to my leg with a vine, but Absalom learned how to untie it. It took all my energy and creativity to keep them safe and, at the same time, help Adam in the fields with the harvesting.

Absalom loved his little sister. He rarely complained about her following after him. More often, rather, he slowed to a walk or picked her up and carried her. Unless she slept in her basket or ate by my side, Bilhah could be found with her brother.

I wondered about the seasons. Which was more difficult—the season of rain with us locked inside; or the season of harvest, which caused extra work to safeguard the children away from the sharp knives and other dangers.

Near the end of the harvest season, Absalom called, "Mama, mama! Look at Bilhah!"

Less than a year old, she stood beside a log, touching it lightly for balance. As I watched, she let go and toddled three steps into Absalom's waiting arms.

"Big girl, Bilhah!" he crowed as he set her back by the log and called for her again.

I cheered her on as she toddled to him once more. She turned and looked up at me, grasping Absalom's hands. I stooped down and held my hands out to her.

"Come to mama, Bilhah."

She let go and toddled five steps to me. We clapped our hands and cheered as she wobbled back and forth between us. Adam heard us and came to see what caused our excitement. He joined in cheering her on and laughing as she became stronger and more stable with each step.

When she tired, Adam swung a giggling Bilhah high into the air. He then picked up Absalom and threw him high. We all laughed until our sides hurt.

CHAPTER FIFTEEN

Drought

With new space in our expanded home for the children, a chamber for us, and a larger area for us to eat and work, we spent a happier and easier time as a family during the raining season. Adam carved small toys for the children. Absalom devoted hours stacking his blocks of wood for Bilhah to knock over. Bilhah rocked and loved her baby made of corn husks, laying it beside her while playing with Absalom. Bark lay watching them play.

The areas were warmed from the fire space built in the first house, now part of the main chamber. The children played in their room, warm and comfortable, though safely away from the blaze. By the time the rains ended, we were ready to walk in the sunshine once more.

As we prepared to plant, Adam turned to me and asked, "Have you inspected the seeds in the storehouse?"

"Not yet. I plan to today as I sort seeds for planting. Why do you ask?"

"It rained extra hard and longer this year." He checked the edge on the tool he used to turn the soil in the field. "I fear the moisture seeped into the food supply."

"Baskets hold everything together, but damp does seep in. We used all the big gourds we found." I lifted a shoulder. "They ban the rain and mice better. I know some of the food spoiled. We gave it to the animals and they enjoyed it."

"Baskets and gourds. Are they all we can use for storage? There must be a better way. Something to prevent spoilage and exclude the moisture." His digging tool hung in the air, ready to be sharpened.

"I am sure there is a solution. Father told us to solve our problems. Let us remember to pray for a solution in our daily prayers." I bent to pick up Bilhah and wiped away the dirt she had scooped up and tried to stuff into her mouth.

Adam nodded and returned to his sharpening. I held Bilhah's hand as we walked to the main room where I started dinner. While it stewed, Bilhah and I went to the storehouse to inspect the few baskets and gourds still loaded with food. Grains and seeds were covered with rot, much more than I expected.

I allowed Bilhah to play outside with Absalom, and Bark, under Pasha's care and went to find Adam in the fields.

"Adequate seed is left for planting, but only just. We have not sufficient for eating and growing. We will be short until after the harvest." I sat with a sigh on a rock near him.

He put his digging tool down. "Is it as bad as all that?"

"It is. Water blew in or leaked through the roof. Much is spoiled."

"I feared this may have happened. The roof must be mended and the overhang extended. Probably should check the roof of our house and the animal house, as well. In the meantime, we require extra care with how we use our food this year. The grains we do not plant will have to be stretched as far as possible."

I felt my stomach contract in fear. "We may be hungry again until after the harvest."

"If we do not conserve our food." Adam reached out and took my hand in his. Together we knelt in prayer for help to survive this coming difficult period. Over the next days, our family prayers were filled with requests of support.

Bilhah, Absalom, and Bark, were inseparable, always supervised by our faithful goat, Pasha. I looked for one and found the others nearby. Absalom's concern for his sister helped them stay safe. Adam and I were able to work together in the fields and gardens with less apprehension for the children.

One afternoon I glanced up to see Bilhah bouncing in the air. I stood and saw her sitting on Pasha's back. The patient old goat had allowed Absalom to lift the little girl onto his back to give her a ride. I watched her blond curls bounce along, head tilted back. Her giggles swelled in the air. Absalom ran along beside them, balancing her.

Many times after, Bilhah rode on the back of the goat, her giggles charging the air. Occasionally, she climbed on Pasha by herself to enjoy a ride.

Early during the growing season, the children discovered thick, heavy clay on the banks of the stream. They loved to play with it, dragging it under a tree to roll and fold and pat into funny shapes. A few looked like Bark or the cow. Others were just blobs of mud. When they tired of their play, they set their creations in the sun to dry. More mud waited for them on the banks of the stream. They brought their favorite creations into the house to play with.

One day, I bumped into a mud toy and knocked it from the table to the floor. I expected it to shatter. It did not. It bounced, still whole. I picked up the toy and wondered about the clay they used. Was this a way to store things? Would it prevent the moisture?

I joined them playing in the clay, hoping to create containers for our food. Flattening it out, I could not make it stand tall, nor would it stand using any of the other methods I tried as I attempted to create a pot that looked like the gourds. At last, I rolled long 'serpents' of clay and coiled them around and around. First, I created small cups, smoothing out the bands of the coils. When these dried hard, maintaining their shape, I moved to larger objects: jugs, cooking pots, and big storage jugs with lids. Some of these worked well in the fire. Others shattered.

Another afternoon, I could not reach a basket, so I grabbed a clay pot. I poured water into it and added maize. I worried it might pick up the flavor of the clay, and watched it cook. I dipped a spoonful of the maize from near the edge to taste. It tasted a bit muddy, but not too bad. I offered it to the children to eat but they refused — too muddy for them.

I set the pot aside with a sigh. We did not have enough food to waste. Adam called me to help in the orchard and I spent the rest of the day picking and preparing fruit to dry.

Days later, I found the pot stuffed with dried maize. Frustrated, I thought I would have to throw the pot away. I scraped out the mess and took it out to wash in the stream. I dipped it in the water and rinsed it out. When I smelled the pot, it did not smell like mud. No muddy taste remained. Most important, water no longer dripped through the pot's sides.

Wondering if I made a mistake, I brought in another, bigger pot and boiled maze in it.

"Not more of the nasty maize?" Absalom wrinkled his nose.

"No, son. You do not have to eat this. This is an experiment. I think the maize clogged the open spaces in the pot. Now it holds water."

"Good. It tasted nasty." He wrinkled his nose.

When I cleaned out the pot, it was less porous, but it still absorbed moisture. I thought back, trying to remember what I did the first time. Then I remembered, the maize sat in the pot for days. How many, I did not recall.

I cooked maize in seven small pots. Each day I emptied one pot, hoping to discover the clay pot sealed. On the third day, the pot almost denied water to trickle through; on the fourth, none dripped past the barrier. Little difference showed in the other pots over the next days. I had my answer, four days of absorbing maize repelled moisture.

I sealed a few more of the jars, before I realized the amount of maize shrunk, with an insufficient supply to seal all the pots and have some to eat. We had enough containers for cooking and a few for storage, it would have to do.

~

Things grew as usual for the first half of the growing season. Then heavy rains began to fall nonstop.

"Look at this squash. It is rotting in this rain." I tromped with Adam through the mud in an attempt to salvage our garden produce after ten days and nights of steady downpour. The storm had receded for a short time. "We have never had so much rain this early in the year."

"It has become a problem in the fields, too." Adam bent to stare at the squash. "We cannot harvest in the storm. Perhaps it will soon slow."

"Look. All the vegetables are spoiling. We must pick everything ripe or nearly ripe. They spoil in this." I lifted a squash that fell apart in my hands, its bottom black and soft. It fell to pieces in my hands. "Yuck. At least the good ones can be put in the storehouse."

Adam pulled a carrot. "I hope we can save enough. These are beginning to rot in the ground. All must be gathered now, or there will be none for the raining time."

We picked all the firm squash and pulled all the crisp carrots, turnips, and root vegetables. We put them on the storehouse floor to dry and returned to the garden to rescue others. I breathed through my mouth to avoid the smell. Adam bit his lower lip in an attempt to avoid the stench.

"Even the melons spoil." Adam glanced bleakly at the clouds.

I raised a vine. "These tomatoes are still green. Those on the ground rot. None are ripening."

I plucked every green tomato and slogged through the mud to leave them in the storehouse. Meanwhile, Adam picked everything else edible and brought them inside.

"I hope these can be salvaged. We need them for next year," Adam sighed. "We have more mouths to feed. With the losses during the raining season and, now, storm caused rot decreasing the harvest, we may be in trouble." He shook his head as he gazed at all the empty baskets and jars waiting for grains or vegetables.

"What more can we do? This has continued for days." I lifted a shoulder and gazed at the black clouds.

"I do not know. We need to check the fields. The grains will not do well in all this."

The clouds opened again, drenching us, running in rivulets across the earth and down our necks. We pulled cloaks over our heads and ran into the house.

"Next time we go out." Adam shook the moisture from his cloak in the shelter of our overhanging roof.

"Perhaps later today?" I wrung water from my long braid. I opened the door and checked on the two little ones. They were snug and safe, napping in their beds, with Bark laying on the floor between them, on watch.

Eventually, we managed to investigate the soggy fields. They were too wet to even consider harvesting the late grains. Even if we could, there was no place for it to dry or to be threshed. We were grateful for the early crops stored before the downpour.

After six seven-days of pelting rain, it stopped.

We only managed to gather a few baskets of late wheat, the rest lay ruined on the ground. Everything not collected rotted. Worse, more than half of the vegetables we picked early rotted with a putrid stench, too nasty for even the goats.

The rains did not return. No gentle rains. No pelting rains. Nothing.

The sun burned the moisture away. In the burning heat, streams dried to a trickle; the river reduced to half its size. Much of our stockpile from the previous year had been planted, some eaten. Now, too many baskets, jars, and gourds sat empty. I feared I may have used too much maize curing the pots and jars.

Adam and I stood together, counting the small number of full storage containers.

"How will we feed ourselves and the animals?" I asked.

"We will manage. Jehovah will provide. Perhaps the animals can graze in the hills or nearby valleys. We will survive if we protect our supplies."

"If I am careful, there should be sufficient." I reached for a new, tall, clay jar. "These should protect our supply. Additionally, we must be sure to save seeds for next year's planting. Where will we be if we eat them? In trouble."

"If we must eat them, Jehovah will provide. He asks us to be provident in our use of all He has given us." Adam gazed at the food. "In times of trouble, we must be wise. All will be well, as we continue to put our faith in Jehovah. We are here to succeed, not to fail, not to die. We will not be required to give our lives, yet. And if we are, that, too, is the will of Jehovah."

We stood together, hands entwined, trusting in Jehovah's care.

With less in our storehouse, we ate less, foraged more, and learned to eat foods we had not tried before. Nuts became important, even the small nuts inside the pine cones were tasty tidbits to subdue our hunger.

In the first days, Absalom and Bilhah considered our plight to be a game, as we ate less than usual each meal. Soon, however, their usual cheerfulness became depressed. They lost weight and began to waste away. I worried about them and searched for alternate food sources. When I detected none, Adam and I gave them our share.

One day I came across a deer dying from thirst. I tried to give him a drink, but it was too late. I helped Adam skin it and dry its meat. Though we sorrowed for its death, we gave thanks to Jehovah for the gift.

The deer fed our family, but many of the animals dependent on us were not as easily fed. Grass dried and blew away. We did not have enough grains to share. Cattle, chickens, and sheep wandered off into the hills and other valleys in their search for food. Even most of the goats left us. Only Black Cat and her mate and Pasha and a portion of his herd remained with us.

We encountered dying creatures and spoke a word of gratitude before taking their meat and skins. I discovered a dying turkey one morning. After cleaning it, I threaded a long stick through its cavity and cooked it over the fire. Fat dripped across it, so I turned the bird each time I passed. When it was cooked, I called the children and Adam to eat.

"What is this you feed us?" Adam asked as he cut a small bite.

"Turkey. I found it foraging in the hills today."

"Like it, mama," Bilhah said. "More, please."

"Me, too, mama." Absalom handed me his plate. "May I have more, too, please?"

I cut another slice for each child. I lifted my eyebrows as I glanced in Adam's direction. He nodded and held his plate toward me.

"Please," he said. "This is good. I did not know a bird would be tasty. Who would have thought?"

"Who would have thought?" Bilhah copied her father like the mocking bird who imitated Black Cat's yowl.

We ate turkey for days. It was all we had to eat during those days. The last of the meat and bones went into a pot for soup, which fed us a few more days until we located something else to eat.

Each seven days we observed the Sabbath and on days of sacrifice, a healthy animal offered himself. His meat added to our ability to stay alive. No rain fell. Still we trusted in our God.

~

We passed the days when rain usually fell, with no moisture falling from the sky. A new year began. Once again, the time came to plant in soil packed hard and dry

Our little family knelt together to pray in faith.

"Father," Adam beseeched, "you know our need for food and water. Satan mocks us, saying our lack of water is his doing. We know you provide for our needs." Adam earnestly begged Father for moisture to encourage the plants grow, to give the animals a needed drink, and that we may live, "If it be thy will."

We fought to break the soil, breaking it with sharp sticks and Adam's digging tools. We were forced to attach long sticks to the digging tools and pound them into the packed earth.

After days of struggle, we managed to gouge ditches from the drying stream to the fields and coax a small trickle of water through the fields. It soaked into the dirt, softening it. The dampness enabled us to break the soil and prepare it for planting. We were reminded of our early days on this earth. We were commanded to work. And that year, we worked harder than most others.

Absalom had been happy to give up his daily bath, but now, even he wished for the chance to wash away the dust and mud. Bilhah, too, wished for a bath. They appeared gray from the dirt in their hair and on their bodies.

Together, the four of us planted a portion of the seeds we had reserved. We held some back, fearful they would be needed for the following year, praying they would not be. The grains and vegetables sprouted, though few of the trees blossomed. With extra effort and work we supported their growth.

"What will we do?" I asked Adam one morning, in the second month of the fifth year since leaving Eden, and near the end of the fifth month with no rain. "The few animals still with us are thin. There has been no rain and little water flows from the mountains. We suffer. They suffer. The only water is muddy water left in the bottom of the deeper holes."

Adam and Absalom found pieces of trees swept down the stream and deposited on the banks by the disastrous floods ensuing from the early storms. These they lay across a bend just beyond the ditch we dug from the stream to the fields, creating a dam. It took many days to fill in the spaces between the wood, much like Adam had tightly woven limbs to prevent the storms from entering our home.

Water began to build up behind the dam. Many days later dirt settled leaving clean water for us to drink. Adam formed a gate to block the water to the trench carrying water to the thirsty plants. In this way, he sent little more than a trickle through the fields. Although not as much as the usual gentle showers, it kept the growing plants alive.

We prayed over every seed we planted and the trees in the orchards. At night we knelt together as a family begging Father and Jehovah to allow the rain to fall from the clouds again. Still, none fell. The trickle in our stream dried.

"It has become time to offer a special sacrifice." Adam raised his eyes heavenward. "We must make special preparations. Fast and pray. I must wash carefully and choose the purist animal. All must be in order, if we are to receive the assistance we need."

"When do we begin?" I stared at the sad looking dry crops.

"Tomorrow, from sunrise to dusk. We will eat one meal, each evening, for the next three days, and on the fourth, we will offer our sacrifice."

Adam and I fasted three days, stopping often to pray with the children. The children were too young to miss their meals, but Absalom insisted on skipping his mid-day meal. On the third day, we walked to the water behind the dam where there was barely enough reserved for us to bathe. The children waited with Pasha on the bank for their turn while Adam bathed.

The next day, a young ram accompanied us on the hike to the altar.

"How is this ram sufficiently healthy for sacrifice— healthier than the others?" I asked.

"He has been protected for this purpose."

Adam took special care to complete the rite, paying particular attention to every detail, much too important, this time, to miss even one small point. Absalom and Bilhah sat still, silent tears flowing.

The rite ended with offered prayers. As we walked down the hill, not even bird songs disturbed our silence. We did not know when rain would come, yet we trusted Father. All would be well and it would fall.

Adam was inspired to clean out the storehouse. When we did, we found baskets full of each kind of grain, four baskets of dried beans, and some dried fruits and vegetables we had somehow missed in our earlier searches. We transferred them into new pots and baskets to reduce spoilage. We now had enough to eat until harvest.

It did not rain for another month.

One morning, close to the end of the fourth month of the year, Absalom lifted his head and asked, "What is that sound?"

I listened. A small plop sounded on the roof, too loud to be leaves. Another plop. I opened the door and Bilhah and Absalom ran outside.

"It is raining, mama! Rain!" Absalom danced in the gentle rain.

"Rain! Rain! Rain!" Bilhah chanted.

She raised her face to the falling shower, looking like a bullfrog trying to catch the drops in her round little mouth. Absalom copied her. I stepped out from under the overhang and stood in the drizzle, allowing drops of mud to splash on my legs as I stood with them in the bullfrog look, catching sweet, cool drops of rain on my tongue.

"What are you doing?" Adam came around the house from the fields.

"Catching raindrops! You should try." I glanced at him before lifting my face once more to the sky.

"You look silly."

"Try it papa." Absalom teased. "It tastes wonderful."

Adam laughed, tipped his head back, and joined us in catching raindrops.

We fell to the muddy ground, grasping hands together in prayers of gratitude before finally returning to the house. Even then, we left the door open, allowing the smell, sound, and vision of the welcome rainfall.

A gentle, soaking rain fell, absorbing into the thirsty earth. Dust washed from the leaves as they straightened, standing tall in the welcome moisture. Birds flitted from the trees, drinking in the moisture and bathing in the puddles. The air, again, smelled clean and fresh.

Things took longer than usual to ripen, but they grew and ripened. Our storage almost gone, we continued to forage for fruits, vegetables, and nuts, remembering the foods we ate the first year, catching fish and sharing a portion of the sacrifices. Through the difficulty, we survived another hungry year.

Black Cat and her family, Pasha, and some of the other goats never left us, happy to eat what little we had to share. After a time, many of the other animals returned, though not all. Our herds of sheep and goats were smaller, as was the flock of chickens that flew into the animal house, returning for protection. The cow, a bull, a yearling calf, and a new little one returned. All were happy for the shelter and sustenance we provided.

But it was not a year without hope. Food was growing. We were saved.

CHAPTER SIXTEEN

Attacked

The next years were years of growth. The animals gave back as they received. In the heat of the year, we found bits of wool from the sheep and goats in the bushes, rubbed away to relieve them of the weight and heat. Adam assisted them in the relieving them of the heavy fleece, using a long knife to cut it off. They lined up, waiting for their turn for the relief of the removal.

I learned to twist and spin it. After much experimenting, practice, and failure, I managed to teach myself to weave the strands together, similar to the way I wove baskets, though in wide lengths. My first attempt formed a loosely woven fabric we used for light blankets in the hot months.

Each attempt brought better and tighter fabrics. Adam carved a special tool with thin teeth to use to push the woven threads tighter and closer. Using thin bones with a tiny slit that held a thinner length of spun wool, I sewed together loose garments for us to wear under our leather robes.

Absalom and Bilhah continued to grow. Each day they did something new and interesting, a joy to watch. Zedoch joined our family the year Bilhah was four and Absalom six. Now we were a family of five.

One afternoon Bilhah screamed. "Mama! Papa! Mama! Papa! Abs is hurt! Mama! Papa!"

I jumped up and ran to find them, carrying Zedoch with me. Adam ran from the fields and we met under an apple tree. There, on the ground, lay Absalom with his right arm thrown out in a strange angle below the elbow. He laid still.

"Oh, Absalom! What did you do?" I cried, hearing the shrillness in my voice.

"Abs fell from the tree." Tears covered Bilhah's face. She leaped into my arms as I juggled Zedoch to make space for her.

I clung to my fear. With my child injured, I could not loosen it. I had to think of the children. Sudden beads of sweat dripped from my forehead onto Zedoch's back. What had Absalom done?

"He is too quiet." Adam felt for bumps. "Lumps rise on his head, more bumps than ever rose on mine when I fell. This is bad." Fear tinged his voice.

My body shook out of control, forcing me to set Bilhah down and put Zedoch into her arms. I inhaled deeply a few times. I could not help Adam treat Absalom if I did not regain control.

After several deep breaths, I tried to speak. "What ..." My voice trembled. I cleared my throat and tried again. "What do you need me to do?"

"Prepare some willow bark medicine. I will carry him home."

I took Zedoch back from Bilhah while Adam lifted Absalom into his arms with gentle care and carried him home. Bilhah followed behind, sniffling and wiping her nose on the back of her hand.

I carried Zedoch with me to the stand of willows to gather the branches necessary for the medicine. Though we usually kept it prepared and ready, I had used the last of it after Zedoch's birth and had not refilled the jar.

I thought about how much Absalom would need. His small body, much smaller than Adam's, would require less than Adam when he injured his head seven years earlier. Tears slipped down my cheeks as I remembered the support I received from Jehovah then. Now that knowledge could help our son.

"Absalom will recover." I heard my words. not aware I had spoken. I nodded and spoke with more confidence, "He will heal."

I set Zedoch on the ground in his blanket and cut several small branches. It would not hurt to have extra medicine. I gathered Zedoch into my arms along with the willows and turned toward home.

Adam had the arm straightened by the time I returned. I looked for Bilhah.

"I sent her to find two, straight, sturdy sticks." Adam held his hands apart the a little longer than the length of Absalom's bent arm. "The arm is broken. I saw the bone brushing just below the flesh of his arm. I am glad you and Bilhah were not here. Even in his sleep, he screamed in pain when I pulled it straight."

"Did you send Bilhah looking for sticks just to get her away?"

He shook his head. "Partly, but no. I need the sticks to hold the arm motionless while it heals. Where is she?"

Bilhah banged the door open and ran into the house, carrying five sticks.

"Will these work?" she asked, holding them out to her papa.

Adam took the sticks from her and examined them. "These two will. Thank you, sweetie."

Adam handed her all but the two straightest sticks which he tied to Absalom's arm with a strong vine. As he worked, he slipped his teeth over his lip, thinking. Bilhah stood on the other side of the bed, holding her brother's hand. Tears trickled unnoticed down her cheeks.

Adam glanced at our son. "I worry for him. He sleeps so deeply. He moans in his sleep and does not waken. He did not even rouse as he screamed from the pain of straightening his arm. I fear this is serious," he half whispered, hoping to keep the knowledge of the seriousness of Absalom's pain from his sister.

"When you were wounded, you managed to stay awake until the worst of it passed," I murmured. "Perhaps that aided in your recuperation." I tugged Absalom's eyelids apart and gazed into his eyes. "You are right. This is bad. His eyes look wrong. I will go steep the willow bark."

"You do that while I care for his arm."

I lay Zedoch in his bed and let him whimper himself to sleep while I put the willow bark in to steep. While the water heated, I walked to the stream to fill a fresh bag of water to cool Absalom's burning body. I took it to Adam to pour it over a bit of wool and wash Absalom's scrapes.

While Zedoch slept, I brought the steeped willow bark to Absalom. He lay still, his face white with pain, and breathing so shallow, I held my hand near his mouth to be sure he lived.

I sighed deeply. "Oh Absalom. Why did you have to climb a tree?" I braced his head and back with my arms and set the cup of willow bark tea to his lips. "Here, son. Drink this. It eases the pain."

A few drops of the brown liquid slipped between his lips. He rested easier after that, though he moaned pitifully in his sleep. Bilhah pulled a stool to the side of his bed and sat beside him. She clasped his hand in hers and spoke to him.

We prayed for him, kneeling by his bed. Adam placed his hands on his head and blessed him that he would mend. I sat with Bilhah, watching him thrash in his sleep, waiting for him to wake. At night, Adam picked her sleeping body up and carried her to bed. Awake, she refused to leave her beloved brother's side.

Adam and I took turns sitting with Absalom, watching him lie so quietly, I feared he no longer lived. Other times he flailed about as he dreamed. I fought to prevent the tears from leaking from my eyes and dropping onto his sleeping body, wiping them away with the edge of his blanket.

Adam found me on the second afternoon, wiping tears from my eyes. "Eve. Absalom lives. He is healing."

"I know," I sniffed them back. "I should have been there. Prevented his fall."

Adam hugged me tighter. "You know our son prefers to explore on his own. At least Bilhah was with him. You cannot prevent every injury our children will have. No more than we can ensure they will always be obedient."

"No. Though I wish we could."

I scrubbed the tears away with my sleeve and blew my nose.

"Better." Adam bent, bringing his lips close to mine and kissed me.

While I prepared a mid-day meal on the third day, Bilhah called, "Mama! Papa! Abs is awake."

I dropped the spoon into the pot, scooped Zedoch from his blanket on the floor, and rushed to Absalom's bedside.

"Sorry, Abs." Bilhah glanced up to me and back to Absalom. "He said my yelling hurts."

"It would." Adam came around the corner. "He injured his head pretty badly. His arm is not much better."

I wanted to grab my child into my arms and hug him tight but knew it would harm his broken arm. Instead, I slumped to my knees beside him, mouthing the words, "Absalom, oh, Absalom."

"What happened?" Absalom emitted a small and scratchy sound. "What is wrong, mama?"

"You fell from a tree and broke your arm." Adam sat on the stool next to Absalom. "Your mama is happy to see you awake again."

"Oh. I thought I dreamed it."

I shook my head and reached for Absalom's cup. It was empty. Bilhah grabbed it and ran to refill it. I sat carefully on the bed and touched his head. It felt cooler. He looked about his room, as if it appeared new to him. The bumps on his head at last began to recede.

Bilhah entered, carrying Absalom's cup full of cool water. She carefully handed it to me. I lifted Absalom's head.

"Mama, I am not a little child," Absalom protested weakly.

"No, but you were injured. Let me help."

Absalom brushed me away and tried to sit on his own but crumpled with a groan. I leaned forward and assisted him, then held the cup for him to drink.

Adam, Bilhah, and I knelt next to his bed to thank Jehovah and Father for helping our son to waken, praying for him to continue to recover.

Absalom woke and slept for days. Bilhah stayed beside him while he healed. She brought cooling cloths for his burning brow, fresh water, and soup. She played with him to help him forget the pain.

Absalom began to move. Adam left the arm in the splint for many seven-days. It was weak for many months more. Even after the lumps disappeared, headaches plagued him for nearly a year.

~

Three months later, between harvests and preserving crops for storing, the children and I sat under a tree working together. Absalom and Bilhah labored over the joys of forming letters and reading words with my help. Reading and writing were important, and we worked together often improving their skills. They were improving every day. While we worked, Zedoch slept in a basket near us. Birds sang, brightening the beautiful, warm day.

"Nice writing, Absalom." I leaned over to view his work. "Slightly crooked, but lovely thoughts."

"Thank you, mama. It is hard to write clearly. My arm is still weak."

"I wondered what happened when you fell?" I stopped working and stared into his eyes.

"It was a man in the tree, mama!" Bilhah cried.

"A man?" I glanced toward her then back at Absalom, my pen forgotten in my hands.

"Yes, mama." Absalom's eyes glazed as he remembered. "I was just standing there in the tree, holding on tight. I knew you did not want me to fall. A yellow haired man with an angry face suddenly appeared next to me." He stared at his hands in his lap.

"He surprised me," he continued. "No men but papa live here, but a man stood there in the tree with me. He just stood there. Bilhah and me talked about it," he waved at his sister. "We never saw him go up the tree. No one stood there before I climbed it. Just suddenly there, spinning his gold cane with a serpent twisting around it. I was so surprised. I lost my hold and fell."

"You saw a man in the tree. A man who just appeared?" I watched him closely, waiting for his answer.

"I knew you would not believe me! See, you do not —" Absalom struggled to stand.

I reached out and put my hand on his good arm, gently pulling him down.

"I do believe you. I know who he is."

He bumped to the ground.

"You do, mama? I did not think you would believe me. Bilhah and me decided not to say anything, but she forgot." He glowered in her direction.

"It is good she forgot." I looked into her eyes and smiled then turned to hold Absalom's eyes with my gaze once more. "We needed to know the Destroyer is still watching us. Your papa will want to know who made you fall."

"Who is the Destroyer, mama?" Bilhah turned and stared into my eyes.

"Yes, mama. Who is he?" Absalom focused his eyes on me, too.

"His name is Lucifer. He beguiled me, told me lies to entice me to eat the fruit from the tree in the center of Eden. He tries to destroy Father's work."

"He wants to hurt papa?" Bilhah's tone became belligerent.

I pulled her into my lap. "Yes, he desires to hurt papa, but he craves the destruction of Heavenly Father's plan. Heavenly Father placed papa and me in the Garden of Eden and gave us everything necessary, asking only for us to obey him and not consume the fruit. Lucifer tried to get papa to eat it, but papa obeyed and did not."

"Why are you and papa both here, then, mama?" Absalom tapped the stick he used to write against his chin. "Did you not eat it? Why was papa sent from Eden?"

"I did, son. Lucifer enticed me to eat it. He told me it allowed us to appreciate the difference between good and evil, light and dark, joy and sorrow. After I ate it, papa did, too."

Bilhah stared at me in wonder. Absalom's stared at his hands and peeked at Bilhah and me under his eyelashes.

"Lucifer hoped to destroy Heavenly Father's plan. Because I listened to Lucifer and ate, the fruit changed us, transformed our bodies and forced us out of Father's presence. We were no longer innocent. And, now we can have you children. We used our agency and transgressed that commandment and are now able to obey the greater law, to multiply and replenish the earth — to have you children."

"Then ... Lucifer is not bad?" Absalom persisted.

"No. He is bad, very bad. He had no right to offer it to us. He tries to destroy everything good. He wants to destroy Father's plans for his children and wants all who come here to be as angry as he is. He covets Father's power."

Absalom worked to make sense of this information. I wondered how he could possibly consider Lucifer to be good.

"How did he get to be so bad?" His lip quivered.

"It happened before we came to this world." My hands moved with my words. "We were taught in a grand counsel that bodies are necessary for our progression, and bodies are only available on a mortal earth."

With wide eyes, Bilhah asked, "Why do we need bodies?"

"Because, little one," Adam said as he joined us and drew Absalom onto his lap, "our bodies give us a chance to learn and do things we cannot receive any other way, like having you three children."

"We are here to gain control over our bodies," he continued, "to prove to ourselves we can make good choices as we understand and use the light and knowledge Father and Jehovah give us. We become like Father as we master loving others."

"Does Lucifer have a body?" Absalom turned to stare into his papa's eyes.

"No, son. Lucifer gave up the right to a body when he fought against Father. Father presented a plan. He warned us some would not obey and announced a requirement for a Savior to complete the plan."

"Why can we not all obey?" Bilhah stood from her seat in my lap, her little fists set firmly on her hips.

"We can, small one, but it is not easy. We all make mistakes. Absalom broke his arm because he did not obey, climbing the tree when he knew he should not. Some who come here will choose to disobey. This is part of our life." Adam pulled Absalom closer and drew Bilhah into his lap.

"Two of Father's sons presented themselves as saviors. Lucifer spoke first." Adam gazed into Absalom's upturned face. "He demanded an alteration to the plan, take away our right to choose, and force everyone to return to Father."

"Why was that so bad? Does not Father desire everyone to return?" Absalom held his hands out, palms up.

"He does. But we require the right to choose if we are to grow. Lucifer proposed to force us home without any growth. In his selfishness, he did not care we would not learn to be like Father, nor be able to be like Him. The Destroyer lusts for all the glory and honor due Father as father of our spirits. He cares about nothing else."

"Who was the other son? You said there were two." Absalom frowned.

"Jehovah. He said, 'I will go and do all you ask, and the glory is yours.' Who do you think Father chose, Absalom? The son who announced he would do the work his own way or the son who agreed to do everything asked by Father?"

Absalom considered a moment, then jumped up. "Oh, papa! It is like the time you asked me to plant the corn in nice, straight rows and I wanted to get finished in a hurry so I could play. I planted it all in just a few hills. Not much of the corn grew. It was all crowded. I understand what you are saying. I would prefer to have my son to obey, do the work as I asked. Father chose Jehovah."

"You are right, son. Father chose Jehovah."

"What did Lucifer do? I bet he was mad."

"Furious. He argued. He raged. And he talked with others. Some thought his to be a better plan. Those of Father's children, who did not choose to be responsible for their actions, preferred an easy progression. However, there is no easy way to become like Father."

Adam gathered the two children close. "We debated. We argued. It became a battle. Some pushed and shoved, but mostly we battled with words. We voted. Two of every three stood with Father and Jehovah. Bilhah, it would be like only you and Absalom, not Zedoch, choosing to follow Jehovah."

Bilhah's little mouth formed a round O.

Zedoch began to whimper. I picked him up from his basket to calm him.

"What happened to the ones who followed Lucifer?" Absalom glanced at his feet.

"Father sent Lucifer and all his followers, from home to this earth never to have a body, never to have children, never to understand the joys and sorrows of a body." I patted Zedoch's little back. "They will never eat or be hurt. They will always be angry. Always demand a body they denied themselves when they chose to follow Lucifer."

"Can they ever taste food?" Bilhah shook a bit and rubbed her stomach.

"No. Nor feel the cool of the stream, or the clay squish between their toes, or the sun on their faces." Adam tipped his face toward the sun.

"How is that fair?" Absalom demanded.

"It is fair." Adam held the older children tight in his arms. "Before they were sent from Father's presence, they were given a last opportunity to change their thinking and follow Father. Few did. Most chose to follow Lucifer. They were too angry, too overcome by Lucifer's arguments and lies to listen to the truth."

"They made their choice," I added as I put a clean cloth around Zedoch's wet bottom. "It can no longer be changed, even if they desired to change. Lucifer and his followers seek to hurt us, but they cannot touch us. Lucifer's sudden appearance startled you and caused you to fall."

"Is that how you were hurt? I should have known." Adam shook his head and frowned. "More importantly, he desires to draw each of us away from Father. He will lie and encourage us to follow him. He seeks for us to be as angry as he is. He urges us to listen to his lies. Following Lucifer will hurt you more than falling from a tree ever did."

Absalom took a deep breath and nodded his head slowly. Understanding began to fill his eyes.

"He believes if we do not obey Father, he wins the final battle. He is wrong. But you, Absalom," Adam touched him on the forehead and then touched Bilhah on the forehead, "and you Bilhah, must be on your guard. You must obey and remember what mama and I teach you. Remember we love you as we love Father and Jehovah. Follow our teachings. Obey Father's commands. Can you do that, Absalom?" He stared into the boy's face and waited.

Absalom hesitated before answering. "Yes, ... papa. ... I can do that." He hurried on. "It is hard! I want to run and chase Bark and climb trees. You request me to work and help mama. It is hard."

"I know, son. It is hard for me, too. I want to run and swim and climb trees. But, if I do not work, we do not eat. I remember the year with no rain. I desire food more than I desire to swim or to climb a tree. Please try to remember to obey."

"I will," the little boy answered. A solemn expression crossed his face.

"And you, Bilhah." Adam gazed into her nut-brown eyes. "Will you do this? Can you listen to mama? Do as we ask?"

She crunched her face up tightly, rubbing her ear. She regarded Absalom and her face softened. "Yes, papa. It is hard, but I can."

~

Nearly five months after Absalom's injury his arm worked as it should in most situations. Adam cared for it so well only a small scar on his arm reminded him of his fall.

We hoped Absalom would be more careful after breaking his arm, but he became rasher, climbing higher, running and jumping with abandon. And Bilhah followed, though not as reckless as her brother. She became the one who watched over him.

One day, the next growing season, Absalom and Bilhah bounced toward us on the back of a young stallion. Our surprise stemmed from our limited knowledge of horses. They lived in the hills around us, stately creatures we honored and enjoyed watching on the occasional glimpses we had of them. Their colts ran and played in the fields as the stallions raced across the hills, rearing and challenging one another. We did not call upon them for help or sacrifice.

"How did you two scoundrels manage to climb onto the back of a horse?" I stared at them as the horse came to a stop in front of us.

"We stood on a rock to get high enough to climb on," Bilhah chirped in her musical little voice.

"But, how ... How did you convince him to allow you climb on?" Fear for my children mingled with amazement as they sat on the back of the marvelous creature.

"We asked for a ride. Red let us climb on his back." Bilhah patted his neck.

"Red?" Adam's voice raised a few tones on the one word.

"Red. Is he not red? That is his name." Absalom reached past his sister to rub the horse's neck.

His coat was a beautiful red with a silken black mane. I reached out hesitantly to touch his nose. He lowered his head, allowing me to scratch his neck and between his ears. His skin, warm and soft, exuded a musky scent.

"Red is a lovely animal." Adam stepped close and lifted his knuckles for Red to smell.

He bowed his head to Adam and nuzzled his hand. The children slipped off his back and wrapped their arms about his neck. Red accepted their love. He shook his skin and whuffed once before turning to trot back to his herd.

Many times after, the children returned on Red. Eventually, the stallion brought a herd of mares to Home Valley to stay. Absalom and Adam, with the aid of the goats, collected enough trees to enlarge the animal building. We were responsible for another family of animals that would require its safe protection from the storms. The horses allowed us to climb on their backs and ride when we needed, making it easier to travel long distances.

CHAPTER SEVENTEEN

New Command

Our home and family grew. Over the next few years, Genisa, Nahab, and Abri had joined our family, filling the rooms Adam and the boys built. Pasha stood guard ensuring the safety of each child.

Adam, Absalom, and Zedoch enlarged the storage house as we added to the size of our fields, garden, and orchard. We added thick vines filled with grapes. More food was needed to feed our growing family and herds of animals. The animal building, now called a barn, was extended to make space for horses, sheep, goats, chickens, cattle, ducks, and alpaca.

Bilhah joined in weaving the wool from the wool-bearing animals, and in sewing clothing for us. We created dresses and robes for the girls and myself and robes, tunics, and riding pantaloons for Adam and the boys. The other girls joined us as they grew big enough.

We continued to use leather robes to keep the rain off and to warm us on cold nights. I placed our original, sacred clothing, carefully wrapped in fine leather, in a chest near our bed only to be used on sacred occasions.

Each child was a blessing in our lives. Each was different, each was special.

The old goat, Pasha, lived into the sixteenth year after Eden. We remembered him there and with us almost from the first. He had grown old as part of our family. He outlived his first sons and daughters.

Nahab came crying to me one warm growing season afternoon while I watched young Abri learn to crawl.

"That old Pasha will not move. He will not get up. Why, mama?"

"He is old."

"Yes, mama, but he will not move. Something is wrong." He pulled on my robe.

"I will go with you to see. Perhaps he needs some warm oat mash to help him regain his strength." I snatched a cricket from Abri before she could stuff it into her mouth.

"Oh, mama, make some mash for him! Make him get up!" the little boy cried, flailing his arms.

I lugged the mash in one arm, Abri in the other as I followed Nahab down the path, taking care not to trip. When we reached the barn where the old goat lay, Pasha raised his ancient gray head and managed a weak bleat. He stared at us with glazed eyes and fought to breathe.

I set my hand on Nahab's shoulder. "Even Pasha must return home to Father."

Adam and the other children heard Nahab's cries and raced to the barn. Each of them loved and had been loved by the old goat. He had kept them safe. Tears fell freely as each child took a turn scratching behind his ears and on his neck, crying into his fur. Absalom took Pasha's head into his lap and hummed a little song. His tears fell on the aged goat's head.

We watched with him until Pasha closed his russet brown eyes a last time and sighed a weary last breath. We lost a friend and member of our family. He had led others to carry heavy loads; watched over our little ones, even allowing them to ride on his bony back; and gave us his love. And, now he was gone.

"We cannot eat Pasha! He is our friend," Zedoch announced, fists set firmly on his hips.

Adam and I looked around at the faces of our children, each with set jaws and firm nods. We ate other, otherwise healthy animals when they died.

"No, we do not eat friends, and Pasha has been one of the best. We will not eat him," Adam agreed.

"We will bury him. I will dig his grave," Absalom declared.

Adam and I gazed into the other's eyes before nodding. Where did they get the idea of burial? No other of our friends received this service. But, yes, Pasha deserved the honor of a burial. Absalom and Zedoch went to the edge of the hills and dug a grave for the beloved old goat. With the grave dug, they returned and found a length of woven wool. Into this, they wrapped their pet and friend.

Silently, they carried Pasha between them to the grave site, the rest of us trudged behind. Carefully, they lowered him to rest in the deep hole dug by loving friends. We each sprinkled a handful of soil over the beloved body.

"We should say something. Remember him," Zedoch announced, hands on hips.

The children stood with their heads down, silent in their thoughts.

"I will always remember the ride Pasha gave me when I was tiny." Bilhah broke the silence. "I was afraid at first. Absalom lifted me to Pasha's back. I thought he might run. Did you, Abs?" She turned to gaze at him. He nodded.

She continued, "But he walked slowly at first, allowing me to get comfortable. When my hands found a tight grip on his hair, he jogged and I bounced along. I will always remember that ride."

"You were small then. I am amazed you remember," I said with a little laugh.

"Time with Pasha is memorable," she whispered.

Zedoch took up the challenge next. "One evening during the rains, I went out to get water. Pasha followed me. I do not know how he did, usually he stayed safe from the storms within the barn. This night, he followed me. The stream flowed high, swollen with rushing water. I bent to dip the bag into the water when Pasha pushed me away."

He raised his hand showing two fingers. "Twice more, I bent for water. Twice more, he pushed me away. Finally, I looked upstream. A huge tree bounced toward me, so close it would have knocked me into the rushing water if I still bent over the stream."

Zedoch shook his head. "I hugged Pasha and moved to a calmer part of the stream." He threw out his arms before hugging himself.

We stood in silence until Absalom spoke. "Pasha had the hardest time keeping me safe. I always wanted to go farther, see more, and do more than he would allow. One day he followed me on a walkabout. I was contemplating something. I do not remember just what. As I stepped forward, I felt the goat's teeth in my back, pulling me backward." He held up a clenched hand like the teeth of the goat.

"I came aware of my surroundings at the edge of a cliff. One more step would have taken me over the edge. We were many hours from home and no one would know even where to look for me. Pasha stopped my fall, the good old goat." The young man shrugged, allowing tears to fall.

Everyone stood thinking of the goat and how he had helped us.

"Last year," Genisa said, "I was in the hills with Pasha, gathering flowers for you, mama." She turned to me and smiled. "I stooped to pick some daisies, but Pasha pushed me back. I was not happy with him, for they were especially beautiful."

A little pout filled her face as she crossed her hands and brushed them apart. "Pasha refused to allow me to reach for those daisies, pushing me back time after time. Then, I saw the serpent lying there waiting for me. I turned and fled, leaving my flowers strewn across the hillside. Pasha ran beside me until we were safely away. I hugged him close, panting with fear, grateful for his protection." She stared lovingly at the goat.

Our eyes followed hers. Pasha had been important to us. How many ways had he helped that I did not know?

"Pasha kept me from falling into the fire," Nahab said. "I was small and wobbly. We were in the mountains on one of our overnight treks. Everyone was busy preparing dinner or something else. I tried to help, but Bilhah sent me away." He glared a moment at her.

"As I stepped near the fire, I lost my balance, falling toward it. Suddenly, a body came between me and the fire, steadying me." The boy reached out, as if he held on to the back of the old goat. "Pasha saw me, knew I needed his help, and prevented my fall. He walked with me, letting me grab his hair until I was safely past the fire."

We sat silently a long moment longer, thinking of the ways the goat had helped each of the children, their friend and protector.

"Pasha loved each of you," Adam said. He lifted his arms as if to embrace us all. "As he loved and protected each of you, Jehovah loves and protects us. Pasha has moved on to a life of joy." He bowed his head and dropped his arms. "In time, we will be with Pasha again."

With red and splotched faces, the boys took turns scooping the remainder of the soil over the body. The girls and I found flowers to decorate the grave. We left the sad and lonely place, knowing we would never have another friend quite like Pasha.

~

Three years later, Absalom and Bilhah found us sitting on the branch of the live oak, where we loved to sit, enjoying a peaceful moment before the birth of another child. Bilhah held tight to her braid and rubbing her ear as she stood slightly behind Absalom, sweat beaded on her forehead. Absalom stood with legs wide apart, planted solidly. He sucked in a breath loudly, and then exhaled.

"Papa, mama," Absalom began. "I love Bilhah."

"We know you do, Absalom." I glanced at Bilhah and then looked into his eyes. "The two of you have been close since you were young."

"Yes, mama. We are close." He lifted his chin.

"And?" Adam waited for an answer.

"We want to be like you. We want to have a family, a family of our own. We want to be married."

"You are still young. Absalom, you are eighteen." Adam turned his gaze toward Bilhah. "And you are but sixteen."

"Nearly seventeen! And we love each other." Bilhah clutched Absalom's hand. "We are eager to be married. We are ready for a home of our own, to be always together, like you." Her voice dropped off as she lowered her eyes.

"It is right for you to separate and marry." He held Absalom's eyes with his. "I did not expect this so early, but it is time."

"What will you do? Where will you live?" I spoke too fast, as I often did when facing unexpected difficult situations. I, too, expected this to happen, although not so soon. How can a mama be prepared for her children to leave and separate into their own families?

"We will build a house." Absalom calmed his voice.

"Your brothers and I will help build your home," Adam said. "When it is finished, I will marry the two of you and you can move in. Can you wait that long?"

"We would like that. Can it be near yours?" Bilhah looked at me, red coloring her ears.

I smiled at her. "Of course. Your sisters and I will help you prepare blankets, baskets, and other necessary supplies to make your new house a home."

"Yes, mama," Absalom turned his gaze toward me. "We want to live close to you and papa." He looked to his papa. "When can we collect logs and begin work?"

"The day following the sacrifice this Sabbath. We will go in the afternoon, when finished with harvesting." He saw the look of distress on Absalom's face and added, "But we will gather logs for your home and work on it each afternoon. Will this work for you?"

"Yes, papa," Absalom and Bilhah said at once, their faces brightening.

I watched them leave arm in arm, chattering together, making plans. My stomach flipped. "Adam, are you sure Bilhah is prepared for marriage? She is only sixteen."

"She will be. She has had her moon times for years. She will be older when we finish their house. By then, she will be nearly seventeen."

"And nearly seventeen is the right age?"

"For these two, seventeen is the right age. For us to multiply and replenish the earth, our children must multiply." He brushed my face with the back of his hand. "They are young, but they will be fine."

His hand moved from my face to my hair, stroking through my long, loose tresses and smelling the lilacs behind my ear.

"Are you sure? Really sure?" I pulled back, staring deep into his blue eyes.

"I am really sure. Relax. All will be well." His hand fell to my back, comforting and warm.

I relaxed and turned into his arms. "I trust you."

Following the sacrifice, we prayed and then the older children took the little ones ahead toward home. Adam and I turned to leave when a messenger appeared. We fell to our knees, listening to his message. We were told to repent of our sins and be baptized in the name of Jehovah, the Only Begotten Son of God.

With his head bowed, Adam said, "Why must we repent? And why should we be baptized?"

I had never heard him question Jehovah's commands. I held onto his hand tightly, fearing a reproach.

Instead, the quiet response informed us we were forgiven of our transgressions in Eden. Repentance was required of us and all our family for our small sins since then. We were commanded to teach them to understand repentance and baptism. I breathed easier as I understood Jehovah's love for us, and our family. He wanted us to return to Him. I felt warmth fill me, confirming this truth.

The Spirit carried Adam away. I stood looking at the empty spot where he had knelt, awestruck by all we learned and his sudden disappearance. Finally, I turned and made my way down the hill toward home, alone.

After a wait, Adam returned somber and thoughtful. Bilhah agreed to watch the little ones while we walked to the apple orchard. There he shared his experience.

"I was carried to our bathing pool." The pool we dammed years earlier. "And buried momentarily under the water. The Holy Ghost filled me. I became one with Father, a son of God."

Adam picked two apples from the nearest tree, gave me one and took a bite from the other. "Such a solemn, sacred experience. The messenger gave me more knowledge and left me overcome for a time, sitting and contemplating on the bank of the pool."

He took a bite of his apple. "I need to add this to our Book of Remembrance. Our family will want to read about this, some day in the future. They will want to learn why we repent and are baptized. You and the children are invited to repent and be baptized, and the younger ones will also be invited when they are old enough."

"Old enough? How old is old enough to be baptized?" I took another bite of my apple.

"Eight. Until then they are innocent. They are not able to make bad choices. When they have lived eight years, the Destroyer may then tempt them."

I finished my apple and tossed the core under the tree. "When can we be baptized?"

He reset the chrysanthemum behind my ear. "I need to teach them about this new commandment. They need to understand the things I learned today. Soon, perhaps. How soon will you be able to be baptized? The babe is due to arrive soon."

"I would like to be baptized, if the older ones are prepared next Sabbath. I have repented already. However, I look forward to hearing all you have to teach us." We turned to go home. "If we had not eaten the fruit, we would not have children or know good from evil. We would not know joy, for we would not know sorrow."

Adam stopped and pulled me into a long embrace.

CHAPTER EIGHTEEN

Rites

The older children joined us in harvesting wheat the next day, using the long curved knives Adam created when we harvested the first harvest. Adam called them scythes. I worked beside them, though heavy with the weight of the unborn child. Nahab watched the younger ones, Abri and Samoel.

Soon Genisa slipped over to me, whispering, "Mama, you are tired. The babe grows and you need rest. Please sit with the little ones and relax. I will do your share." She saw me waver. "Please, mama. I can do it."

I allowed an awareness of my exhaustion to fill me. "Yes, you are right. I am tired and need to lie down."

"Your time is near. The baby will soon be born. Sit awhile."

I moved to the edge of the field, grateful to sink to the earth beside the younger children. Little Abri had made a doll of sticks and leaves and sat rocking it. Samoel had some small sticks he found and knelt on the ground stacking them.

"Mama! Building house. Like Absalom and Bilhah," he crowed.

"What a nice house, Samoel. If Absalom and Bilhah build a house as nice as yours, they will be happy." Exhaustion overwhelmed me.

"Thank you, mama," the little boy chirped, returned to his house and gently set a roof in place.

"You need flowers." Nahab tugged his brother to stand. "Mama has them around our house. Bilhah will want some, too. Can you find some we can use?"

The boys searched the grass. They returned with tiny star shaped blooms and stuck them in the dirt surrounding the little stick house. It soon had flowers and little trees surrounding it.

Abri lay in the grass near me and fell asleep. I lay next to her, watching the boys. As I began to drift into sleep, I felt the stirrings of the babe and a twisting cramp. It would come sooner than expected.

I dozed and woke to a sharp cramp. The sun had not moved far across the sky. The birthing pains started closer together than ever before.

"Nahab. Nahab."

He looked up from playing. "Yes, mama?"

"Please go find papa in the field. Tell him it is time."

"Time, mama?"

"He will know. Do not dawdle or play. Go quickly. I need his help now." I winced as another pain crossed my stomach. I groaned. Much faster than earlier. "Hurry, please, Nahab. That is a good boy."

A look of concern crossed his face and he turned and ran toward the fields. I watched his little red-brown head bounce through the fields and listened to him call, "Papa! Papa! Mama needs you! Papa! Where are you?"

I closed my eyes to relax. I would not again for hours.

"Papa, mama says to tell you it is time!" Nahab's voice floated across the field.

Adam would soon be here. The pains returned, faster and harder. I clasped my hands in tight fists across my stomach and clenched my teeth, not wanting the younger children to be frightened by my pain. Thankfully, Abri slept and Samoel continued to build and poke flowers into the dirt.

Please hurry, Adam!

Adam arrived, lifting me into his strong arms. Genisa's voice lilted as she gathered the little ones, carrying sleeping Abri and shepherding the boys toward the house. She would care for them. I appreciated Genisa and my other older children.

Another strong pain ripped through my stomach.

"Adam, the child comes swiftly!" I tried to be calm, but misery colored my voice.

We reached the house and Genisa opened the door for us to enter.

"Your stomach hardens — the babe is ready to be born. Genisa, please set water on to boil and bring me clean cloths.

Perhaps you can send Nahab and Samoel to collect dry moss for us?"

I harvested moss and stored it in the storehouse, earlier. Adam knew I had. He wanted the boys busy and out of the way.

He lay me down on our bed. Bilhah slipped in and washed her hands in some of the hot water Genisa had brought. Adam washed and prepared for this birth as he had for each of our other babies. I had no time to be concerned with Adam's actions. I focused inward and on the hard work ahead. My work. My sorrow. My pain. My joy.

Little Abigail arrived in a rush, bawling as her little body slid from mine. Adam and Bilhah cleaned us and took care of the bloody mess. Only then did Adam allow the others to crowd in to greet their newest sister. She stared into her sibling's eyes, trying to tell them something important.

"Your mama has faced the trials of giving birth once more," Adam said to the gathered children. "This little one is a gift from Father, like each of you. Is she not beautiful?"

Her older brothers and sisters leaned close to see her, speaking in soft tones of her beauty. Adam used the moment to begin to teach them of choice, repentance, and baptism.

He lifted Abri and Samoel onto his lap. "A part of this life is learning to love as these little ones' love. Everyone will make mistakes, sometimes without knowing. Sometimes we choose disobedience."

He taught them things he learned the day of his baptism. You can read them in his Book of Remembrance. He taught them of repentance, using Samoel's tearful story of eating the last apple. He ran sobbing to me.

"I am sorry, mama. I did not know you needed it."

I tousled his golden hair and bent to kiss his forehead. "I know, darling. I forgive you."

Adam nodded toward us, "This is repentance and forgiveness." He scooped the sobbing boy into his lap and soothed him.

Absalom leaned forward with arms on his knees. "I remember when I broke my arm. Papa told me not to climb trees. I wanted to look at a bird nest, so I climbed the tree anyway. Even though both papa and mama forgave me when I fell, my arm still aches during the rain season."

Adam nodded, "Sometimes we must continue to feel the consequences of our actions, even after we repent. Your mama and baby sister require rest. Birthing is always difficult for mama and babe, and Abigail's was particularly difficult. We will discuss this in the other room. Let them sleep."

The family trooped out, quietly talking of Abigail and the things Adam had shared.

Adam stooped to kiss me. "Did they understand?"

"I hope so. They seemed to understand. Teach them more, make your discussions short and simple, especially with the young ones. They will learn."

He kissed me on the forehead. "You and Abigail need rest. We will bring you food. Until then, sleep."

~

While I recovered from Abigail's birth, Adam taught the children more of the things he learned from the messenger. We taught our children from the time they were tiny, but the command to teach repentance and baptism intensified his instruction.

"The children understand the commandments," Adam began one evening. "They ask questions and respond to mine, but I worry. Absalom and Bilhah are concerned for Lucifer. They think he was wronged somehow."

"Lucifer? Wronged?" My jaw tightened.

"They say he did a good thing offering you the fruit of the tree. They say he is also a son of God. Where did they get such nonsense?"

"I wonder. Have they been talking with the Destroyer? Only he would put such things in their minds." The heat of anger rushed through me. "No. They could not have spoken to him." I shook my head, trying to grasp their point of view. "We gained so many blessings when we were forced from Eden. The disobedience came when I listened to the serpent. Lucifer attempted to usurp Father's plan. Jehovah told us there would have been a better way. How can Absalom and Bilhah believe the Destroyer did the right thing?"

I stood and paced. "Why does the serpent have to destroy every good thing we try? He makes me angry."

Adam caught me by the hand and pulled me into an embrace. "Calm yourself, Eve. Your anger has no purpose beyond helping the Destroyer."

He held me close until I regained my calm.

"I will visit with Bilhah tomorrow, see what she has to say. You keep teaching them, please." I said.

He kissed me. "Please do, Eve. We are losing them, already."

For him to be shaken concerned me. It happened so rarely. Still, I appreciated his calm.

We held each other that night, praying we could find a way to keep our family close to Father.

I did not get an opportunity to talk with Bilhah until the next evening when we were preparing dinner. "Will you be baptized this Sabbath? I will."

Her answer came slow and hesitant. "I ... think ... I ... will be prepared. Are you healthy enough?"

A stirring spoon slipped out of my hand and fell onto the ground. "Yes, I am healthy. I am prepared and excited. I planned to be baptized before Abigail decided to be born early. I am eager to have my sins washed away." I picked up the spoon and cleaned it. "I want to be clean again, like this spoon. Do you not want the same thing?"

"I do. I want to be cleansed. But," she hesitated, and then continuing in a rush. "But, I am not sure I am prepared. I must visit with papa, be sure I am ready." She clutched her knife a long time before beginning to chop vegetables.

"It is important to be sure, to be prepared, but do not take too long."

"No, mama, I will not. I will talk more with papa."

We worked in silence for some time.

I broke the silence with a topic I knew she would want to discuss. "How are things coming with your house? Have you managed to get any of the wood you need?" I stirred the soup.

"We went during the past seven-days, after we finished harvesting wheat. We should have plenty. Red went with us and pulled a large raft of wood. We brought many more logs than we expected. Red is a strong horse. I remember the rafts of wood you gathered with the help of Pasha and the goats. This raft was larger than all those together." She reached for a pepper, sliced it open, and cleaned out the seeds to be saved for the planting. She then sliced the peppers and set them on a plate.

"I am glad you have your wood." I tucked the last of the cleansed dishes into the chest. "You are closer to getting your house built."

Abigail woke hungry and I sat to feed her.

"Mama, what is it really like to give birth? I helped papa when both Abigail and Abri were born. I heard you cry out in your suffering. But, what is it really like?"

"You heard me moan and cry out, for that was given to women, to have sorrow and pain in childbirth. I will not tell you it is easy. You have been with me. It is not." Abigail pulled away and gazed into my eyes. I patted her until she latched on once more, eating with vigor. "The joy after the birth is greater than the suffering. Because of the intensity of childbirth, the joy of welcoming a new life is as exquisite as the agony. It makes everything worthwhile, in a way different from other pains."

I massaged Abigail's little back. "As I watch each of you grow into a lovely young women and men, it becomes forgotten. I remember it only for a short while, until the wonder of the new child takes over, erasing it. Even now, the pain from Abigail's birth is slipping away."

"The pain is terrible and still you forget? Abigail's birth was more difficult than Abri's. You worked hard and suffered much. How can you forget?" Anguish filled her voice.

"It lingers in my memory, returning in a rush with the next birth, but the suffering is forgotten in the pleasure of holding her, nursing her, seeing her smile, watching you and your brothers and sisters meet and love her. All this helps to erase the recollection. If I had not forgotten, I would not have had more children after Absalom." I lifted the babe to my shoulder and patted her back. "This great joy overcomes the pain and sorrow of birth."

"I am beginning to perceive your meaning. Even when I know it will hurt to put my hands into nettles when I gather leaves for tea, the tea is worth the necessary discomfort to gather them. The need for the leaves is greater than the pain they cause."

I nodded. "You start to understand. Birth is not easy, for mama or child. The pain for both is beneficial. Life is more important than the pain."

Bilhah ducked her head. "I guess I follow. Someday I will have the same sorrow and joy."

Adam baptized me on the next Sabbath, along with the older children, all but Absalom and Bilhah. They chose not to join us, yet. We hoped they would choose to do so soon. I rose from being buried a moment in the water, feeling clean in a way I had not felt since Eden. The blessing Adam gave me when he bestowed the Holy Ghost on me, comforted me. It was too sacred to write, but one I will always remember.

~

Late in the year, nearly time for the rains to come, the harvests were safely stored and waiting to be eaten. The new home for Absalom and Bilhah rose tall and ready for them. The girls and I harvested dried gourds and fashioned dishes and pots from clay. These we painted with colorful designs using a mixture of clay and color mixed from flowers, ground chunks of colorful rocks and fat. We applied the paint with thick hairs from the end of Red's tail. Clean, fresh bedding filled their bed, warm furs and woven coverings lay on it.

Absalom and his brothers built the bed, a table and stools. They also whittled dishes and spoons. They built a safe fire space inside for heat and cooking.

Adam and the boys cleaned out the barn and moved in tables. The girls found the last of late flowers to brighten it. The barn looked and smelled wonderful. We dressed in our best clothes.

Bilhah sewed special clothing for Absalom and herself, decorated in colorful porcupine quills. She wore a lovely dress and Absalom wore soft tunic and pantaloons.

The other children and I settled in along the sides to observe the ceremony. Adam stood with Absalom and Bilhah in front of him. He spoke the sacred words of the marriage rite, beautiful and simple, ending with a sweet kiss.

We celebrated the rest of the day, talking, eating, and laughing, enjoying being together. Joy filled our day. After the young couple retreated to their new home, we emptied the barn of human additions and allowed the animals to return. Adam and I carried the little ones to bed, asleep from the excitement of the day. Zedoch, Genisa, and Nahab companionably cleared away the dishes.

I sat with Adam on our live oak branch, enjoying the twinkling evening stars as they emerged in the darkening sky.

"The day went well," I said. "Absalom and Bilhah looked lovely. You remembered all the words. Did you get help?"

He nodded, suddenly pensive. "They all behaved, helping the day to go well. Only ..." His voice drifted off. His teeth surrounded his lower lip.

"Only? Only what?"

"The Destroyer joined us. He lazed by the door, staring at our children with his usual sneer on his face. His clothing was resplendent velvet in golds and reds. The design rippled across his body. A gold trimmed cape fluttered in the breeze. The serpent around his cane twisted and hissed at me," Adam said in a rush.

"Lucifer? Lucifer, here? On our day of joy? In what way can he ruin our happy day?" I glanced about, half expecting to see him even now.

"Who knows what he thought. He will try to find a way. He always seeks to destroy."

"He destroyed the good mood of our day."

"He will continue to try to ruin our happiness," Adam sighed and slid a comforting arm around my waist. "All we can do is teach our children and pray for Father's protection. They will have His protection, as long as they choose to obey. He will not take away their agency, but they will make mistakes. Absalom and Bilhah are already struggling. They chose not to be baptized when you did."

I lay my head on Adam's shoulder. "I wish it were not so. It is hard to be parents."

"No harder than it for Father," he reminded me. "He lost a third of his children in the battle with Lucifer. Thousands and thousands of souls chose to rebel, even in His presence. Away from Him, it is difficult to have faith. It will be hard for us, as it was difficult for Father."

We sat together in the dark, watching the stars. They were cheerful, contrary to our mood. The Destroyer had pushed himself on our happiness.

Lucifer did not wait long. Only months after the wedding, he managed to intrude into our lives once more.

CHAPTER NINETEEN

Defection

The storms ended, allowing us to go out into the warmer air once more. One morning I took Abigail to the bathing pool outdoors. She had started to crawl and found ways to get into everything. She squealed as she splashed and played.

"Mama." Bilhah's voice broke into my thoughts, startling me.

I jumped. "Bilhah! You surprised me. I did not expect you to be here now."

She slipped off her clothing and joined us.

"Mama, I need to talk"

"What do you need to talk about, dear?" I reached to draw Abigail back.

"Abs talked with Lucifer." Though she spoke quietly, her words tore through my soul and filled me with fear.

232

"He did what?" My shocked voice rose. I took a deep breath and managed to calm it. "Did he not remember the things we taught him?"

"Yes, mama, he does. But he communicated with Lucifer last night. Lucifer told Abs he is also a son of God. Papa says we are children of God. Lucifer lived with Father in heaven. Would he not also be a son of God? Mama! Grab Abigail!"

I started and stretched out for the baby who paddled in the water and bobbed under. I grabbed her and pulled her out of the water into my arms. She giggled, unharmed by the dunking, and tried to wiggle herself back into the water.

"Bilhah. He beguiles us. Tells us things close to the truth, but not true. Lucifer gave up all right to the privilege of being a son of God when he rebelled. He wants us to believe he is the god of this world. He is not." Again, my voice rose in pitch and volume.

"I know, mama. I only tell you what Lucifer instructed Abs." Bilhah's eyes began to fill with tears.

I worked to control my emotions, to speak calmly. "Jehovah is the God of this world. He gave us the right to choose. Not the Destroyer."

My voice continued to rise in volume and I spoke too fast. I struggled but could not control myself. "The Destroyer desires to take away our rights to choose. We learn to obey, gain light and truth to gain joy,"

Abigail began to wail. I stopped and took a deep breath, hugging Abigail tight while I brought my voice and emotions under control. I spoke slower and quieter. "Lucifer wants us to be as angry and hurt as he is. He wants to surround us with darkness and lies. What should be clear is not always obvious."

"No, mama, it is not. I am confused. Abs is so persuasive. He has decided to listen to Lucifer. Mama. He is my husband! I love him. I do not care about Lucifer. but I love Absalom."

"Yours is a great challenge. You must be strong." I reached out and cupped her chin in my hand. "Stand firm for Jehovah. Stay in the light."

"I want to, mama. I do." Bilhah put her arms around me, hugging me and Abigail.

We stepped out of the pool and I wrapped a piece of woolen cloth around Abigail and myself. Bilhah wrapped her cloak around her. We walked together toward our homes in silence. I hoped she had the strength necessary to not give in.

Later in the evening Adam and I sat alone under the stars on our live oak tree branch. "You will never believe what Absalom announced to me this afternoon." Adam ran his hand through his hair. "That boy does not understand the grief that awaits him!"

I turned from the stars to face him. "I heard. Bilhah shared with me this morning. He is talking to Lucifer. The Destroyer declared to Absalom he is also a son of God. I talked with her, tried to help her comprehend the beguilement."

"He believes the lies." Frustration crowded into Adam's voice. "He insists we are wrong to believe Jehovah, to worship Him, and to sacrifice to Him. The Destroyer tells him we should be worshiping him as god of this world. Do you remember when he tried that on us?" The muscles in his jaws and shoulders tightened.

I nodded, remembering the horrible day. We walked away then. Adam had not even engaged him in conversation. After then, the Destroyer did all he could to make our life difficult.

"He has waited for a break in our faith." I clenched a fist.

"And found one in Absalom. Did we not teach him better?" Adam's voice broke in grief. "Did he not listen?" Did he not understand the danger to his joy and his hope for eternal life?"

"We feared the Destroyer would find a way to cause us pain. He has beguiled our child, drawing him away from Jehovah. What greater way to hurt us?"

Our tears mixed together in an embrace. Eventually, we dried our tears and looked up. A star streaked toward the earth, landing in the valley over the hill with a loud explosion. Even the stars felt it.

Absalom and Bilhah drew farther from us each day. Absalom tried, unsuccessfully, to quarrel with Adam, who did not respond to his anger. Bilhah listened to his arguments and saw some twisted reasoning. She began spouting them as her own, trying to change my way of thinking. She did not know the love and trust I held for Father and Jehovah that I developed in Eden.

"Absalom was surly in the field again," Adam said another evening as we watched the stars and shared events of the day. "When I refused to discuss his views on choice and responsibility, he stomped to the other side of the field, sullenly jerking weeds from the ground. It is getting difficult to work with him."

"It is difficult to hear them spout words we know were given to them by the Destroyer. Bilhah continues to try to involve me in discussions. I will not join in. I have learned to turn my mind to other things or sing a song. She gets frustrated with me. I will not be involved in her arguments."

"Nor will I listen to Absalom's diatribes." Adam gazed into the stars as he regained his composure.

"I fear they will draw the others from Father," I whispered.

Adam stared past me, hurt in his eyes.

"How did we lose them? We taught them." I stood and paced. "What more we could have done? What more to tell them?"

"We observed the Sabbath each seven-days. We taught them at every opportunity." Adam joined my anguish. "Could I have taken him alone more often, shared with him the blessings of Jehovah?"

"What can we do to protect the others? How can we stop this? How can we help Absalom and Bilhah?"

"We can love them," Adam said, suddenly calm. "We have taught them. We cannot argue, we can only love. Arguments and hate will be a win for the Destroyer."

His voice soothed me. I stopped pacing and stared into his brilliant blue eyes.

"It is essential they have agency to choose, as we did." Adam placed his hands on the swell of my hips and brought me near. "We cannot force them. We must pray they return to the light and love them. Always love them. They know this, though their choices are opposite from the way we prefer."

I slumped onto the tree limb beside him. "I thought my sorrow was giving birth. Now I find it comes when our children make terrible choices. It is much harder to stand aside and watch them, unable to do anything. Perhaps the love they feel when their little one arrives will help them remember."

"I know, dear." He pulled me close, smelling the jasmine in my hair. "Who knew life would require this of us? Yet, somehow, we should have known. How can we be different from Father? A small part of His pain hurts me now."

"I pray we will not lose that many children."

If it had only been one-third, I would have been happy.

~

We loved them, invited them into our home for meals, and tried to be kind, though we obtained little relief. Absalom continued to press his wild beliefs on us, insisting on the friendship of the Destroyer as the god of our world.

Bilhah's growing body brought her to me, asking questions about what to expect and if her aches and pains were normal. I hoped the questions would help to rebuild our closeness. I hoped their baby would bring them back to us, or at least soften the harsh words.

Some days, we made progress, though those days were few. We watered our pillows with our tears many nights after they pressed their beliefs onto us harshly. Our visits became less frequent, less friendly.

Absalom rushed into our house one evening shortly after the end of the storms, after a month of no communication. His blond hair stood on end and his emotions were in a stir.

"Papa! Mama! Help me please! Bilhah is in great pain! She bleeds. The babe seeks to be born with no success. I do not know what to do. Please help us."

Adam looked at me. Although I expected to deliver another baby within days, I agreed. We did not agree with many of their decisions, but these were our children. Our first grandchild fought to be born. We loved them.

"Absalom, you must help us." Adam set his palm on Absalom's back to calm him. "You may need to do this alone, as I did when you were born."

"How did you do it alone? How did you know what to do?" Absalom, distracted by fear for his wife, brushed his hands through his hair.

"Later. Now we must go help Bilhah," I lay my hand on his arm. He did not flinch away as he did so often. It gave me hope. "Do you have dry moss? A warm piece of wool to wrap him in?"

"No," he wailed turning around, searching for those items in our home. "I did not know he would come this early. I lost count of the moons."

"Go to the storage building," I said. "There you will find moss gathered by your sisters, hanging in the corner near the door. Look in the middle drawer on the west side, along the wall. There are lengths of wool stored there. Choose one Bilhah wove. She will like that. Bring these to your home."

"Hurry, Absalom!" Adam encouraged.

"Your papa and I will go there now. We will do what we can to help Bilhah." I pushed him out the door toward the storage building.

I gathered together a pot for boiling water, one Absalom made years earlier, and some scraps of fabric. Adam picked up his sharp knife and a ball of thin yarn sitting near my loom. Genisa entered and watched our preparations. "Is it Bilhah's time?"

I nodded.

"I will care for the little ones, mama. You should be there for her. Do not worry."

"Thank you, darling." I touched her cheek then hurried out the door.

Bilhah lay in her bed soaked in sweat, blood pooled about her middle. My heart raced. This had never happened to me. We moved to her side.

Adam touched her face. "How long has this been going on?" he murmured.

"Since last night," she moaned. "The pains began, getting harder and harder. I started to bleed this afternoon."

"I can tell." Adam turned to ready his supplies.

"All will be well, Bilhah. Your papa is here. He knows what to do." I did not know for sure he did, but she did not need to know. Not now.

Adam touched her stomach and Bilhah moaned. He handed me a bowl of cool water to me with one of the cloths we brought.

"Use these to cool her. She is too hot." He spoke quietly.

I mopped her forehead and the back of her neck, remembering how I did the same for her papa, using cut off strips of leather. She moaned. I dipped the cloth in the cool water, wrung it, and set it on her forehead. I gazed into Adam's eyes, silently asking, 'Will she be all right?'

Adam nodded before pouring water into the pot and setting it over the fire to boil. He gently spread her legs to examine her.

"The head has crowned. No wonder things are a problem. They should have called someone much sooner." He patted Bilhah's thigh to get her attention. "Bilhah. Bilhah."

She groaned. "Unh?"

"Wait a moment. The next pain will come soon. It will be difficult to not push. Wait, dear, just a second. I must move the babe's head."

"Yes, papa," she groaned.

He reached down, turning the head a bit before a contraction rippled through her belly.

"Push now, Bilhah. Push!" he cried.

She pushed and pushed. Adam's gentle hands turned the tiny, dark head and it started to move.

"Wait a bit," he called.

I touched her arm to get her attention. He ran a finger around it, releasing a shoulder. I watched in amazement. As the one in the bed, I never saw the things Adam did for me. It was beautiful—and messy.

Another contraction rippled.

"Bilhah, push, one more time and it will be over."

She pushed and the infant slipped out.

The door opened and Absalom rushed in, carrying moss and a length of beautiful fabric Bilhah wove the year before. He stood staring at the bed. His face blank.

"Absalom, Bilhah, you have a son," Adam said holding the baby up for them.

He laid the tiny boy on Bilhah's stomach while he completed preparations to separate the babe from his mother, tying two bits of yarn two finger widths apart around the cord connecting him to his mother.

He handed the knife to Absalom. "Cut between the ties."

Absalom set the knife between the two ties and cut it with a soft thunk. He dropped the knife on the bed and moved to grab Bilhah's hand and gaze into his wife's eyes.

"A boy, Bilhah! We have a son."

"I hoped to have a man child." Her hand waved weakly toward Absalom. "What will we name him?"

Adam took the babe from Bilhah's stomach, cleaned him and then wrapped him in the length of wool Absalom brought. He placed the child in his papa's arms. Absalom stared into his little face in wonder. He lifted the infant and brushed his lips across his little one's cheeks, breathing deeply. He bent to set him into Bilhah's arms with a look of tenderness. He searched for her breast. She helped him find it and smiled. Love filled her.

"Lev," Absalom whispered. "Remember, we decided if he is a man child we name him Lev."

"I remember. Lev," she crooned.

The birth was more difficult than she had imagined, more difficult than any I experienced. I knew how she felt, remembering Absalom's birth. I lifted the cloth from her forehead, rinsed it, and handed it to Absalom.

"Use this to cool her face and neck. It will help."

Absalom took it and wiped her cheeks and forehead. Bilhah looked at him and smiled.

While Adam worked to expel the afterbirth, I poured warm water into a tall cup and added a generous dollop of honey. When it mixed together, I handed it to Absalom.

"She needs this to replace all the blood lost. When she drinks it all, mix honey in warm water and insist she drinks it. She lost too much blood."

Adam and I changed her bedclothes and he placed the dried moss between her legs to soak up the blood, as gentle with his daughter as he had always been with me. He gave Absalom instructions on how to encourage Bilhah' healing, then we bent to kiss Bilhah's forehead, hugged Absalom, and walked out the door. The new family needed time to be alone.

"Will Lev heal the rift between us?" I asked as Adam slipped his arm around me.

"We can hope he will."

~

For a time, Lev bolstered good feelings between us and his parents. His dark brown curls and deep blue eyes that changed to a deep brown delighted his parents and us. His parents loved him. They allowed us to see him and hold him during those early months.

They refused to allow a Thank Offering for Lev, nor would they allow Adam to give him a Name Blessing. Our hopes that his birth would help draw us closer together were dashed. Absalom and Bilhah continued to listen to Lucifer's lies and to distance themselves from us.

Our Jared arrived a month later. Genisa and Adam helped me. I appreciated Adam's gentleness even more after watching him help Bilhah. Eight days later, we hiked to the altar on the hill and offered thank sacrifices. Adam brought two perfect young rams to sacrifice. The first as thanks for Jared's safe birth, the second for Lev's. All our family, except Absalom, Bilhah, and Lev, were there.

Before the next rains, Absalom and Bilhah took Lev and moved into another valley. They packed as much as they could place into baskets, tied to two long trailing poles attached to Red. Adam gave them baskets filled with seed.

Absalom took the baskets and growled, "I earned this. You should give me more."

I ducked my head slightly to prevent staring at him.

Bilhah grabbed the food I prepared for their journey from me and shoved it into the packs on Red's back. Her lips formed a thin line. I could not tell if the cause of the line came because she did not want to talk to me or if Absalom had ordered her silence.

They stood before us, prepared to leave Home Valley and make a home of their own, all the while Absalom raged at

Adam and me because we "forced them to leave" because we were unable to "understand and accept" their position. I suppose we did, for we expected obedience to Jehovah's commandments. Neither Adam nor I returned their insults.

As they turned to walk away, we called, "We love you, Absalom. We love you, Bilhah. We love you, Lev."

With no indication they heard us, we watched their disappearing backs until they crossed the ridge.

Within a year, Genisa and Zedoch were married and our family began to multiply in ways we did not believe possible. Sons and daughters married, adding grandsons and granddaughters to our number.

Our children's disobedience to Jehovah's commands expanded, along with our sorrow. More of them were drawn to follow Absalom and Bilhah, listening to the Destroyer. As they chose to follow the Destroyer, they became uncomfortable in our presence and left Home Valley.

"Do you remember Father's loss?" Adam asked one evening as we sat on our live oak limb, enjoying the stars.

I nodded, numb at the thought.

"I have been thinking of our family. We have lost more than half our children and all of our grandchildren."

"We thought one-third to be grievous for Father," I sighed, shoulders drooping. I hoped to lose less than one-third."

Adam reached for my hand. "Some of the younger children show promise. There is hope."

CHAPTER TWENTY

Hope

We had lived almost a hundred years on this earth. Many children were born to Adam and me. They continued to be born, beginning to fill the earth. In my sorrow over their loss from the love of Jehovah, I wanted to be near the end of my responsibility to multiply, except we had no righteous sons. None to follow Adam in preaching the gospel nor to honor Jehovah's priesthood.

Too few of our family listened to our teachings. Too many left. Too many chose the Destroyer. I worried they were too prideful and stubborn. I feared they all would turn away. Would any of my posterity obey?

We added one more son to our family, a beautiful, dark haired son. We hoped he chose to be righteous. I accompanied Adam and some of the younger children in the thank sacrifice and naming blessing. Adam offered a prayer and named him Cain.

"He cries too much." Benoni thrust his lip out, folded his arms, and held them close to his body.

"He does cry," I agreed. "I pray he listens to the word of Jehovah and becomes happy. I pray each of you will listen to His word." I stretched my arms out to gather in our young ones who stood near the altar.

Cain protested louder than the others. He sobbed during his blessing and frequently during the day and night, stirring up the household. I woke tired each morning from rocking him trying to soothe him into sleep. He bawled for most of his first three months.

As soon as he grew big enough, I spooned a thin mixture of millet and oats into him. His teeth broke through the gums soon after, causing his nose to run and more tears to flow, from both of us. We howled each time he ate until he learned to nurse without biting me. I helped him to suck the juice from fresh plums and peaches. He began to gnaw the fruit to the pit. As he ate different foods, he stopped crying, and life became easier for everyone.

A quick learner, Cain crawled early, tasted everything in reach, and babbled to us. By the first anniversary of his birth, he toddled from one chair to the next and laughed at everything. He had become a joy to be around. It did not take him long to learn to tease. He offered an apple to his older sister, then pulled it back and ran. Others received similar treatment.

One day he watched me shake dust from my foot coverings. The next morning, I slipped my foot into the foot covering.

"Ouch! What is in this?" I cried.

I pulled the covering off and shook it. Out plopped a pine cone. I heard giggling from behind the chair.

I followed the giggling and discovered Cain. I grabbed him up and hugged him close, tickling him until we both giggled so hard we could not breathe.

After then, we made it a regular practice to shake our foot coverings, or we would step onto a pine cone, a stone, or a stick. From a different room, his resounding cackle echoed with glee. He found other ways to tease. He favored pulling the cat's tail and trying to ride the cow. He shook his dark curls at us and begged forgiveness. Forgiveness was given, though we were certain he would find trouble somewhere else.

Another quiet, thoughtful child who we named Abel joined us about three years after Cain did. Unlike Cain, his blond hair and blue eyes described him as appearing much like his papa. I hoped to discover in these boys the one to carry on Jehovah's work of the kingdom. We had three of them, now, who could follow Adam in the priesthood: Benoni, Cain, and Abel.

The boys assisted me in the garden when they were not working with their papa and older brothers in the fields. While we worked, we remembered to be aware of Cain's pranks and questioned which of us would be his victim. He carried wood for me or sat still, observing a plant grow or some other wonder of nature. I often thought his stillness indicated his planning new ways to tease his older brothers and sisters.

Though younger than the older sons, Benoni worked hard in the fields beside his papa and brothers, always ignoring Cain's teasing. He never rejected the gospel as he aged, but he did not desire to carry on the battle with those who had. He discovered his joy in raising horses. Some of them were the same beautiful color of Absalom and Bilhah's Red.

Abel grew differently than his brothers. He loved his papa and developed a character like him—quiet, gentle, and obedient. Whenever they would let him, he trailed the men in the fields, assisting in every way he could. When I searched for him, his blond hair bounced behind his papa in the fields or racing to bring me water.

One afternoon I could not find Abel. I searched the fields and did not discover him. I tramped through the gardens and did not see him. I looked by the woodpile, not there either. I called and called with no answer.

At last, I pushed open the barn, shouting, "Abel. Abel. Where are you, Abel?"

"Shhh, mama," Abel whispered. "Butternut is birthing."

I tip-toed into the barn and sat beside the small boy. Together, we watched in wonder as Benoni aided the mare, Butternut, birth her foal.

"Look, mama. There are the back legs. The foal will be out soon." Abel reached out for my hand as he whispered.

"There are its front legs. Oh, look, mama." his excited whisper intoned. "It is a stallion. And look at its nose. He has a white star on it!"

"What color will he be, Benoni, do you think?" Abel asked.

Benoni stood up from behind the colt as the mare cleaned it. "He will be a chestnut color, like his mama, I think. His papa had some white in him, so he could have some white."

"Like the white star on his nose?" the little boy stretched his hand toward the colt's star.

"Yes, Abel, like the white star on his nose. He may have white in other places. You will have to watch him. Do you want to give him a name?"

Abel nodded and thought for a time. I could see him mouth names, then shake his head. I thought for sure he would name the colt Star. The name fit, but Abel rejected it.

"Light Bright," he said at last. "His name is Light Bright."

"Light Bright?" Benoni asked. "Yes. I see the bright light on his nose. Good name for him. Will you stay and help me with him?"

"Can I?" Abel looked into his brother's eyes in adoration. Benoni nodded.

"May I, mama?" he turned his eyes to me.

How could I deny him his joy? "Yes, son. You may. Come to me when you are finished. I have a treat for you and your brothers."

"Yes, mama."

After that, when not with his papa, I found Abel with the animals. He played with the young, assisted the injured, and participated in the birthing of most animals. He spent his spare time with Benoni and his horses. All living creatures fell within the bounds of his love. Animals and people loved him. Especially Cain.

Cain and Abel lived and loved each other. They wrestled in the dirt, carried water and wood for me, and joined in harvesting and threshing. It became a contest between them to see who could harvest or thresh the most baskets of grains or beans. Sometimes Cain won; other times, Abel did. Strength and stamina were well matched in these two brothers.

~

In the days since we left Eden, the animals became smaller and weaker. Plants grew less hardy, requiring a greater amount of land to produce the same amount of food.

As the boys aged into their teen years, Cain's energies diverted from teasing to cultivating plants. He hiked into the hills where he discovered new seedlings. He learned to increase the yields of the familiar grains and vegetables and improve taste, somehow crossing a new one with a variety from our fields. Many times, he brought me a new plant he worked on to taste.

"Is it good, mama?" he asked. "I want only to produce good tasting, healthy food."

Frequently, I answered, "Yes, Cain. This is very good. Better than the older variety. Almost better than those we ate in Eden."

Cain smiled and give me a hug.

On a few occasions, I replied, "I am sorry, son. This does not taste as good. It is mushy (or bitter, or something). You may want to try again."

"Thank you, mama. No one else will give me an honest response. Now I know I must return to work on this."

Again, and always, he smiled and gave me a hug.

New foods, with new and wonderful flavors, delivered excitement. We cheered and hugged one another when these were tasted and enjoyed. Diversity of food increased the health of our family in Home Valley.

Abel continued to love and show interest in the creatures. While Cain spent time in the fields increasing the yields of crops, Abel worked to build the flocks. He, too, introduced stronger wild animals into the flock. The sheep, goats, and cattle grew stronger. They flourished on tougher grass that sickened them earlier. Abel labored to rebuild the health and size of our flocks and herds.

Both young men grew in favor with Adam and Jehovah. Perhaps, at last, we had sons who would become righteous priests of Jehovah. With the three boys and their sisters, love and laughter filled our home during those years.

Adam and I sat on the live oak branch one evening, as we frequently did, discussing our children, as we had over the years.

"They are obedient sons." I tilted my head to the side.

"Yes, all three boys are obedient." Adam worried his bottom lip with his teeth. "I wish Benoni would choose to follow the calling to the priesthood, although Cain and Abel are honorable, now."

"You worry for them?"

"I remember their brothers. How many sons have we thought would accept the call, or be obedient past their teen years, only to learn they would not?" I heard sorrow and frustration in his voice.

"I remember. Absalom's desertion hurt the worst. After him and Zedoch, the desolation decreased."

"It did. It hurt when his brothers followed in his path or refused the calling. So many refuse, I almost fear to hope." Adam's voice broke.

I encircled his waist. What could I say? I lay my head on his shoulder and sighed.

As we did every day, we prayed for them.

Adam maintained his teaching them of the priesthood and the fundamentals of sacrifice. He was careful, for other sons had received this honor and later turned their backs on it to follow the Destroyer.

"How are Cain and Abel doing in their training?" I asked another night, nearly a year later. "Will either boy be ready to hold the priesthood?"

"I am not sure. Cain does all I ask him to do. He participates in the learning and joins in the rites, though there is little enthusiasm. He goes through the motions. I fear for him." Adam's voice was flat and sad. "There is a glimmer of selfishness and greed deep within his soul."

"And Abel? Does he show interest?"

Adam became animated. "Abel, ah Abel. He participates. He asks questions. He searches for answers. If any of our sons are worthy, it is Abel. He is such a loving, giving young man.

How can we not love him? How could Jehovah not love him?" The joy dropped from his voice. "Perhaps, this is the reason Cain harbors darkness within him. Is he jealous of the love Abel draws to him? I hope not. Abel does not seek attention. His love draws it to him."

We watched our sons, both of them now with dark hair like Adam. Cain's eyes were dark brown, as mine are. Abel's eyes were a startling blue, like Adam's. Each boy accepted more responsibility, Cain cultivated the experimental plants. Abel cared for the goats and sheep, herded them to the hills, and protected them from wild animals.

Men from other villages found their way to Home Valley. They did not seek the knowledge and joy of Jehovah but came to learn from Cain and Abel. Abel freely shared and then returned to the hills and his creatures.

Men came to Cain, begging a handful or a basket full of new grains or a start of one of his plants. He traded, happy to accept anything they brought for trade. He built a separate, larger storehouse to hold all the grains everything he gained in trade.

Cain began to brush past me and his papa, hardly noticing us.

"Those men are turning his head," Adam said after an encounter. "They are filling him with pride, cheering on his exceptional plant knowledge."

"He has begun to withdraw from us. I cannot remember the last time he came to dinner with the family, happy and clean." I ran a shaky hand through my hair.

"It has been many Sabbaths since he joined us without bragging about his trades or his new plants." Adam took my hand.

I grasped his. "He chooses other's company over ours."

Abel united with the family for dinner when in the valley. He kept track of the healthiest, first-born animals, usually without writing. These were offered as sacrifice. Abel presented them to his papa each time a sacrifice was needed. He participated with Adam in sacrifice and offering prayers for our children and grandchildren.

Cain avoided the altar.

I trekked to Cain's fields on a warm afternoon to visit him. I wandered through several different ones before I found him kneeling in the amaranth. I stayed back a moment, watching and listening.

"Father," I heard Cain say, "I want to be close to you. I want to obey. Please help me."

I waited and watched until he stood and picked up his digging tool.

"Cain?"

He spun around. "Mama?"

"You have not been home for days. I am worried for you. Are you well?"

"I am, mama." He brushed away tears from his cheeks.

"Will you join us for dinner tonight? We miss you."

"Uh, sure. I can probably do that."

"Good. I will cook your favorite meal."

Cain came to dinner more often for a few seven-days. Then, his appearances became less frequent, his attitude belligerent. He stopped coming us for Sabbath worship and refused to attend sacrifices. We could see him failing.

Abel shared his attempts to talk with his brother, his calls for him to repent. He came to me to clean his wounds one afternoon.

"Mama, I fear for Cain's soul. He expresses anger with me. Me, his little brother. What have I done to cause such anger?"

"I have no idea. What happened between you two?" I washed his cuts with warm water.

"Our friendly wrestling matches have become violent. He seeks for me wanting to beat me. I try to stay away from him, but he searches for me." Abel winced.

"Sorry. Did you inflict similar wounds on your brother?" I daubed aloe on a cut.

"Do not worry, mama. I will live. And, no, mama. I accept his beatings without returning the violence." He grimaced as I daubed the wound on his shoulder.

"Why allow him to cause this without fighting back?"

"I gain nothing by fighting. These injuries to my body are nothing compared to Cain's pain." Abel picked up his tunic.

"Cain hurts?" I watched him and allowed surprise to course through me.

"He is filled with agony. He believes he has lost the love of Jehovah." He shrugged into his tunic.

"Has he forgotten the power of repentance and the gift of forgiveness?" I closed my mouth.

"He has. I fear for him. Cain is not the brother he used to be."

I put my arms around Abel and we shared tears for his brother, my son.

I lost the association of both my sons after that. Abel spent more time in the hills with the sheep and goats, far away from Cain. He returned only for Sabbath worship and on sacrifice days. One Sabbath, Abel joined us in worship. As usual, Cain did not.

"Where is Cain?" I asked.

No one answered.

"I will go find him, mama." Abel pushed his chair back, rose from the table, and took his cloak from the hook behind the door.

"Abel. You cannot go alone after Cain. You know he is angry with you."

"I know, mama. The Lord is with me. I will be fine." He bent to kiss me on the cheek before striding through the door.

"Adam! Do not let him go. It is not safe. Stop him!"

Adam shook his head and surrounded my hand with his. "He is a man, dear. He must do as he thinks is right."

Abel did not return.

CHAPTER TWENTY-ONE

Death

I waited all night for Able to return. I walked the floors, praying for his safe return. My head ached, I could not breathe, and my stomach hurt. As the night passed, my misery increased.

I shook all over when Benoni's youngest son, Jed, returned from searching for Abel in Cain's fields the next morning. He ran back to our home, the front of his robe soaked in tears and blood.

"Grandmama! Grandpapa! Cain is not in his fields, but Abel is! He is not moving. His head is bloody, and he will not answer. Grandpapa, come with me! Please!" he cried tugging on Adam's sleeve.

I grabbed a length of clean wool and dry moss for his bloody head and followed Adam and Jed at a run to Cain's fields. We were all panting when we arrived. Jed led us through the field, and then pointed to a bit of flattened rye in the middle.

Abel lay there. Our beautiful, obedient, loving son lay with his head smashed. A big, bloody rock lay next to it. Adam bent to check. No breath of life filled him. He looked up and shook his head. Abel was dead.

I dropped my bundle of healing supplies and fell to my knees, sobbing, "Abel. Oh, Abel! What has happened to you? Who did this? Oh, Abel. Why did you come here to find Cain? You knew Cain was angry with you. Oh, Abel!"

Adam knelt beside me and held me close, whispering into my ear, "Eve, Eve. He is gone. Every indication suggests his brother killed him. Jehovah warned me something would happen. I did not expect this. Could I have prevented it? Abel, our obedient son. Oh, Eve."

He, too, began to sob. Jed knelt in front of us and wrapped his arms around us, his tears fell onto our necks. We sobbed until our robes were drenched, our tears gone. When we finally separated, Adam wiped my face with a bit of the hem of his robe, then wiped his own while Jed scrubbed his tears away with his hands.

Jed and Adam carried the broken body home, cradled in the length of wool I took with me, between them. We were met with cries of wonder and sorrow. Brothers yelled that they wanted to find the one who did this and find out why. The cries swelled in anger.

Adam turned to them. "No! No more sorrow or pain of death. It will only cause your souls to be darkened like his.

Let him alone. Jehovah will handle this. Your brother is in His hands."

Though they mumbled and grumbled, the men listened to Adam, their papa and grandpapa, turning, instead, to help with the burial grave, dug as we dug a grave for Pasha so long ago, on the hillside.

Abel's sisters helped me clean the broken body and wash away all the manifestations of his injuries. The broken skin and bruising showed starkly against his pale face. Chava, an older sister, dug through his possessions and found a clean tunic, pantaloons, and robe in which we dressed him.

As we prepared the bruised and broken body, Adam directed Jed and the others in digging a grave near the edge of the hill. Young grandsons ran to tell others in Home Valley and in the surrounding valleys. Many came to join in our sorrow and to honor Abel.

I noticed Cain did not join us, nor did many from Samoel's family. I understood Cain's desire to stay away but did not understand why Samoel stayed away. I brushed the thought away as we attended to the burial of my youngest son.

Adam, Benoni, Jed and Danel carefully lowered Abel's body into the grave. Many who loved him shared examples of his kindness, his obedience, and his great love for his family and animals. Adam reminded us of the future resurrection of Jehovah, to be known as the Christ.

"All will die. All will be resurrected. We will live eternally with Jehovah and Father if we repent. Abel did these things.

He repented, he obeyed, and he will live eternally. Each of you must do all you can to do the same."

My sad and sorrowing High Priest husband taught us more. As he spoke, tears flowed down his face and onto his robe. Many others also drenched their robes with tears. My own red face felt swollen. My head throbbed. Young Deborah sobbed uncontrollably. I stepped to her side and pulled her into a close embrace.

"Why so full of grief, my dear?"

"We wanted ...to be ... married. We ... planned to ask ... permission ... tomorrow," she managed to stammer out through her sobs.

My heart broke once more, for Deborah, and fresh tears joined hers as Adam began to cover the body with earth. Deborah and I each took a handful of soil and sprinkled it over Abel's broken body.

I tugged at her elbow. "Let us find a way to honor him."

"How?" She looked up through her tears.

"We can cover his grave with the beautiful flowers he loved."

While the men completed the heart-breaking task of filling the grave, Deborah and I walked to my flower garden and cut roses, iris, and gladiolus. We placed them in beautifully painted gourds with water. We found tiny white star flowers, blue bells, and lupine and dug them up. We carried them all back to the grave, along with a bucket of fresh water and a cup. Deborah set the cut flowers near Abel's head. The plants we buried atop the grave, to grow and remind us of his beauty.

We passed the water bucket and cup around among the mourners. We needed water to replace the moisture we lost with our tears. I learned long before it would help sorrowing headaches.

"Now, what do I do?" Deborah whispered, tugging on her braid. I wondered how we could be expected to survive this grief.

~

Many evenings later Jed found us on our live oak branch. We still sorrowed for our lost sons. His red face radiated embarrassment and he could not be still. He stood, then sat, and then stood again.

"Grandpapa. Grandmama. I have something I must tell you."

"What is it, Jed?" Adam's eyes latched on to his.

"I, um, I know more about what happened ... to Abel." He rocked on his feet and rubbed his hand across the back of his neck.

"Tell us." I grasped his hand and tugged him toward us.

He sat on a bench and recounted his story.

"Cain tried to convince me to join him in his disobedience. He talked with me about the things the Destroyer told him. I am sorry. He insisted I keep all this to myself, but I cannot. I must tell you."

Cain met the Deceiver in his fields. The wicked one appeared as an angel of light, commanding him, 'Worship me. I am the god of this world. I, too, am a son of God. I was there during the formation of this earth. Worship me!'

'You are not the god of this world,' Cain replied. 'My papa told me you are a liar.'

"Cain knows is papa is an honest man," I yelped.

Adam put his hand on mine. "Hush. Hear the boy's story."

Jed continued, speaking as though he were seeing what happened.

'I stand in light. I am God!" the Destroyer said.

"*Give me the tokens so I may know you are from Father, or you are a liar and your light is false." Cain demanded.*

Lucifer offered some token.

Cain did not know the correct tokens. He had not yet been taught. He only knew there should be a token.

'I am not the liar. Your papa deceives you.'

Cain looked away from the Destroyer's intense stare.

'He is jealous of the attention you receive from men who come to learn from you. He desires for them to learn from him. Your papa does not like for you have such a following.'

'Papa would not do that.'

The Destroyer's voice boomed, 'I speak the truth. Give honor and respect to me. Bow down now. Worship me!'

Cain attempted to refuse, but the pattern on Lucifer's clothing changed and the serpent on his cane hissed.

'Perhaps you are right. I will discuss this with my papa.'

'Do not share any of this with Adam. He will only force you to repent.'

Three times Cain received the disturbing visits. The last time, the terrible voice echoed off the hills, causing Cain to fall to his knees.

'Forgive me. I am wrong. My papa must be wrong as well. I will teach him.'

'No! Adam will not believe. It is my challenge to teach him. You have no need.'

'What shall I call you?' Cain whispered. 'You are not Jehovah. Who are you?'

'You may call me Lucifer or Satan. It matters not to me. I only demand you obey.'

'What is your wish, Satan?' Cain asked.

'Take grains from your field and sacrifice,' the Destroyer demanded, pointing to the altar on the hill.

Jed stood and paced.

'Yes, Satan, but we were commanded to sacrifice the first of our flocks—'

'You will do as I require,' the Destroyer shouted. 'Sacrifice from your fields. It will be honored.'

Cain ducked his head in agreement.

'Adam has taught you the words of the rite?'

'He has.'

'Then, you know how to do it. Gather your grain and offer sacrifice.'

The vile Destroyer whipped his glittering cloak around him, lifted his cane by the serpent's throat and withdrew. Cain walked through his fields, gathering the required items into a basket and carried it with him to the altar on the hill.

Cain knew you, Grandpapa Adam, expect to oversee all sacrificial offerings, in order to ensure all is done as directed by Jehovah. However, his fear of Lucifer throbbed greater *than his desire for obedience to Jehovah or you,Grandpapa Adam. He performed the rite alone, praying to Satan before setting it on fire.*

Days later, on a day of sacrifice, Cain joined us as Abel brought the commanded ram, firstborn and unblemished. He performed the rite in the proper way, with your supervision. Jehovah's voice pierced our ears. 'Abel's offering is acceptable.'

"Jehovah's voice surprised me, pleased me to hear it once more. Cain showed surprise, as well, for I remember Cain's face darken with rage as he stood beside me." I remembered the day only months earlier. "He had not attended for many months. I asked him why he harbored such great anger toward his brother, who sacrificed according to the law. Cain growled, 'No reason,' spun on his heel and rushed down the hill."

"We did not know of Cain's earlier offering." Adam shook his head. "We did not understand his anger came from hurt pride. He wanted Jehovah to honor his."

Jed sat and put his chin in his hands. His voice broke as he resumed his somber story.

When Cain returned to his fields, the voice of Jehovah came to him, saying, 'Why are you angry? When you obey, your offering is accepted. Sin overtakes you. Lucifer desires your body. Obey my commands, or he shall have you. You will be his, though you be his ruler. Beware. This is not an honor.'

'Why should I not want it?' Cain shouted. 'I offered sacrifice. Why did you not accept it? I did as I was commanded.'

'You prayed and sacrificed to Lucifer. He accepted it. You were deceived. Lucifer commanded the sacrifice. He knew it would not be acceptable. Repent, or you will be father of his lies forever.'

'Because I sacrificed my grains? Without the supervision of my papa?'

'Because you listened to Lucifer and followed his commands.'

Jehovah withdrew, leaving Cain alone to ponder. He worked hard, wanting to do right. After many days of struggle, his digging stick slammed into the soil beside the plants. Some were viciously yanked from the earth.

Cain went to his brother, Samoel, and requested for his youngest daughter, Urit, to be his wife. Cain promised Samoel wealth and power if he would follow him. They celebrated the marriage that day and entered into a blood covenant, unknown outside their family.

"Oh, Jed. It must have been hard for you to hold this story inside." I reached over and touched his arm.

"It was, Grandmama." Jed sat with his head bowed. Then he shook himself and looked up. "Cain threatened to kill me, too, if I talked. I am afraid of him — afraid he would beat my head in as he did Abel's. I did not enter into the covenant with him, but I saw it happen. Abel thought I did. I knew danger followed me, until Cain and Urit disappeared, with Samoel and those of his sons who joined in the covenant. They have been gone for more than a seven-day now. Perhaps, I am safe." He squared his shoulders. "I cannot hold all this in any longer. I had to tell you. You needed to know."

Adam put an arm around Jed's shoulders, pulling him close.

Adam spoke at last. "I have heard some of this from Jehovah. He told me of the pact with the enemy, Cain, and Samoel and his family. The Destroyer suggested the pact before Cain killed Abel. They covenanted to die rather than share any information with us. They coveted the power and wealth Cain and the Destroyer promised."

"How can things be of greater worth than a brother?" My jaw tightened and my head ached. "They did not receive anything from Abel. They never will."

"Cain believed he would become master of the grand secret. He murdered for property. He desired glory. After the murder, Cain believed he gained freedom and wealth, that Abel's flocks were his."

I sat in shock, listening to words I never wanted to hear.

Jehovah came to Cain, asking, 'Where is thy brother, Abel?'

'Am I my brother's keeper? I do not know where he is.'

'What have you done? Your brother's blood cries from the ground. The earth opened her mouth to receive your brother's blood and now curses you. She will not give you of her strength. You will be a fugitive and a vagabond. I will not hear your pleas. Go to your new master for that.'

Adam stood to pace. Walking back and forth in front of the live oak before continuing.

266

Cain cried out, 'Satan tempted me with my brother's flocks. He said they would be mine. I suffered anger because you accepted only Abel's offering. My punishment is greater than I can bear. You have driven me away. You will not hear my voice. My brothers will destroy me.'

   'Be still. I will set a mark on you, so no man will kill you.'

   Cain took the family of Urit and fled to the land of Nod in the east.

   "Our sorrows multiply." I shook my head. "Father told me I would have sorrow in conception, but I did not understand the sorrow would be greatest with the murder of one son by another. How could Cain take the life of his brother? Why did he have to listen to the Destroyer? I am heartbroken by Cain's actions, but angry with the Destroyer. Why does he desire our sons? Why could he not just take one? Why was he determined to take both of them?"

   Adam pulled me close, calming me. "The Destroyer desires to steal love and light from this world. He could only do this by taking a life, the life of a son most prepared to follow Jehovah. The destroyer could not stand the hope Abel brought us."

   "Hope? Yes, and joy. Will it ever return?" I fell into his arms. My tears drenched the front of his robe.

~

It took months for me to overcome my sorrow. Adam spent more time with me, as did the women of our village. When a child flashed me a smile, my heart lifted. The loving arms of my sweet husband, daughters, sons, and grandchildren comforted and aided me in overcoming the sadness within.

Adam led me outside one evening to sit on the live oak tree branch. There, he held my hand and spoke to me in a gentle voice.

"Eve, my darling. You are allowing the Destroyer to win."

"Me? Allowing that vile thing to win? How?" I asked.

"Your sadness." I started to interrupt, but he hurried on. "It is right to sorrow for lost children, but when you let it go on this long, seeing only darkness, the Destroyer wins. Father and Jehovah placed us here to have joy. We cannot permit the actions of others to cause us such pain and sorrow."

"He murdered our son!" I wailed.

"He did and murdered his own soul. His life and eternity are for Father to determine. It is your responsibility to be joyful once more. Look into the eyes of children and find hope. Feel the support of your family. Know you are cherished by Father and Jehovah. Remember the great act of love Jehovah will perform for each of us, allowing our repentance."

Unwanted tears slid from beneath my eyelashes. "Adam, I need help. Please give me a blessing."

"I thought you would." Adam stood and moved around behind me, lay his hands on my head, and gave me a sweet blessing.

After this, my heart lightened, and I found joy once more in my life.

Our family continued to grow. Some denied the faith, leaving Home Valley in search of something different. Others listened to Adam's teaching, building a community within our valley. This community of believers began to spread beyond the edges of the valley.

Adam began to travel among the faithful, teaching and exhorting them to remain faithful to Jehovah. A small number of our children of those who had denied their faith returned to listen and to learn. A smaller number felt the stirrings of faith and came to the waters of repentance and baptism. In this we found comfort.

Danel returned to the faith and worshiped Jehovah, among other young men. He courted Deborah and they were married. Danel honored and loved Deborah. Their marriage and family brought me great happiness.

After much contemplation and many tears, I shared my sorrows in a letter to Cain, hoping someday I could find someone to give it to him.

~

Oh Cain, my child!

I grieve for you. We had bright hopes for you. You were full of compassion. You had the most to gain from Father's love. You had the opportunity to stand for truth, to share His word with your brothers. You lost your greatness.

You turned from the light to find darkness. It never has provided as the light does, nor will it ever. When you are no longer needed, it will throw you away. Pray to the dark, pray to your false god. It will never give you light or joy, as given by Father.

You fell for the trap of power and fame. You wanted something that was already yours. All the Father has was yours. And you gave it up. For what?

Satan urges you to seek for and obey other gods. Do you not remember Father is a jealous God? His jealousy is not like your god, not jealous of another's good deeds and obedience. All good comes from Him. He jealously guards and protects his children.

Gods you create cannot solve your problems, whether they are made of wood, stone, or beautiful jewels. They cannot heal your babies or fight your battles. Will they provide you with love and tenderness? How can they? You created them.

To you, a woman is a slave to tread beneath your feet, to answer to your every command, to be beaten and abused. She no longer stands by your side. Why? To prove you are bigger and stronger? How sad for you. She could help you, if you allow her.

Your women create goddesses to give them the solace Father would have given them. False gods give them nothing, when the one true God would gladly hear their plea, and yours, and provide light and love.

Oh, that I could help you understand. Oh, that I could once again hold you close, as I did when you were a child. But, this is never again to be.

I weep for you. I weep for my grandchildren. I weep for your losses.

Farewell, my son. I will always love and remember you, as you were.

Your mama,
Eve.

CHAPTER TWENTY-TWO

Expectation

Children ran wild and unprotected in Home Valley over the next few years. Parents were occupied—growing food, building, and attending to the myriad of other necessary activities of active adults. On my travels through the village, I stopped several and asked if they could read or write.

Most responded with a shy, "No, grandmama. Mama does not have time."

This important skill, one that allowed our people to remember their heritage and the words of Jehovah, would soon be lost in the busyness of life. I taught these skills to our children and helped many grandchildren, mamas and papas of these children who now ran wild and illiterate.

I brought my concerns about the lack of instruction to Adam's attention when he returned from his latest journey.

"Their mamas and papas are engaged in working. The land no longer provides as easily as it did for us earlier." He pulled a book from his bag and set it in its place on the shelf. "I am concerned they will not be able to read your Book of Remembrance. They must be taught. And their parents are involved elsewhere." I sat on the bed to watch him.

"Reading and writing are as vital as eating, for if we do not remember Jehovah's teachings, we cannot obey." Adam dumped the last of his pack on the bed. "But, what can we do? This is their parents' responsibility."

I thought about the problem through the day and into the evening. When I went to the well for water the next morning, I found little Avram alone, walking along the inside edge of the well. My heart paused momentarily with a small gasp. I sat on the edge of the well near him.

"Hello, Avram. Where is your mama?"

"In the fields, helping papa." He stepped past me on a circuit around the well.

"Your sisters and brothers?"

"Working with mama and papa. They sent me away."

The little boy stopped beside me and sat down. "I can do it. I am strong. But strong is not enough for mama."

"Mamas are like that sometimes. They do not want their little boys damaged. I tried to protect mine. He was still injured."

"Really Grandmama Eve? Who got hurt?" He looked at me with his big brown eyes peeping out from behind long, dark brown curls.

"Absalom. He thought he was big and strong enough to climb the tree. He fell and broke his arm."

Avram's eyes opened wide.

"We mamas consider our boys to be small and precious. We do not always know when they grow strong like you." I stood and offered him my hand.

Avram held on a moment, then jumped off the well and kicked at a stone. "Mama will not allow me in the fields when they are harvesting. What can I do to change her mind?"

"With good reason. Scythes are sharp and you are small," his face dropped and I added, "though you are strong. It would be easy to swing the scythe and hit you. It hurts to be cut by them." I kicked the stone before leaning down conspiratorially to whisper in his ear, "They keep me out of the fields, too."

"You, too?"

I nodded. "They do not want me injured. Do you want to do something with me?"

Avram looked up, wonder filled his eyes. "Do something with you, Grandmama Eve?"

I nodded solemnly, "Yes. I would appreciate company. You are just the right boy to help."

"Help you? How?"

We stopped under the live oak tree near my house. "Could you help me practice reading and writing?"

"I cannot read or write." His excitement diminished, he scuffed his feet in the dirt. "Mama says she does not have time to teach me."

"Oh? Maybe we can work together. Perhaps I can remember a thing or two. Would you like that?"

"Could we? I have wanted to read and write like Yagil and Ora, but no one has time. Would you really help me?" He frowned, then grinned shyly at me.

"I will. Shall we sit here?" I waved at the soft grass near us.

Avram grinned and sat beside me. "What will we read?"

"We can make our own words first here in the dirt. Later, I will bring a story I wrote telling the story of our dog, Bark and his horse friend, Red."

We doodled with sticks in the dirt, talking about words and letters. Other children joined us. They listened for a while before joining in the discussion. When mamas began to search for missing boys and girls at midday, eager boys and girls surrounded me, happily learning to read.

"Avram! Are you disturbing Grandmama Eve?" The little boy, jolted from his study, stared into the face of his impatient mama.

"No problem here, Els." I glanced up to see her frustration. "I invited young Avram and his friends to assist me in recalling how to read. We are doing a good job, too."

"You, you invited him?" Her rigid body began to relax.

"Yes. I invited Avram to help me. I have not practiced for some time."

"You are not bothered by all these children?" Incredulity raced across Nasya's face.

"Why, no. I love helping them." I placed my finger by my chin. "Do you not remember learning at my side?"

Her face softened as her memory brought back those times.

"I have been concerned our girls and boys are not gaining this critical skill." I added.

"We are working, tending fields, caring for families, keeping our houses in order —" Mikele began.

I held up my hands forestalling arguments. "I know. You are all busy. You must leave young ones home while you work. It is difficult to handle all the responsibilities of women. Things today are more difficult than they were for me when as a young mama. There are more families, more children, more for you to do each day. I decided to assist you by teaching them to read."

The noise from the women was like the cackling of hens. I let them gabble, knowing they would soon understand.

"Are you sure you have time to teach?" Adam asked that evening.

"You do not allow me in the fields during harvest. I have less to do. I prefer to teach them correctly. I still remember reading and writing from before."

"Who will you teach?

After a long moment of contemplation, I said, "Every child who joins me. If they join me, they are excited and interested in learning."

"And how long?"

"I will keep them only a part of the morning. Leave them time to help their mamas. During this harvest, I will work with them in the morning while everyone else is busy."

Adam reached around my waist and pulled me close. "What will you have them read?"

"I will do as I did with Absalom and Bilhah. I still have the stories I wrote for them about Bark and Red. Then, they will be writing their own stories."

We sat in comfortable silence. Adam's arm warm encircled me.

"Oh!" Adam jumped when the baby within me leaped. "Will you feel well enough to teach while you carry a babe?"

"I always have. I will begin the project. Some young women may join me and take over later." I massaged my newly bulging stomach. "My, this little one is active. Perhaps this will be the obedient son."

"Perhaps. Too many times over the last years our sons chose disobedience or other activities. I cannot force any to follow my path. A child will be born. A son will be found. I trust Jehovah."

~

Children eager to learn flocked to join me each morning. On sunny days, we sat together beneath the live oak. Stormy days found us in my kitchen, crowded together, laughing and learning. The littlest children worked with sticks, tracing letters in the dirt and brushing it away. Older children used a large, flat piece of bark and sharpened a hardwood stick with the point burned black.

They learned rapidly. They enjoyed learning. Time passed quickly as we worked together.

Young women, who learned these skills earlier, joined me after the harvest. They took on the task of teaching when my babe grew too big to bend over the children's work. I continued to check in with them and listen to the little ones read though I no longer actively taught. This, too, gave me joy. The day for this new child to be born drew near.

One hundred thirty years after we left Eden, our plea for another son was answered in Seth's birth. We hoped he would be the son who could withstand the temptations and lies of the Destroyer. Adam believed him to be the son. I trusted his belief.

Like Abel before him, Seth's features were the exact image of Adam's, with the same brilliant blue eyes, same dark brown hair, and his nose had the same straightness. Even his smile echoed his papa. Most importantly, Seth loved Jehovah and strictly obeyed each commandment. Sabbath worship became joyful once more, with Seth joining in song and prayer.

He tagged after Adam everywhere. He followed him through the fields, helping where he could. He joined us at the altar, intently watching in preparation for the day he, too, would receive the Priesthood of God. He was a true son of God and we cherished him.

The members of our community cherished Seth almost as much as Adam and I. Benoni brought him a young stallion for his fourth birthday.

"A horse, Benoni?" I exclaimed. "You really think he is big enough for a horse?"

"Yes, mama, I do." Benoni watched the boy and young animal together. "See. They love each other already."

The horse, taller than the little boy, bent low to receive love and attention. Seth scratched his ears and pulled him tight for a hug.

"What will you name your horse?" Adam squatted next to the child.

Seth squished up his little face in thought.

I stood next to the glistening black horse and ran my hand through his silky coat. I expected the small boy to call him 'Blackie.'

"Pacer. Do you like that name, boy?" Seth spoke softly to the colt, his face near.

The colt nodded his head and leaned his nose into Seth's face and whickered.

"Pacer it is, then." He patted the colt's nose. "Papa, his name is Pacer."

"Pacer?" I raised my eyebrows.

"Yes, mama. His name is Pacer. He likes his name, huh, boy. You like your name?"

The horse snorted and bumped into Seth.

"See, mama."

"I see, Seth. Welcome to the family, Pacer." I patted his nose.

The colt shuddered and stood still once more.

"Come with me, Seth," Benoni said. "We need to take him back to his mama. He will be hungry again soon."

"Can I help brush him?"

"Of course. He is yours now, your responsibility."

The two brothers, one an adult, the other a little boy, walked toward the paddock. Pacer followed, his head leaning over Seth's shoulder, his black hide only a few shades darker than the boy's hair.

"Joy on four legs," Adam said.

"And on two. I do not know who is more joyful, the boy or the colt."

Adam laughed and hugged me.

Not many months later, Seth wandered home, a bundle of yellow fur asleep in his arms.

"Mama, see what Danel gave me," he whispered.

"A dog? Did you beg for a puppy?" I asked, matching the level of my voice to his.

"No, mama. I watched the mama with her puppies. This little one is small. She cannot push past the others to eat. Danel said if I would feed her, I could have her. He says she may not live, if someone does not assist her. May I help her? Please?" A tear slipped down his cheek.

"Of course, Seth. This little ball of fur would not be the first pup we helped to stay alive."

I put my arm around his shoulder and guided him to the barn. We found the bucket and a stool near the door and called to the cow.

"I know you gave milk already," I patted her withers. "Can we get a little more warm milk? This little pup is in need."

The cow turned and mooed. I sat next to her and squeezed enough warm milk into the bucket to fill a small dish, then patted the cow and stood.

I remembered a time, many years ago, when Absalom brought home a pup needing our help to live. We had such big hopes and plans for Absalom.

I shook my head. This was Seth, not Absalom. Many hopes were laid on the little boy's shoulders, and he hardly even knew it.

I showed Seth how to dip his fingers into the warm milk and allow the pup to lick it off until he learned to lap the milk from the bowl.

"It tickles, mama," he giggled.

Seth named the dog Scamp. Like Bark of a hundred years earlier, she became part of the family and close to her friend, Seth. When Seth grew old enough to take the flocks to the hills on his own, the dog and horse went with him.

"Will he be safe in the hills?" I asked Adam the night before his first trip alone. "The Destroyer has attempted to destroy all our sons — and has succeeded in nearly every case."

"I do not fear for Seth," Adam replied. He leaned back on the live oak branch and smelled the early lilacs. "Jehovah told me he will guard this obedient son."

"Will not Cain and his children come to destroy Seth as he destroyed Abel?"

"Cain does not know about Seth. If he does, he will not take the chance to come here. Seth has loved ones who watch out for him. I do not think Pacer would allow an attack on Seth. Between him and Scamp, our son is safe."

"I have never seen a horse so protective of a boy," I laughed. "Even I must be wary when Pacer is around."

"And Scamp is the same. Do you remember when Absalom and I left you alone before Bilhah's birth?"

"I will never forget my fear, Lucifer lazing insolently against the tree, and the animals who came to stand guard between me and that vile creature. Jehovah sent animals to protect me then. The memory makes the hair on my arms and neck stand up."

"And in the same way He sent animals to preserve you, He will protect Seth. Can you believe otherwise, when his horse and dog already watch over him?"

"No. But, why did Jehovah not safeguard Abel? If he can defend Seth, why did he not shelter our other son, our first son to be obedient?"

"You know the answer." Adam lifted his arm up from the tree branch and encircled my waist with it. "Father gives everyone freedom of choice. He had to allow Cain the right to choose good or evil, even when it meant Abel would lose his life. In choosing evil, Cain chose to lose all opportunities to return to Father's presence. He clearly knew. He chose to turn from truth and light to the darkness of Master Mahan."

I shivered at the name, Adam pulled me closer and nuzzled my ear, crushing the purple and white petunia in my hair, releasing its strong fragrance.

"Do not worry. Seth will be protected."

As Adam held me, a star streaked across the heavens, leaving a light in its path. A sign from Father? I hoped so.

CHAPTER TWENTY-THREE

Changes

Years later, when Seth was less a boy and beginning to be a man, he returned from herding the animals with a glow about him, one Adam and I recognized. "You have heard from Jehovah." Adam leaned toward our son.

"He spoke to me. Me, a boy! He knows I am obedient and do my best. He honors me. I am to assist with the sacrifice this next Sabbath day. Papa, will you help me?" He stood quietly, the glow emanating from him.

"Yes, Seth, I will. It will be an honor. I have not had a son participate with me for many years."

"When do we begin?" No little boy excitement, only confidence of an honorable future Priesthood holder.

"Tomorrow. One of the older children can watch the herds for you. Choose one. You are an adult, now."

"I choose Tovi." Deborah and Danel's youngest grandson. Their home was near ours. Danel's sons and some of his grandsons cared for his flocks.

I allowed my eyes to widen at the mention of Tovi, who had been a rascal and a tease.

"Tovi often comes to the hills with me. He understands the sheep and they listen to him. Even the goats listen to him. He will be perfect to watch over our animals." Seth defended his choice with quiet words.

"Tovi is a fine boy." I lowered my eyes. "I did not know he loved our animals as you do."

"His mama forgets he is a good boy." Seth shifted his weight on his feet. "I think I will give him some animals to make up a small herd from ours. He deserves it, with all the help he has given me—if you agree, papa?" Seth looked to Adam. "After a few days alone with them, he will have earned a flock."

"Good plan," Adam answered. "Tovi is a good one to watch our herds, and he will have earned a flock for himself."

"How will you decide which ones to give him?" I lay my hands in my lap.

"He can choose. He knows which are friendly with each other. He will make a good choice." Seth stomped dust off a foot.

"You do not worry he will take your best?" I remembered the arguments of other sons when large herds were divided.

"No, mama. Even if Tovi does, Jehovah will increase our flocks. I do not worry."

"Few are willing to give their best to aid another," Adam leaned back and set his hand behind me.

"I am not like other men." He drew himself a little taller, a little straighter.

"No, son, you are not." Adam patted his shoulder. "Do you know which ram to use for the rite?"

"I have one in mind, but I must inspect him to be sure he is unblemished. After I talk with Tovi about herding our goats and sheep, I will bring him to the barn. Is that the right place for him, papa?"

"Yes. You will want to keep him close. We have much work to do in the next five days before then."

"I thought so. I will speak with Tovi now."

Seth left quietly, no loud noise, no cheering. He had a quiet respect for the Priesthood he would soon receive.

"I am not surprised he heard from Jehovah," I said. "He is a good man."

"Father promised us an obedient son, if we waited. Since Abel's death, grandsons and granddaughters obey. It is good to have a son who is so completely obedient." Adam stood and stretched. "I need to record this moment in my Book of Remembrance."

I nodded. "At last, something joyous to record."

Adam took down the sacred book from its place on the shelf, opened the drawers of his desk and found pen and ink, and sat down to write.

Seth's nimble mind quickly learned. Before the rite, in front of all who came to observe, Adam lay his hands on

Seth's head and gave him the Priesthood, allowing him to participate in sacrifices, teach the word of Jehovah, and call others to repentance.

Seth continued to grow physically and spiritually. He drew close to Jehovah. A younger copy of his papa, in look and action, he obeyed strictly all of Jehovah's laws.

Adam took him on his trips to reclaim our children. Sometimes they were successful. Usually, only a man and a woman, with a small family listened and obeyed. Seldom did they manage to teach a whole community to remember the teachings of Jehovah.

We heard news of Cain. In his fear that his brothers would find and kill him as he killed Abel, he and his people moved a long way away from us. Hatred developed, and those brothers no longer searched to destroy Cain for his murder, rather they searched to learn from him.

His sons stopped roaming, settling in a land they called Nod. Others who sought their knowledge and eschewed the righteousness of Adam, fled there until people filled the land and Nod became a great city, filled with filth and wickedness. Other cities followed.

Stories spread of Cain's cruelty to his women and their eventual search for peace and hope. Tales of goddesses they worshiped caused me sorrow. It is a sad thing to be right about such things.

Seth became a man, a strong, gentle, obedient son of God. One evening as Adam and I sat on the live oak, observing the last rays of sunshine glow across the mountains in reds, violets, and golds, Seth joined us. He sat watching the stars appear and the owls and bats swoop over the cloud of midges above us.

Eventually he whispered. "Papa, I am to ask you for my mission."

"Mission?" My voice squeaked in surprise.

"I knew you were coming." Adam sat with a smile playing across his lips.

I looked to him with upraised eyebrows. Then I dropped them. He had the look of one who spoke recently with deity.

"What am I to do?" Seth stared into his papa's eyes in earnest.

"You are to travel with a companion to teach all who will accept your teachings. They no longer listen to me, perhaps they will attend to you."

"A companion?" Seth let his mouth drop open.

"A woman. It is past time for you to find a good woman and marry her. Together you will seek those who search for truth and light. Is there a woman you have considered?" Adam gestured toward the houses in the village.

Seth stared at his papa, his mouth open.

"Is there a young woman who interests you? Perhaps Ganet?" I leaned forward.

Seth snapped his mouth shut and stood up.

"Yes, mama, I do love Ganet and she loves me. We have talked of marriage. Will she be right for this mission, Papa? It could be dangerous."

"It could be, but you will be protected. You will serve Jehovah with the support of a good woman." Adam reached for my hand and held it tight. "A good woman makes our challenges become something special. Sometimes we try to protect our women in ways they do not want." He looked at me and winked.

"Too true," I said. "You should ask her."

"Do I have time to wed before I leave?" Seth rocked between his feet.

"Go find Ganet. If she will have you, explain your mission and allow her to choose whether to go or stay. Then request her parents' permission," Adam said.

Seth brightened. "Thank you, papa."

He left us in a rush in the direction of Ganet's parent's home. He reminded me of the days of a little boy rushing off to play with his animals.

"Will Ganet marry him?" Adam asked as we watched him go.

"She watches him wherever he goes. I think she will. My question is whether her parents will allow her to join him? She is their youngest. I am not certain they will, only to have her leave them so soon."

"For Seth's sake, I pray they will agree." Adam turned toward the night sky. "Seth will need a good woman on his mission."

Seth and Ganet were married in a quiet, sacred ceremony. Adam spoke the sacred words of the covenant, the same ones Father used when we were married.

As we ate the marriage meal Ganet's mother, Bethel, prepared, I turned to Adam. "Do you remember the day of ours, so long ago in Eden? Father used those same beautiful words."

"Of course, I remember that day. How do you think I remembered them?" He grinned at me.

Seth interrupted our kiss, "Your marriage used the same words you used today?"

"Yes, son," Adam said.

"They are beautiful. A perfect pattern," Seth said.

"In this and all things, Father gives a perfect pattern. Sad others do not know the joy of obedience." Adam turned back to kiss me between the eyes.

Seth nodded solemnly. "I look forward to sharing with those who have lost it."

The young couple left the next day, serving Jehovah.

~

I missed Seth, his quiet ways, and his gentle smile. I knew he worked for Jehovah and the knowledge helped. I often found myself thinking of him and Ganet, wondering what they were doing. Were they safe? I trusted Jehovah to keep them safe.

Sometime after Seth and Ganet left, I went to the stream, alone, to dig clay for more storage jars. Rather than digging, I sat with tears running down my face. For years, I carried a child within my body or in my arms. All were grown now. My arms felt empty.

"Why, Father, do I no longer conceive? Am I still worthy? Have I been disobedient in some way? Are there no more children for me?"

I sat contemplating, praying, and wiping away the tears.

"Eve. What is wrong?" Adam put his hand on my shoulder and turned me to face him.

"Oh, Adam, it has been years and I no longer conceive. Is it something I did? Have I displeased Jehovah in some way? Why?"

"Are not thirty-six children enough?"

"I do not know! We were commanded to multiply and replenish. Have I done enough?" I flopped my arms out away from me.

He brushed my graying hair from my eyes, running his hand through its length. "Father loves you as much now as always."

"Are you certain? My arms are so empty."

"Shall I ask? Would you like a blessing?"

I remembered the blessings he gave to me and to others and knew I would receive a gift from Father. I bowed my head in agreement. He placed his hands on my head and gave me the blessing I needed.

Among the wondrous and sacred words were, "Eve, you are loved of your Father. He accepts the offering of your body in bringing children into this world. Many still listen to your teachings and have gained joy in obedience. Others disregarded your guidance and now follow Satan. They used the agency I gave them. You are no longer required to bring sons and daughters to this earth. Your daughters and granddaughters will continue to multiply and replenish."

I am loved. I am not disobedient.

We stood together after the blessing, wrapped in love. Adam's strong, gentle arms around me comforted and protected me. He bent to kiss me, long and deep.

I now understood that my responsibility to bring children into this world had been apportioned among my daughters and granddaughters. This relieved me in unexpected ways. Younger parents could care for active little ones easier than me in my older years.

Instead, I learned to love and teach my grandchildren as often as the opportunity presented. I advised, demonstrated, and instructed them in reading and writing, and other life skills, when needed. I loved to see the light of learning fill their eyes.

We loved watching our children grasp new ideas and grow. We sorrowed when their choices drew them away from us and Jehovah. Now, we find great happiness in those of our children and grandchildren who chose obedience. As they learn that happiness comes from obedience, our joy grows.

Living here with Adam in this beautiful world, bringing children and grandchildren to join us, and teaching them of Jehovah's love has made my life wonderful. I still wonder how our lives would have been different had I not chosen to eat of the fruit when I did. Then I think of the blessings of our bodies and all my children and grandchildren. Such great joy could never have been encountered within Eden.

Were it not for my transgression, we would never have had children. We would never have known good from evil. We learn so much from the opportunity to make choices. Our knowledge of Jehovah, who will provide redemption and exaltation, comes because of our obedience to Father's and Jehovah's laws. How great and wonderful has been our life.

Epilogue

The old woman looked up. The clearness in her eyes attending the memories of her earlier years began to fade with exhaustion.

"Is that what you wanted to hear, Ruth?" Her voice broke suddenly, once again ancient and small.

Women and children stirred with a sigh.

"Yes, very much, grandmama. I, we, did not know how difficult life was for you." Ruth spoke for the congregated women.

"And worth all the struggles. Look at my posterity." Eve spread her arms out to include all the women and children. "We were blessed. How could I have known how wonderful this life would be the day Father and Jehovah introduced me to Adam? Our life together has been fulfilling, full of joy and sorrow. Leaving Eden to receive all this is my greatest blessing."

The women gathered together blankets and babies. A buzz of sound rose above them.

"Who is next? Who will tell her story tomorrow?" Ruth called.

Names were called out, as Eve stretched her frail arms and legs. "That is easy," she said. "It should be Ganet."

Words of agreement filled the hill.

"Prepare to report tomorrow, then, Ganet." Ruth lifted a shoulder.

Ganet nodded and bent to help the ancient woman stand. "Thanks, grandmama." She leaned close to be heard amid the growing sound of women gathering together children and possessions. It sounded like a hive of bees had been opened.

A twinkle of pleasure filled Eve's eyes. "Of course, Ganet. There is much these young women can learn from your life. Better start thinking on it. Be prepared."

"Of course, grandmama."

Ruth joined them, taking Eve's thin arm on one side while Ganet helped from the other, walking past the other women, through the trees, and toward the fires of cooking dinner.

Did You Enjoy This Book?

Thank you for joining me in the story of Eve with Adam, and her family. I hope they touched your soul the way they did mine. As I wrote, it felt as though she whispered in my ear.

If you enjoyed this book, will you do something for me?

I'm and independent author, publishing my books without the backing of a major publisher. That means no six-figure advances and no advertising budget. This makes it difficult to promote my novels and put them in places new readers can find them. But you can help me.

Honest reviews and genuine "word-of-mouth" advertising makes all the difference. I'm not asking for one of those awful bookreports I used to try not to sleep through, as a teacher. What will help me is if you would leave an honest star rating and a couple of sentences on Amazon or Goodreads. Or a short review on your blog. Or tell your friends about it on Facebook or Twitter.

Let people know what you liked about this book and why they might like it. Maybe you could buy a book or two for your friends. If there was something you didn't like, you can say that, as well. Constructive criticism helps me write a better book next time. But please, send criticism to me. I look forward to your email. But, please. No spoilers!

Thanks for reading.

Angelique Conger

Http://AngeliqueCongerAuthor.com

Contact me at angelique@AngeliqueCongerAuthor.com

Would you like to know more?

If you enjoyed this story, you may enjoy a **Free Micro Story**, written about Eve in her travels with Adam, later in their lives. Eve must find a way to rescue Adam after he was taken by servants of the Destroyer. No one else is near and it is up to her.

Avenging Angel is **free** and only available when you subscribe to my **Ancient Historical Fiction group** newsletter

Go to: http://www.AngeliqueCongerAuthor.com to get your **free copy.**

Acknowledgments:

It is necessary to give thanks to Eve, who sat next to me, sharing her story through my fingers. Hers is a story lost to the ages, though this may have been purposeful. She wanted her story told now.

A big thank you to my sweet husband, Jack, who has supported me as I sit beside him, ignoring him and all his movies as I write. His support made it possible for me to write this. Thanks, too, to my parents, whose love and support have always been dependable.

Thank you, too, to my sister, Tina Gilger, who talked me into joining National Novel Writing Month in 2013. I could never have done this without her encouragement, insights, and suggestions.

Thanks to my editor, Danica Paige, who helped me with my focus. Because of her, I was able to tighten my writing into something worth reading.

Huge thanks to my artist friend, Heather Thuerer, who took time out of her extremely busy schedule to paint my cover for me. If you are interested in her other work, go to http://www.HeatherThuerer.com. Her art is amazing!

Other Books by Angelique Conger

Books by Angelique Conger

Ancient Matriarchs:

Eve, First Matriarch
Into the Storms: Ganet: Wife of Seth
Finding Peace: Rebecca, Wife of Enos
Moving into Light: Zehira, Wife of Enoch

Lost Children of the Prophet

Lost Children of the Prophet
Captured Freedom
Abandoned Hope
Brotherly Havoc
Betrayed Trust
Convicted Deliverance
Trouble Escaped
Impassioned Grief
Love Defied
Hidden Purpose

ABOUT THE AUTHOR

Angelique Conger writes historical fiction about the earliest days of our earth between Eden and the flood. Many consider her books Christian focused, and they are because they focus on events in the Bible. She writes of a people's beliefs in Jehovah. However, though she's read in much of the Bible and searched for more about these stories, there isn't much there. Her imagination fills in the missing information, which is most of it.

Angelique followed her Navy husband around the world and later worked as a teacher in the years her children were growing. Writing about the earliest days of our earth, those days between the Garden of Eden and Noah's flood, helps in her efforts to change the world.

Angelique lives in Southern Nevada with her husband, turtles, and Lovebird. Her favorite times are visiting children and grandchildren.

AngeliqueCongerAuthor.com

Made in the USA
Las Vegas, NV
07 February 2023

67094180R00174